CATSTRONAUTS
DIGITAL DISASTER

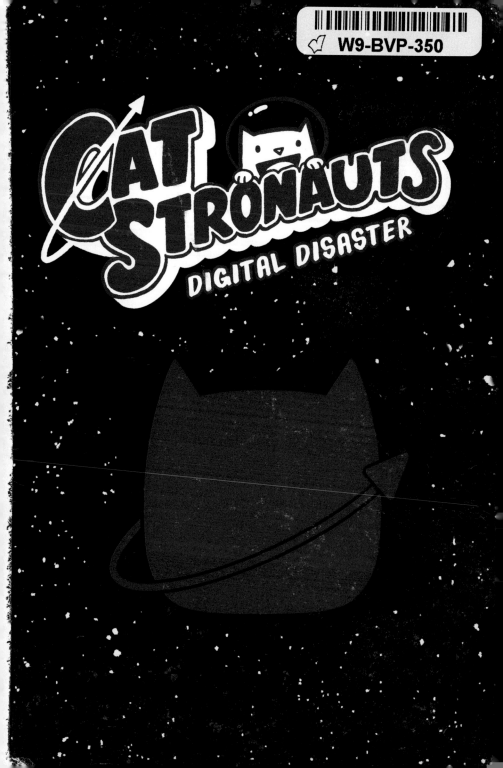

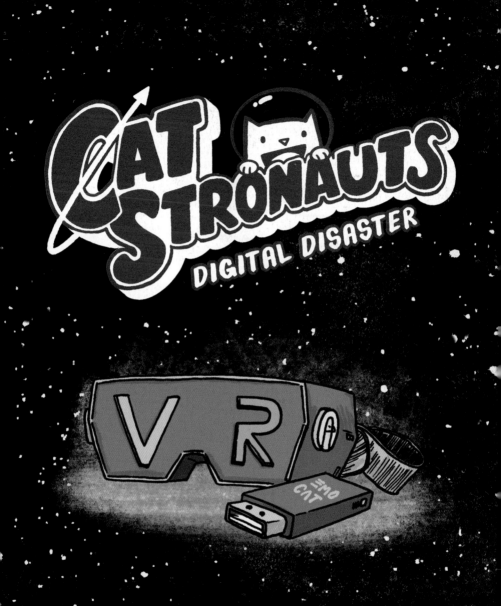

CatStronauts

Digital Disaster

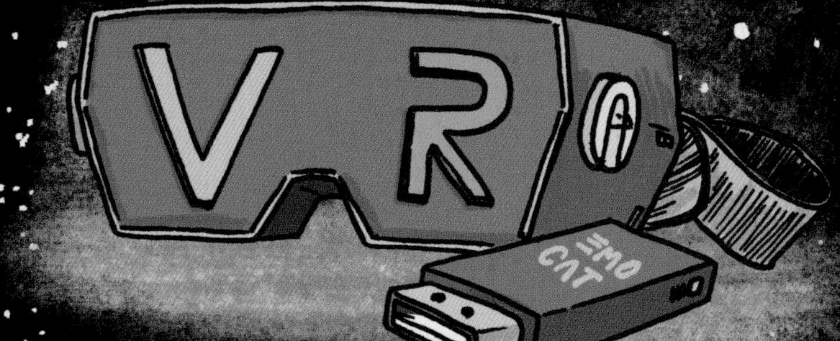
VR
EMO CAT

BY DREW BROCKINGTON

LB
Little, Brown and Company
New York Boston

About This Book

This book was edited by Russ Busse and designed by Ching Chan. The production was supervised by Erika Schwartz, and the production editor was Lindsay Walter-Greaney. The text was set in Brockington, and the display type is Brockington.

Little, Brown and Company
Hachette Book Group
1290 Avenue of the Americas, New York, NY 10104
Visit us at LBYR.com

First Edition: August 2020

Little, Brown and Company is a division of Hachette Book Group, Inc.
The Little, Brown name and logo are trademarks of Hachette Book Group, Inc.

The publisher is not responsible for websites (or their content) that are not owned by the publisher.

Library of Congress Control Number: 2019021967

ISBNs: 978-0-316-45132-1 (hardcover), 978-0-316-45127-7 (pbk.),
978-0-316-45130-7 (ebook), 978-0-316-45129-1 (ebook),
978-0-316-45128-4 (ebook)

Printed in China

1010

Hardcover: 10 9 8 7 6 5 4 3 2
Paperback: 10 9 8 7 6 5 4

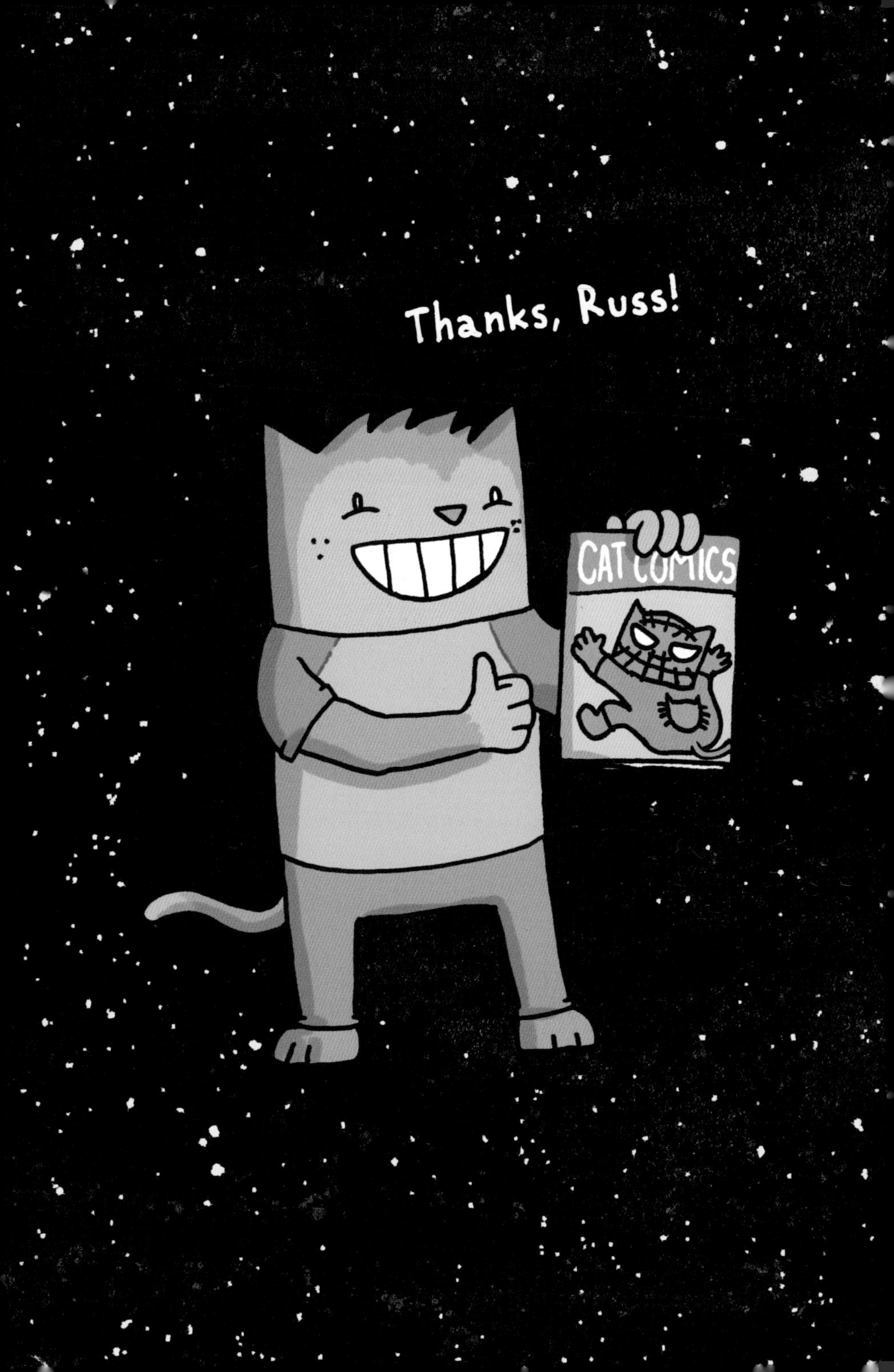
Thanks, Russ!
CAT COMICS

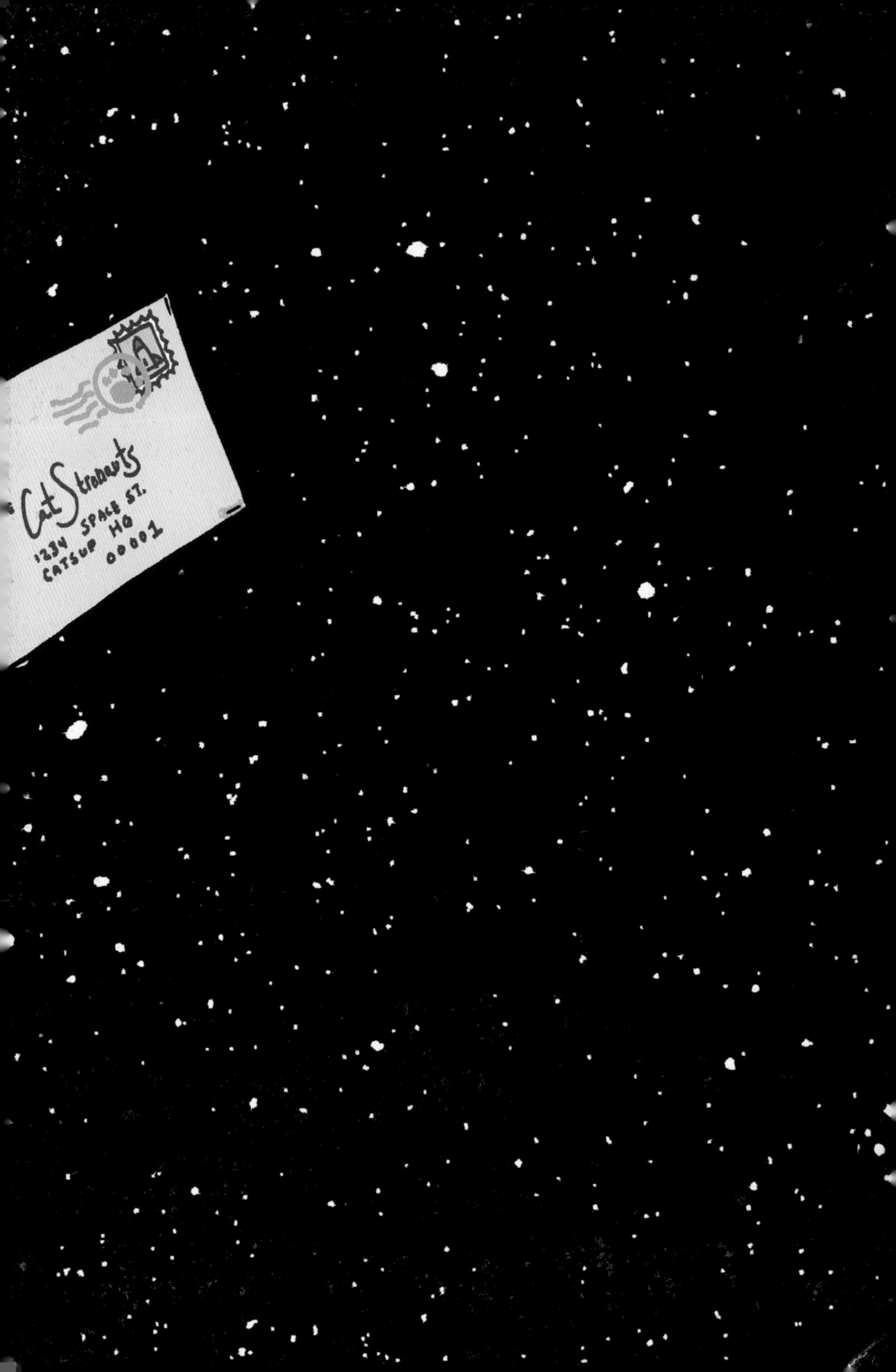
CatStronauts
1234 SPACE ST.
CATSUP HQ
00001

CHAPTER 1

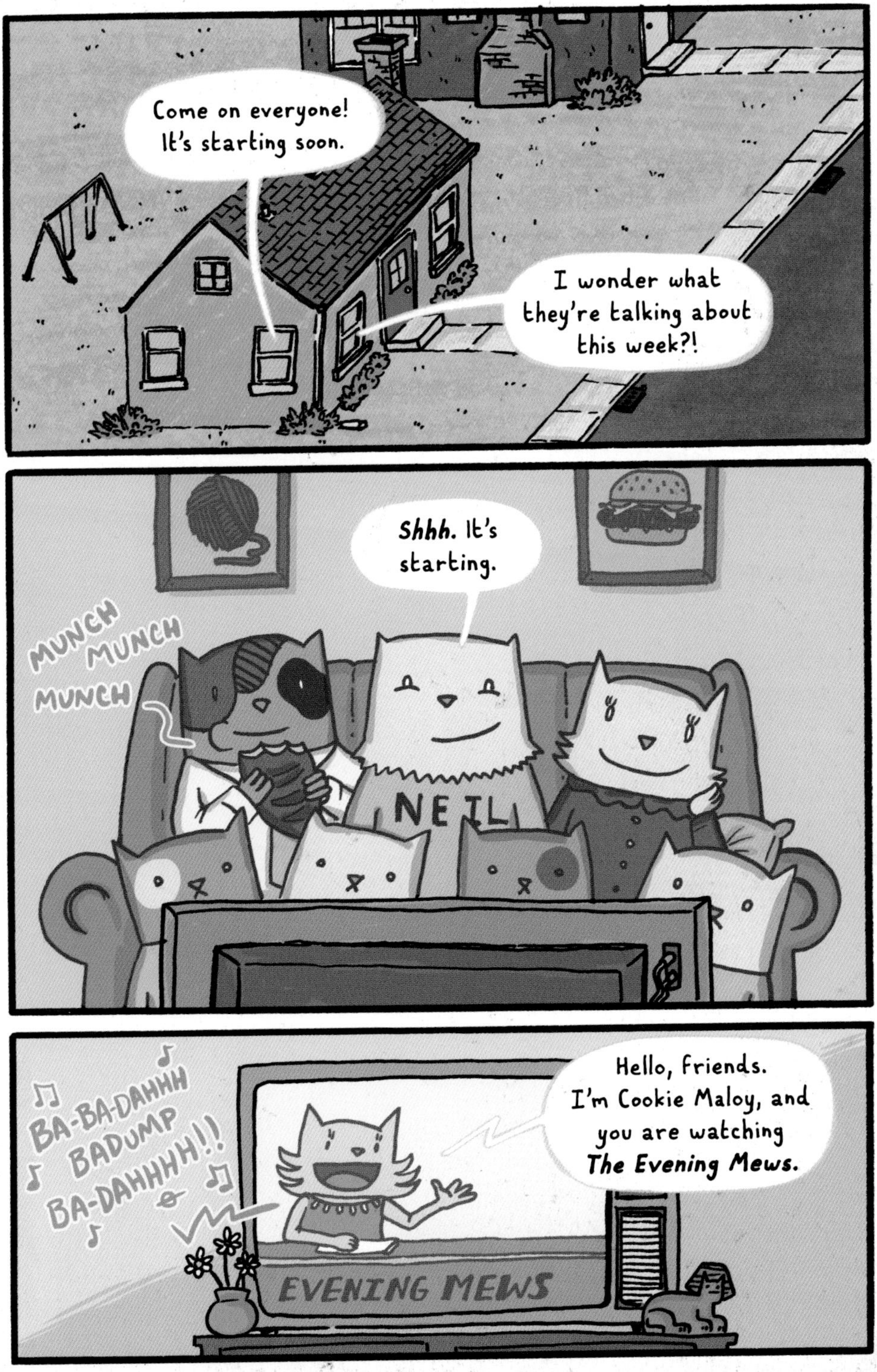
Come on everyone! It's starting soon.
I wonder what they're talking about this week?!
Shhh. It's starting.
MUNCH MUNCH MUNCH
NEIL
BA-BA-DAHHH BADUMP BA-DAHHHH!!
Hello, friends. I'm Cookie Maloy, and you are watching The Evening Mews.
EVENING MEWS

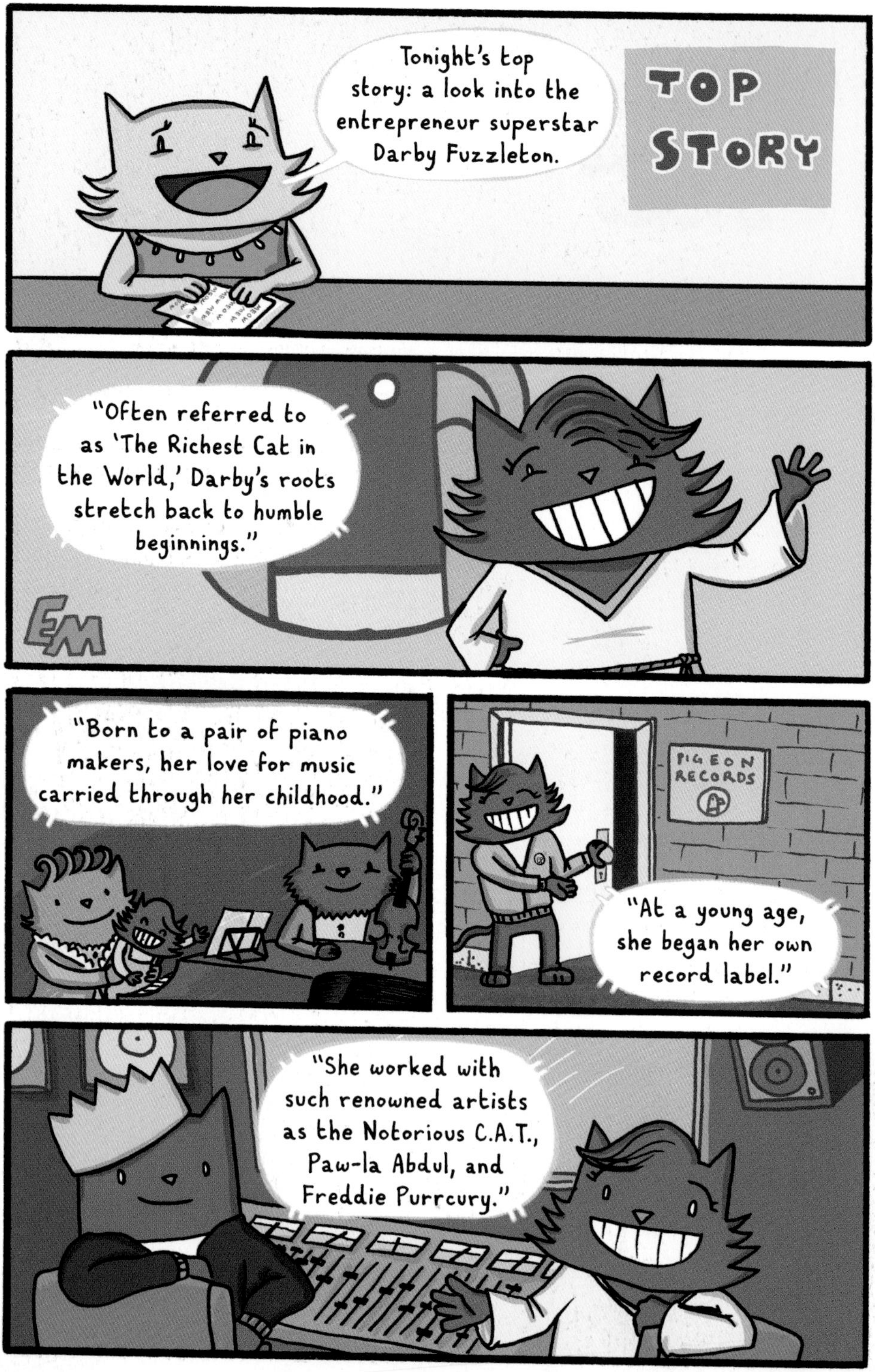
Tonight's top story: a look into the entrepreneur superstar Darby Fuzzleton.
TOP STORY
"Often referred to as 'The Richest Cat in the World,' Darby's roots stretch back to humble beginnings."
"Born to a pair of piano makers, her love for music carried through her childhood."
PIGEON RECORDS
"At a young age, she began her own record label."
"She worked with such renowned artists as the Notorious C.A.T., Paw-la Abdul, and Freddie Purrcury."

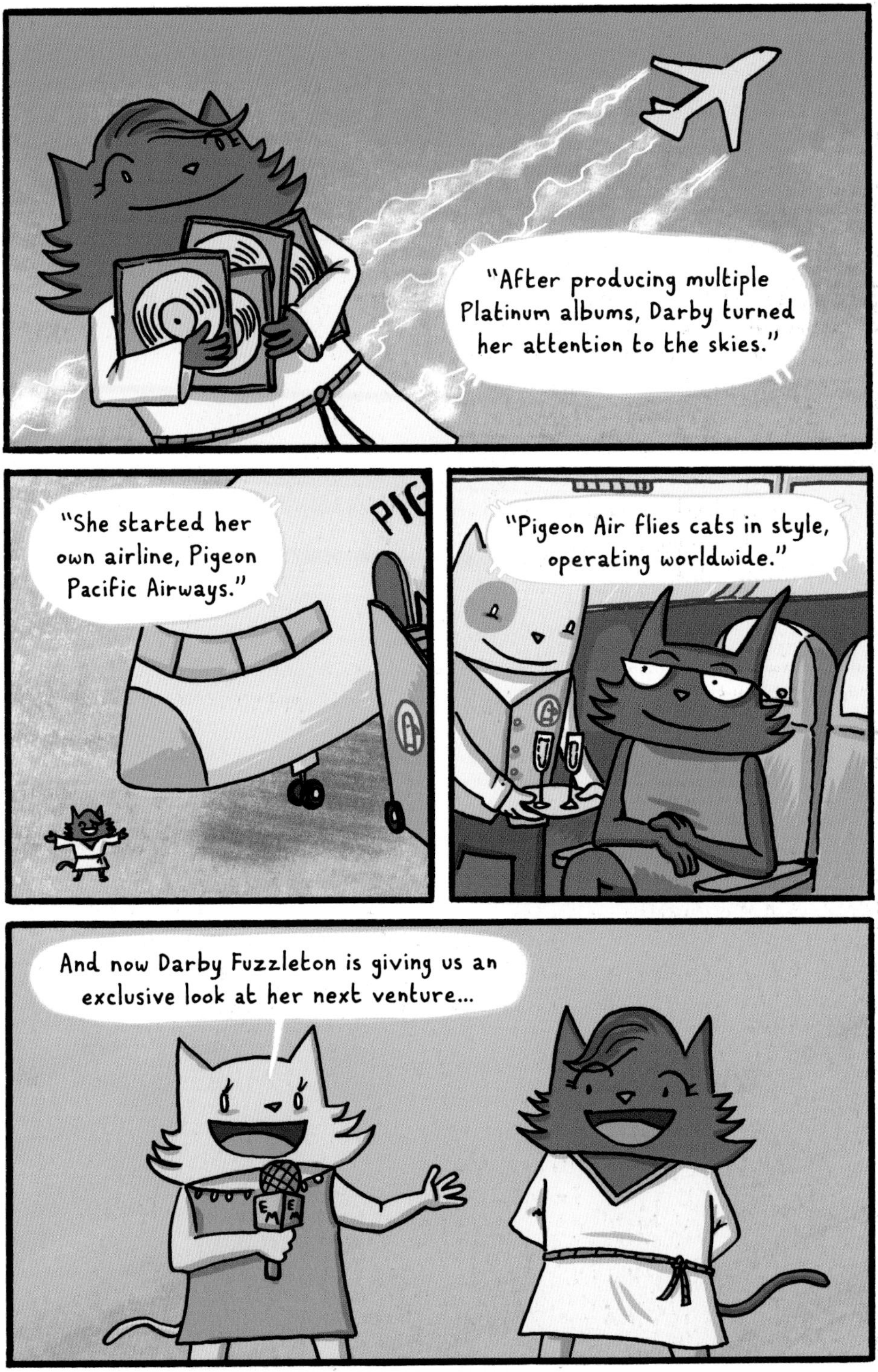
"After producing multiple Platinum albums, Darby turned her attention to the skies."
"She started her own airline, Pigeon Pacific Airways."
PIG
"Pigeon Air flies cats in style, operating worldwide."
And now Darby Fuzzleton is giving us an exclusive look at her next venture...

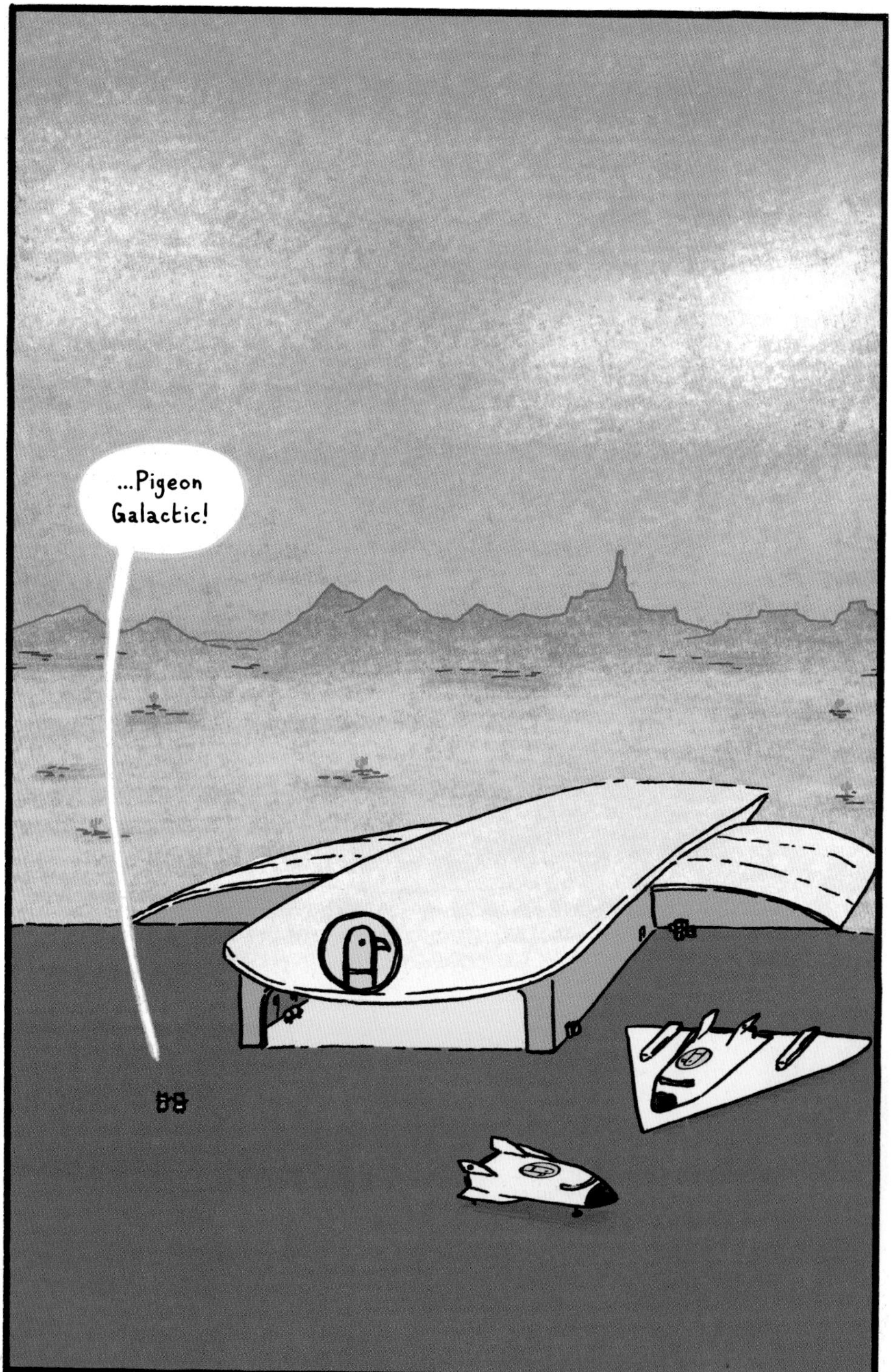
...Pigeon Galactic!

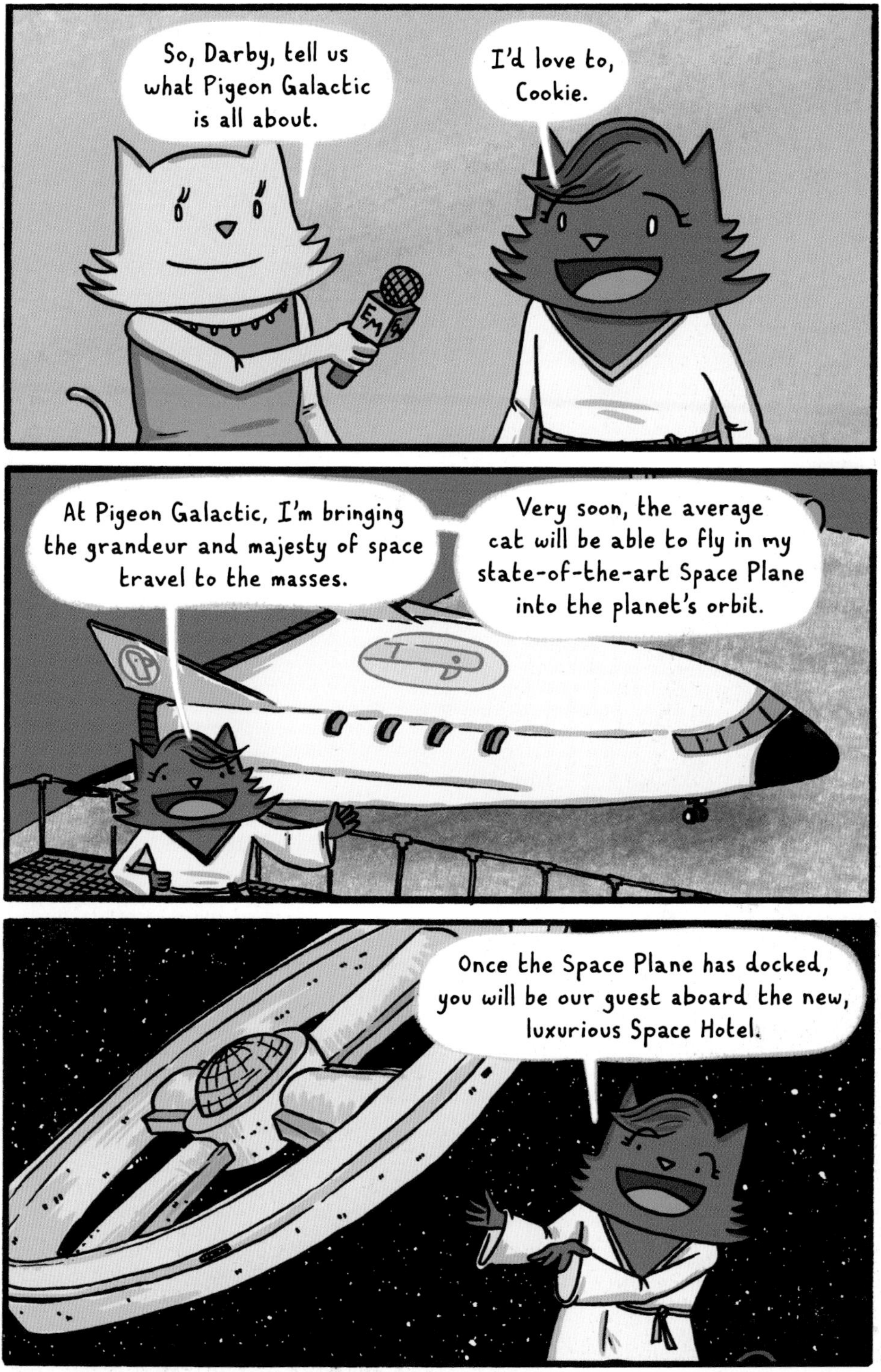
So, Darby, tell us what Pigeon Galactic is all about.
I'd love to, Cookie.
At Pigeon Galactic, I'm bringing the grandeur and majesty of space travel to the masses.
Very soon, the average cat will be able to fly in my state-of-the-art Space Plane into the planet's orbit.
Once the Space Plane has docked, you will be our guest aboard the new, luxurious Space Hotel.

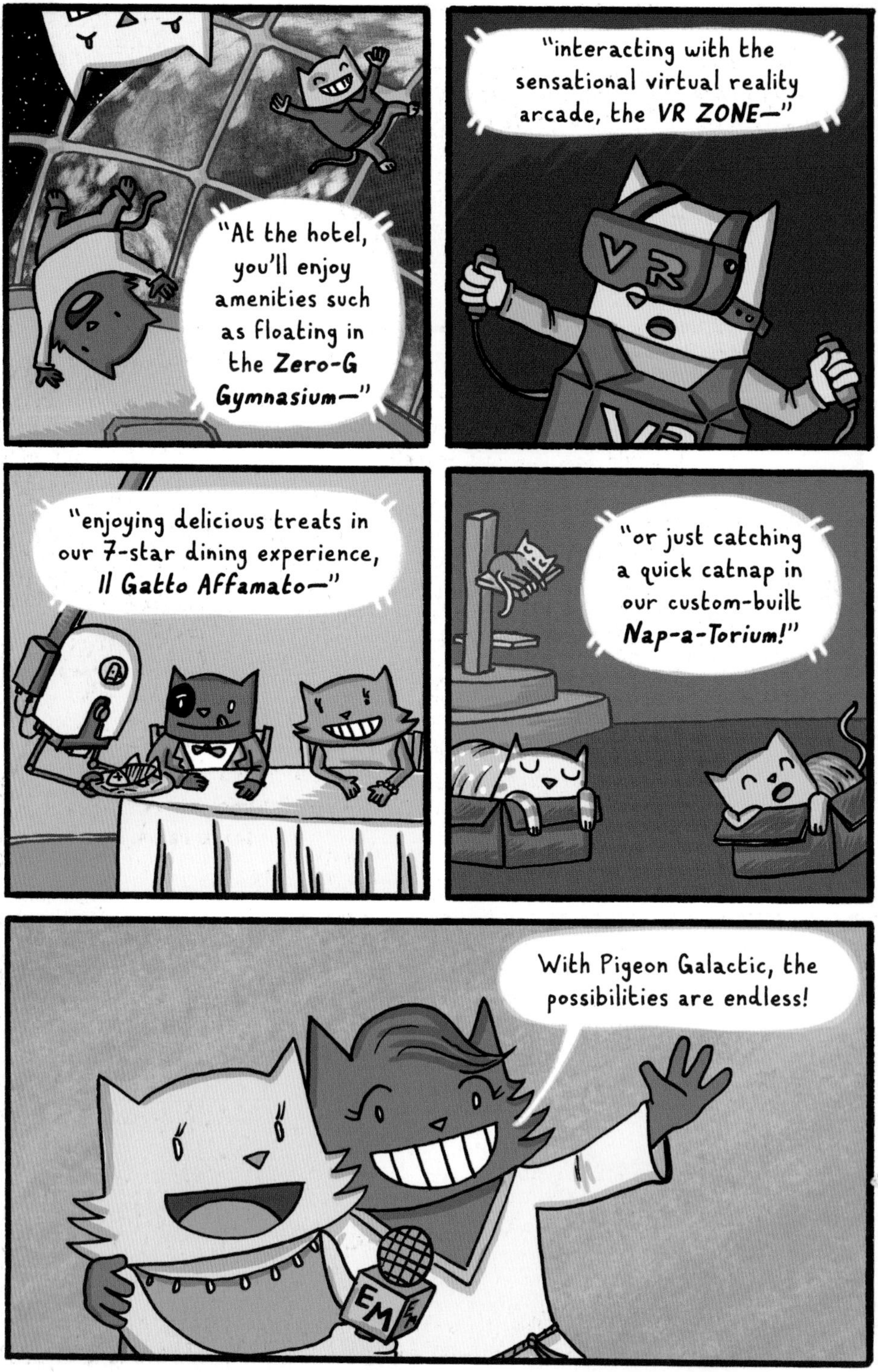
"At the hotel, you'll enjoy amenities such as floating in the **Zero-G Gymnasium**—"
"interacting with the sensational virtual reality arcade, the ***VR ZONE***—"
VR
"enjoying delicious treats in our 7-star dining experience, ***Il Gatto Affamato***—"
"or just catching a quick catnap in our custom-built ***Nap-a-Torium!***"
With Pigeon Galactic, the possibilities are endless!
EM

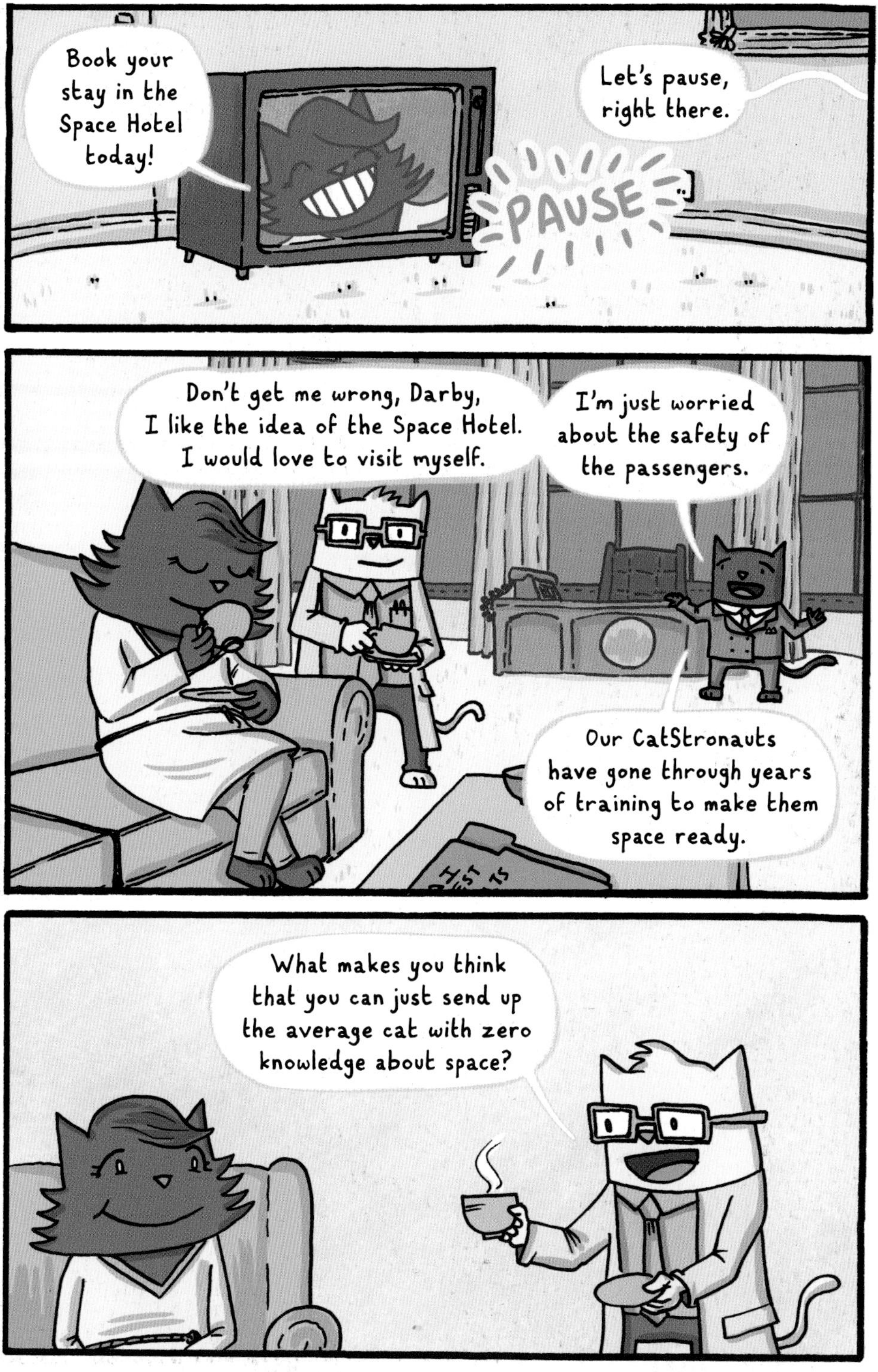
Book your stay in the Space Hotel today!
Let's pause, right there.
PAUSE
Don't get me wrong, Darby, I like the idea of the Space Hotel. I would love to visit myself.
I'm just worried about the safety of the passengers.
Our CatStronauts have gone through years of training to make them space ready.
What makes you think that you can just send up the average cat with zero knowledge about space?

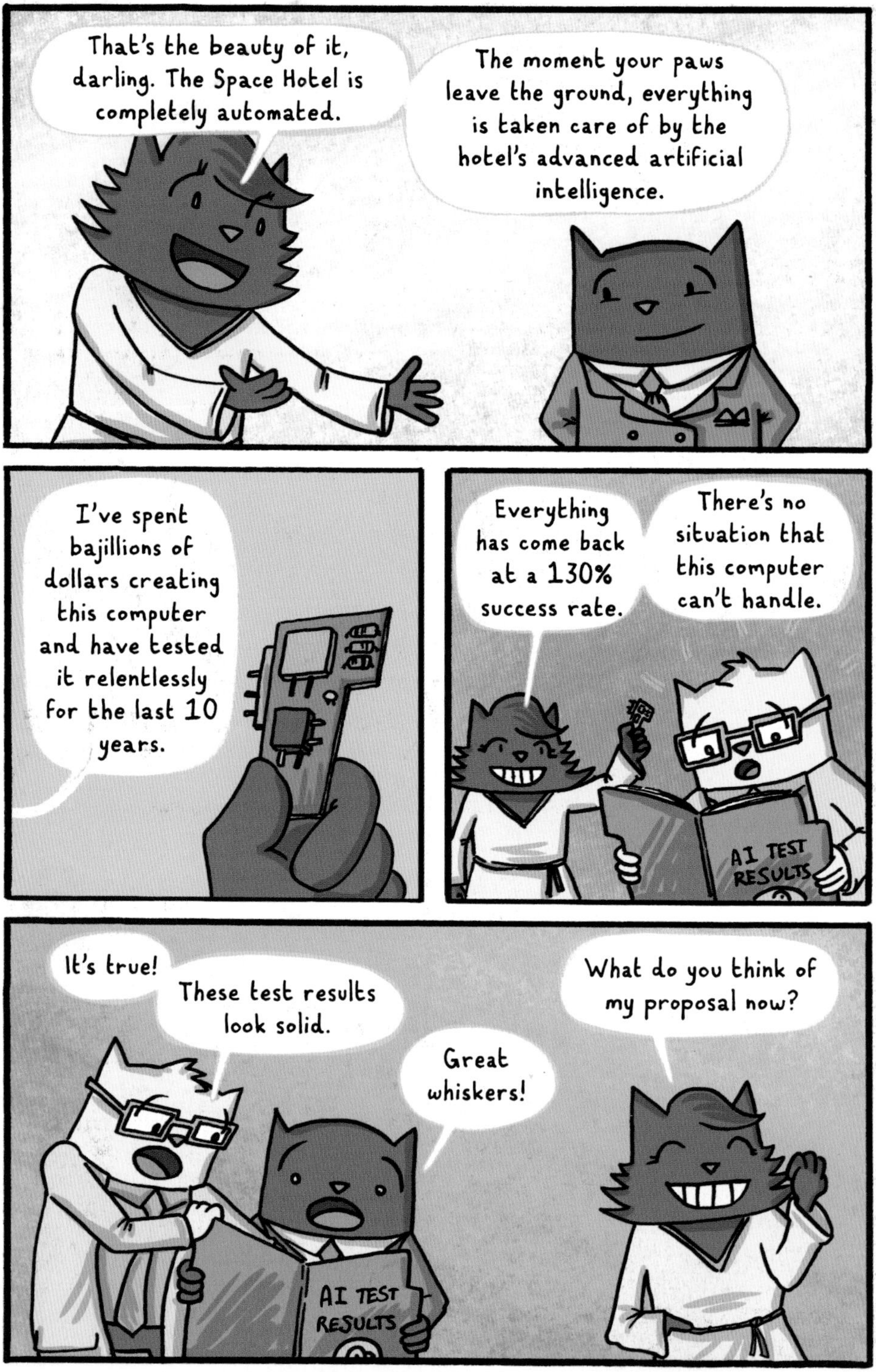
That's the beauty of it, darling. The Space Hotel is completely automated.
The moment your paws leave the ground, everything is taken care of by the hotel's advanced artificial intelligence.
I've spent bajillions of dollars creating this computer and have tested it relentlessly for the last 10 years.
Everything has come back at a 130% success rate.
There's no situation that this computer can't handle.
AI TEST RESULTS
It's true!
These test results look solid.
Great whiskers!
What do you think of my proposal now?
AI TEST RESULTS

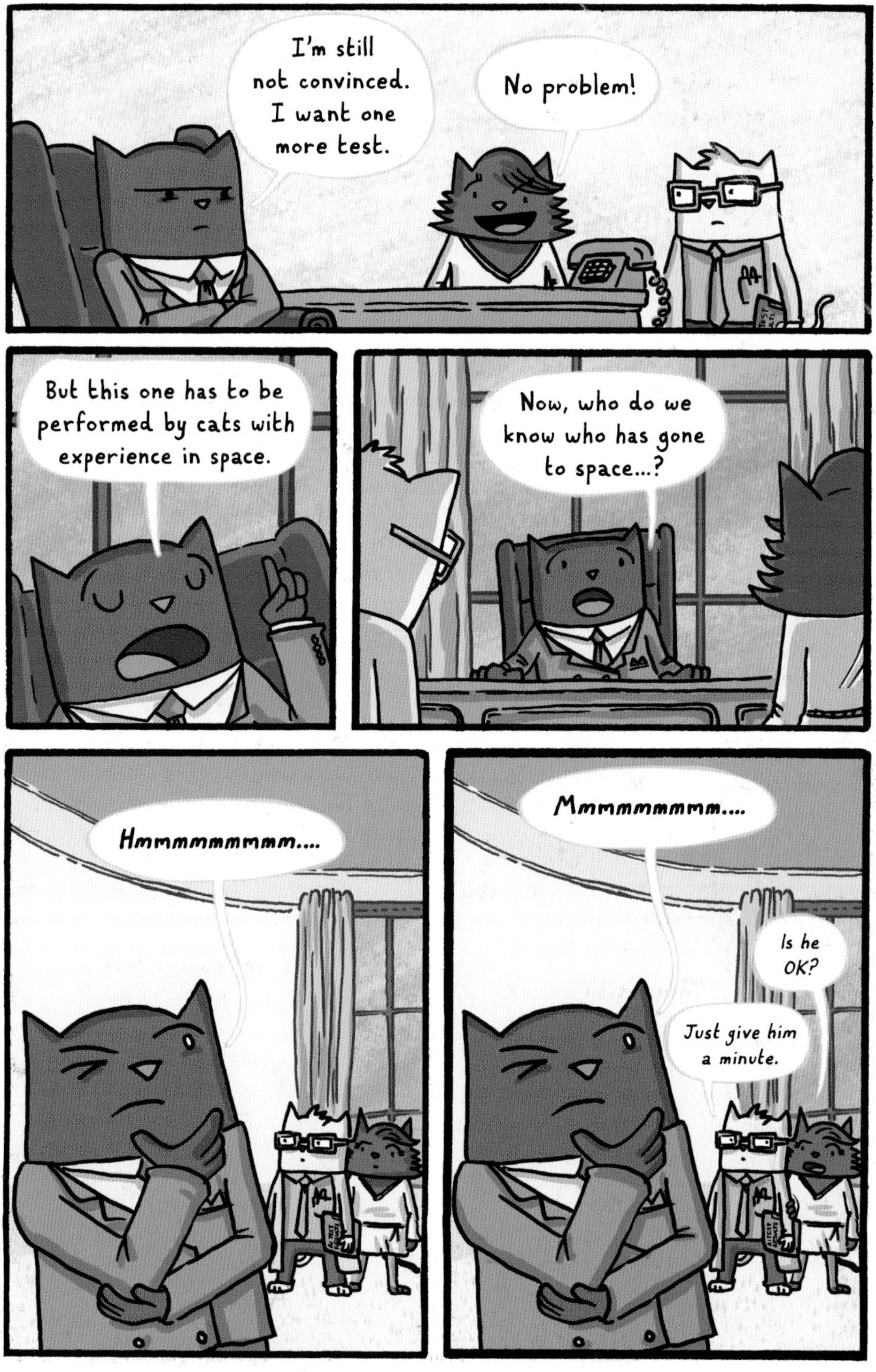
I'm still not convinced. I want one more test.
No problem!
But this one has to be performed by cats with experience in space.
Now, who do we know who has gone to space...?
Hmmmmmmmmm....
Mmmmmmmmm....
Is he OK?
Just give him a minute.

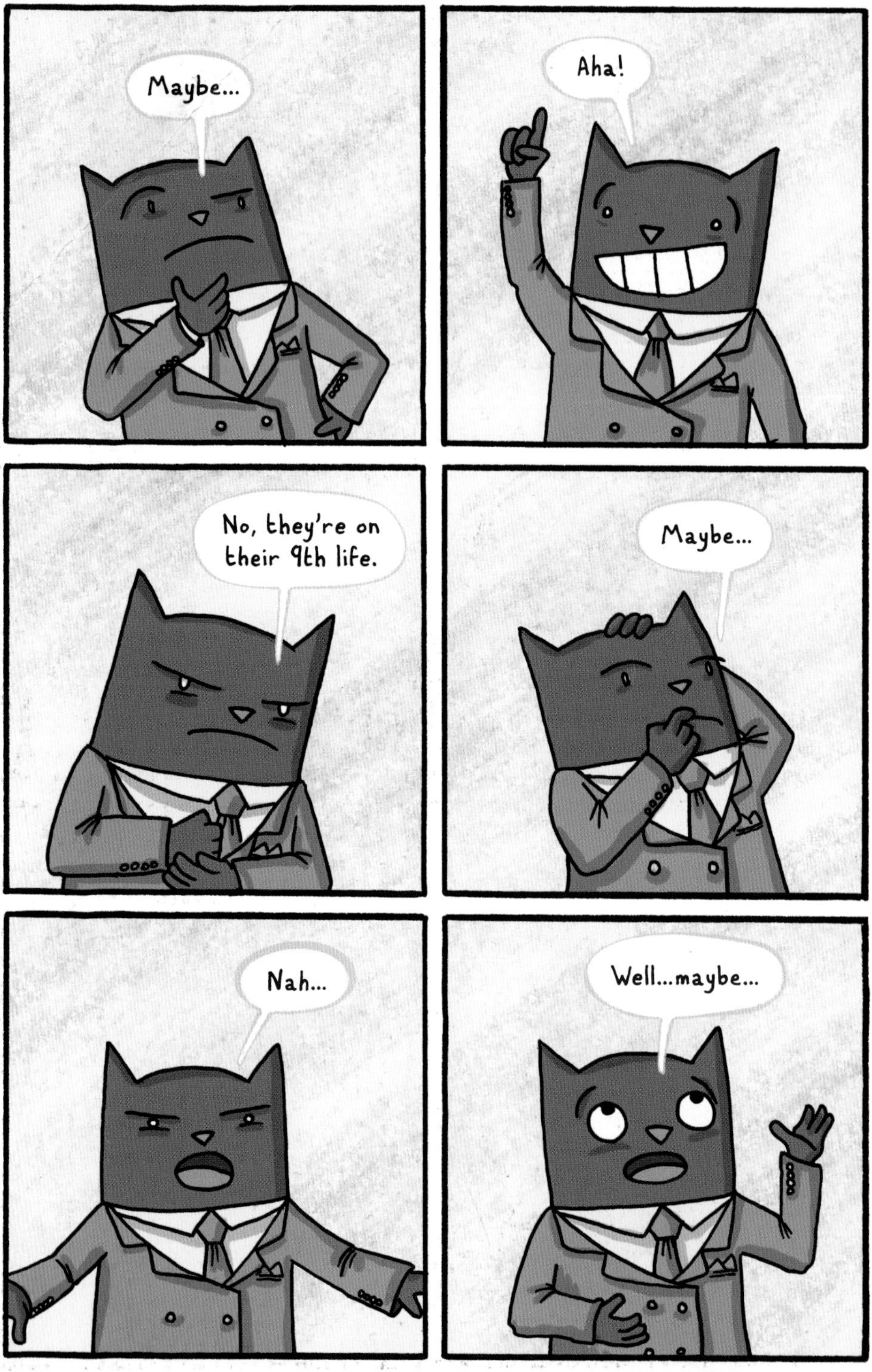
Maybe...
Aha!
No, they're on their 9th life.
Maybe...
Nah...
Well...maybe...

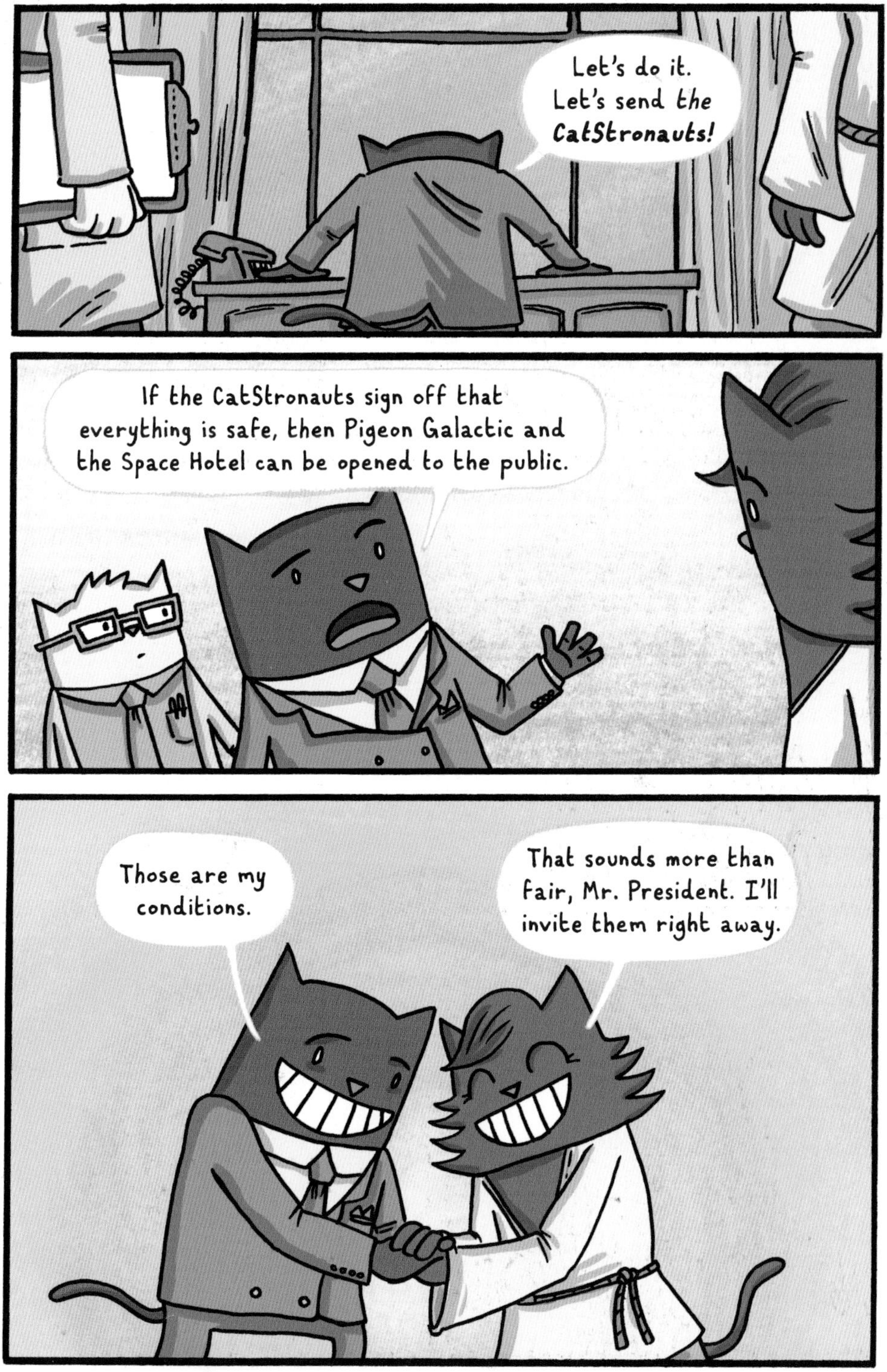
Let's do it. Let's send *the* **CatStronauts!**
If the CatStronauts sign off that everything is safe, then Pigeon Galactic and the Space Hotel can be opened to the public.
Those are my conditions.
That sounds more than fair, Mr. President. I'll invite them right away.

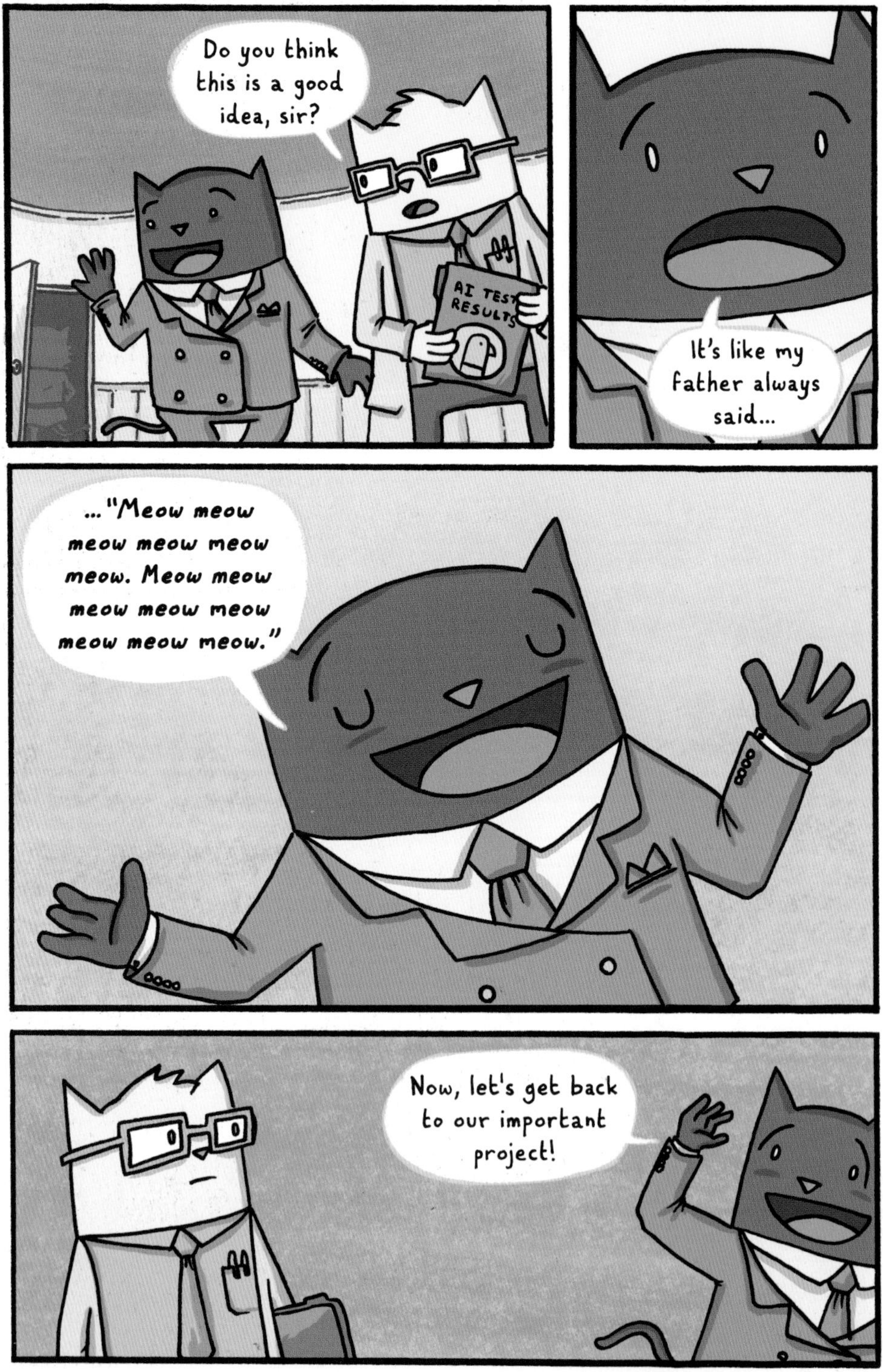
Do you think this is a good idea, sir?
AI TEST RESULTS
It's like my father always said...
..."Meow meow meow meow meow meow. Meow meow meow meow meow meow meow meow."
Now, let's get back to our important project!

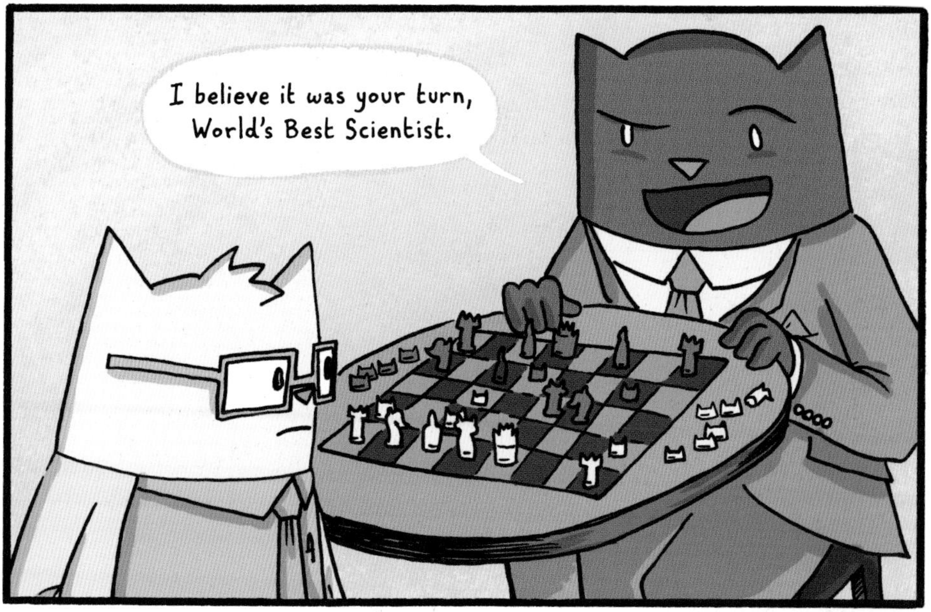
I believe it was your turn, World's Best Scientist.

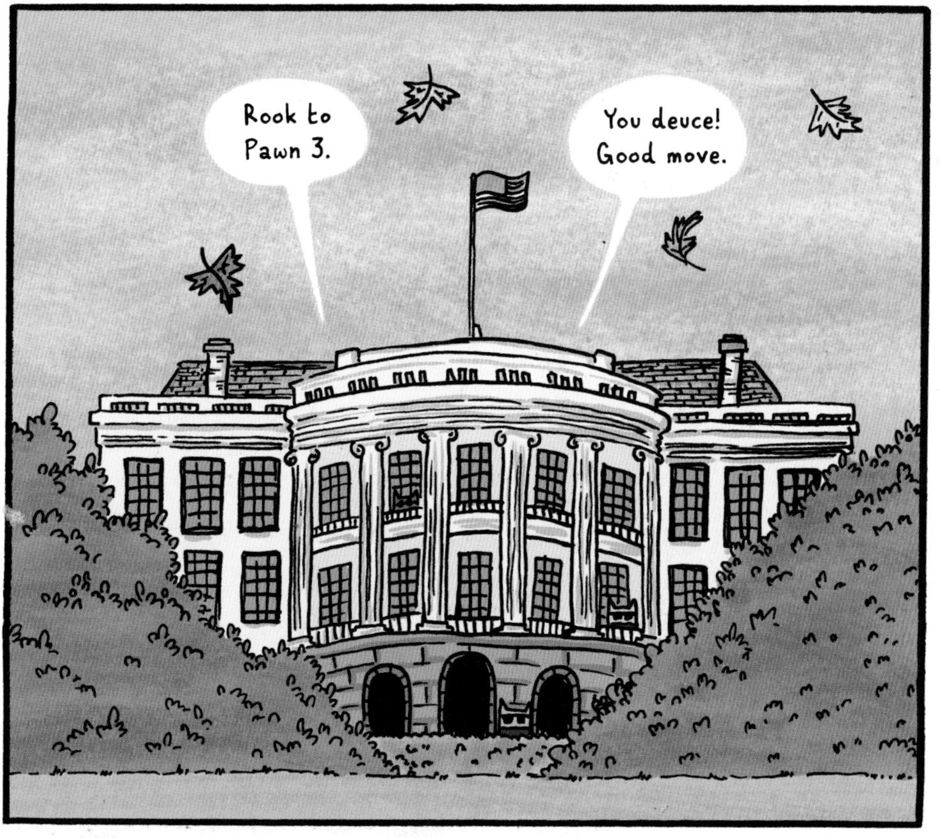
Rook to Pawn 3.
You deuce! Good move.

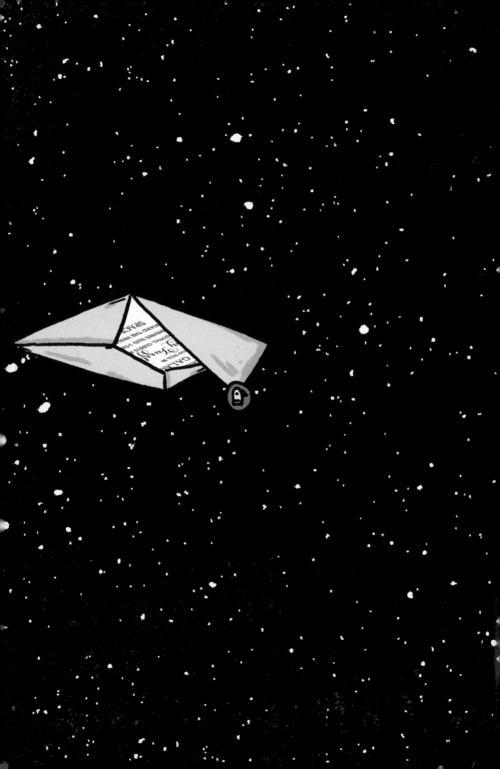

CHAPTER 2

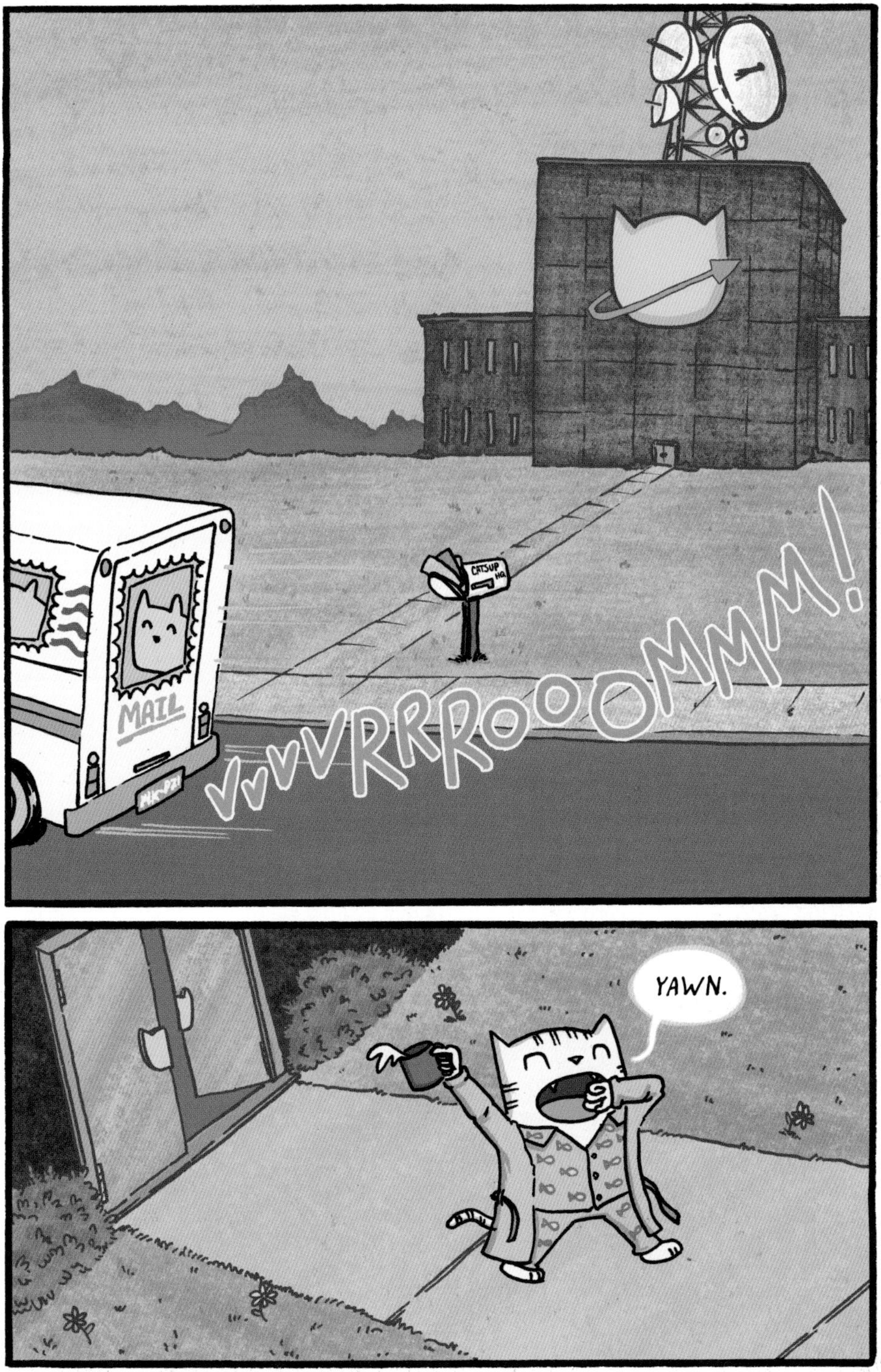
CATSUP HQ
MAIL
VVVVRRROOOOMMMM!
YAWN.

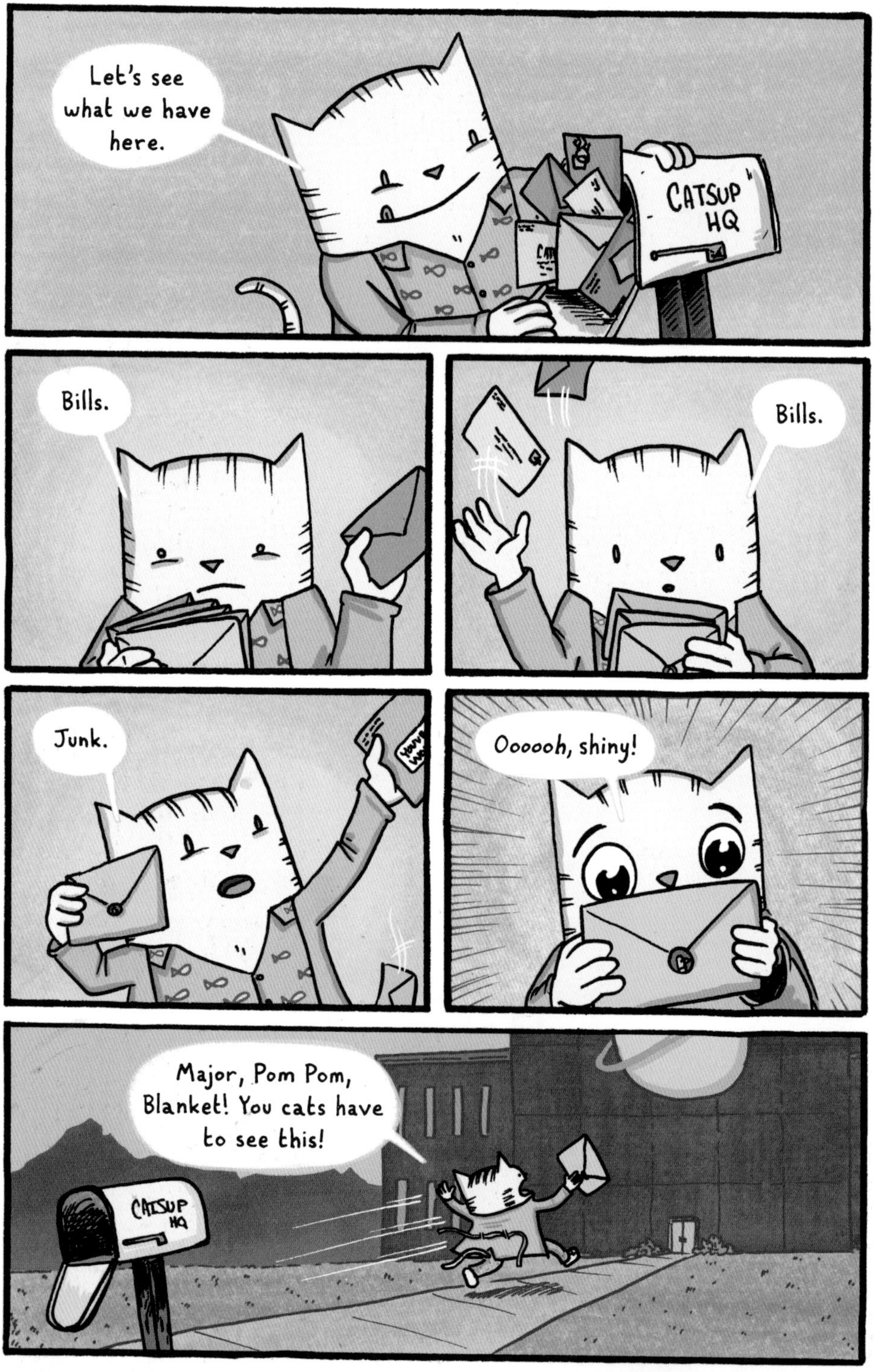
Let's see what we have here.
CATSUP HQ
Bills.
Bills.
Junk.
Oooooh, shiny!
Major, Pom Pom, Blanket! You cats have to see this!
CATSUP HQ

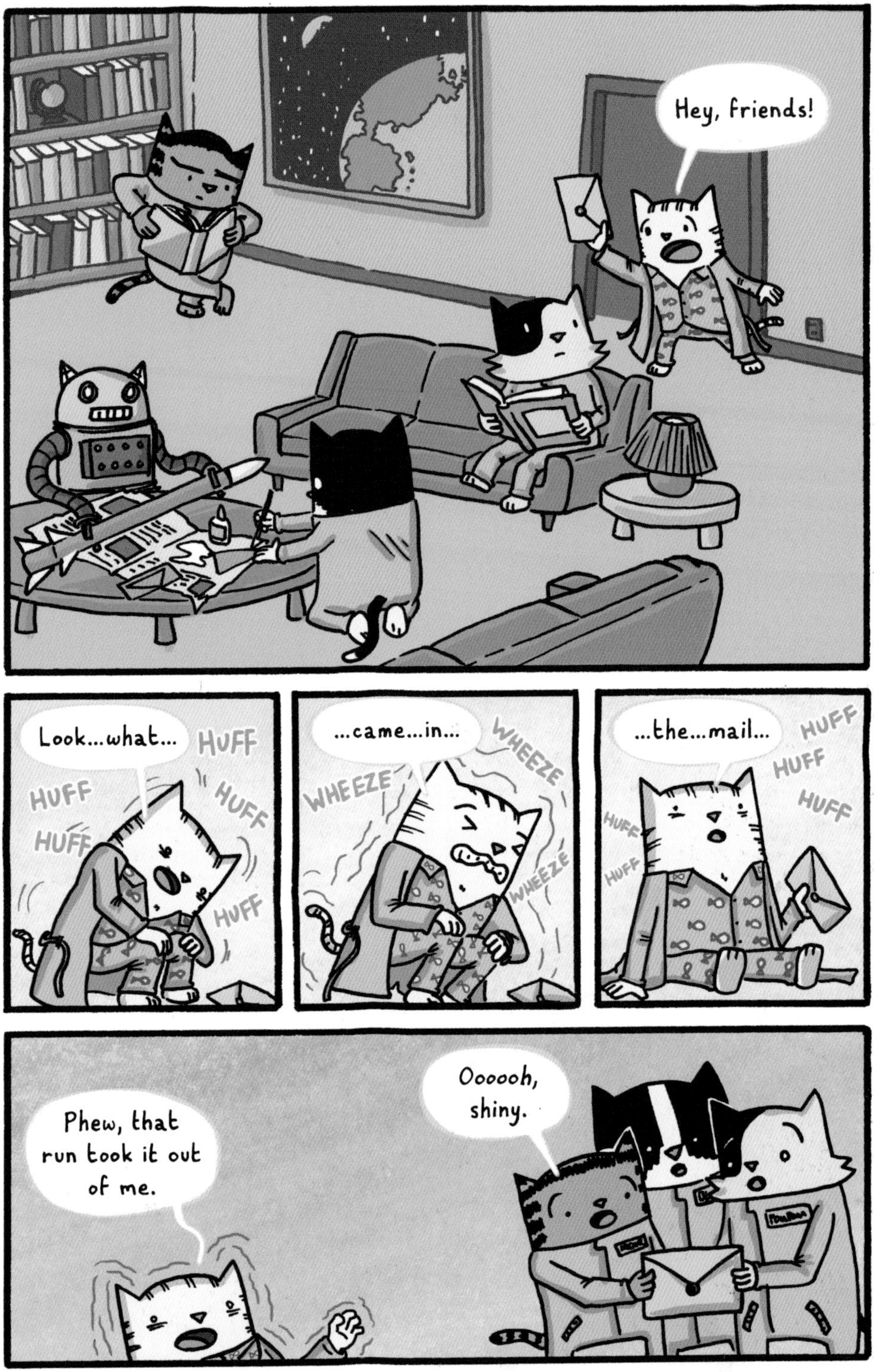
Hey, friends!
Look...what...
HUFF
HUFF
HUFF
HUFF
HUFF
...came...in...
WHEEZE
WHEEZE
WHEEZE
...the...mail...
HUFF
HUFF
HUFF
HUFF
HUFF
Phew, that run took it out of me.
Oooooh, shiny.

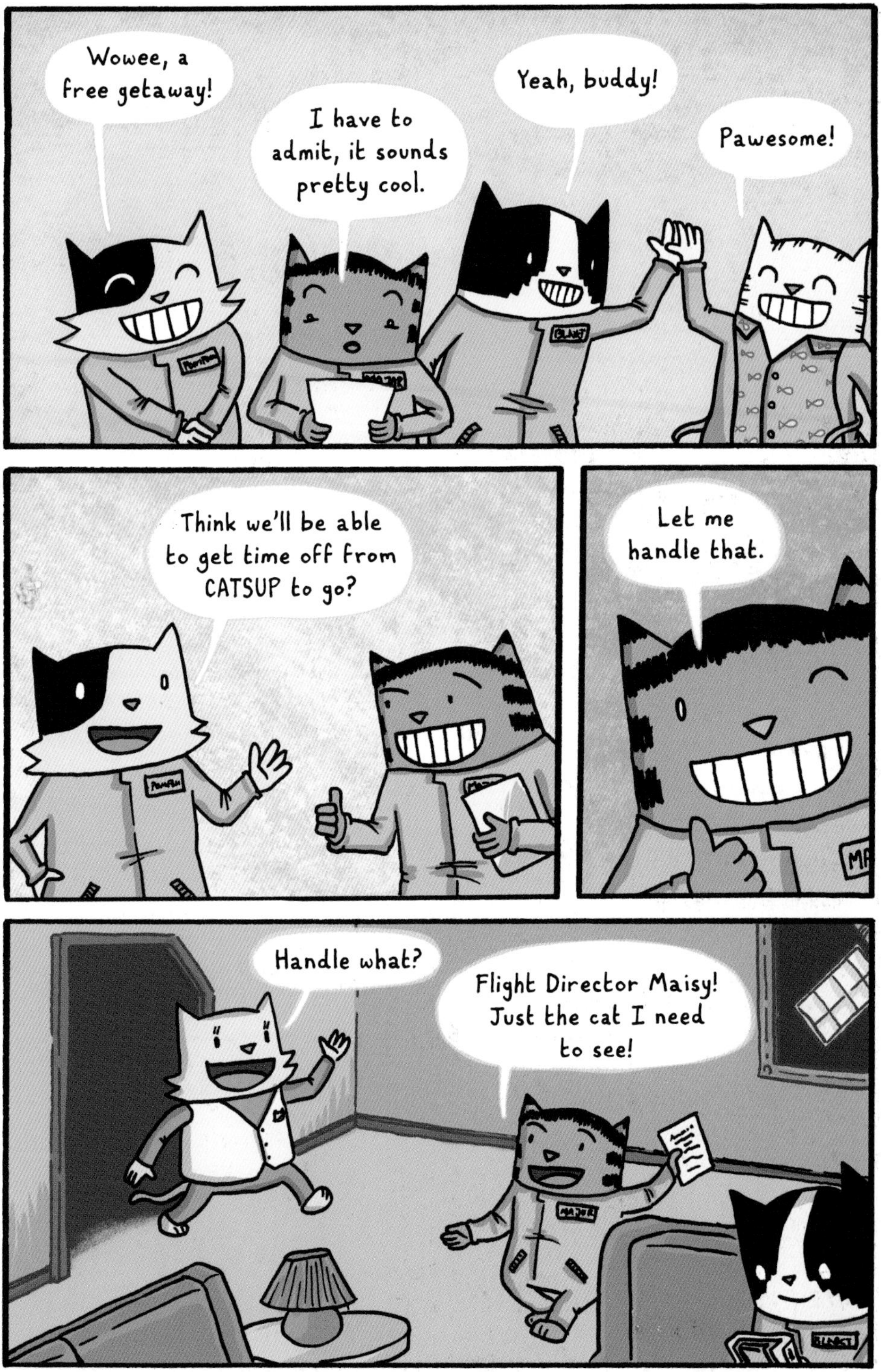
Wowee, a free getaway!
I have to admit, it sounds pretty cool.
Yeah, buddy!
Pawesome!
Think we'll be able to get time off from CATSUP to go?
Let me handle that.
Handle what?
Flight Director Maisy! Just the cat I need to see!

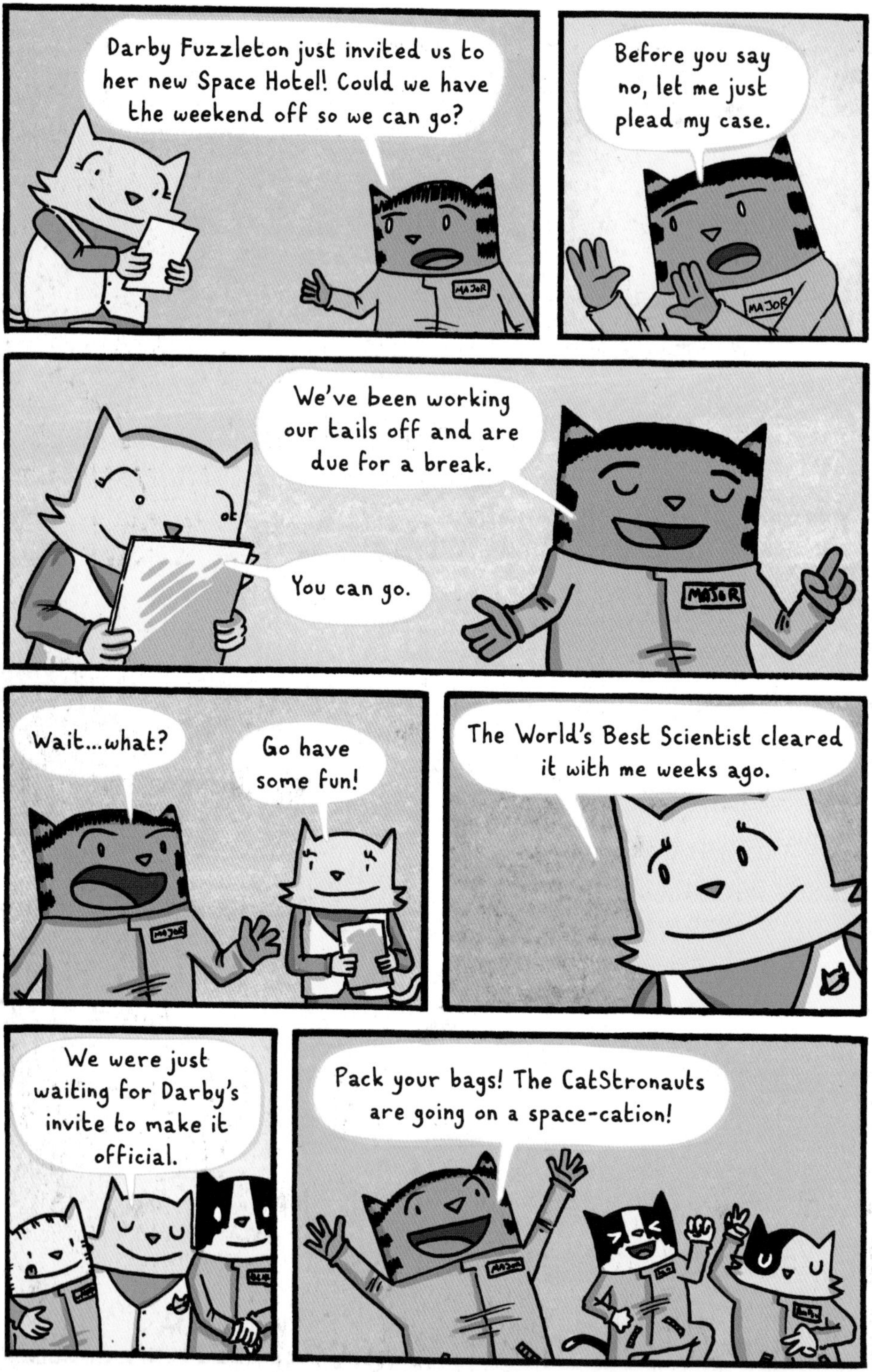
Darby Fuzzleton just invited us to her new Space Hotel! Could we have the weekend off so we can go?
Before you say no, let me just plead my case.
We've been working our tails off and are due for a break.
You can go.
Wait...what?
Go have some fun!
The World's Best Scientist cleared it with me weeks ago.
We were just waiting for Darby's invite to make it official.
Pack your bags! The CatStronauts are going on a space-cation!

THREE DAYS LATER.

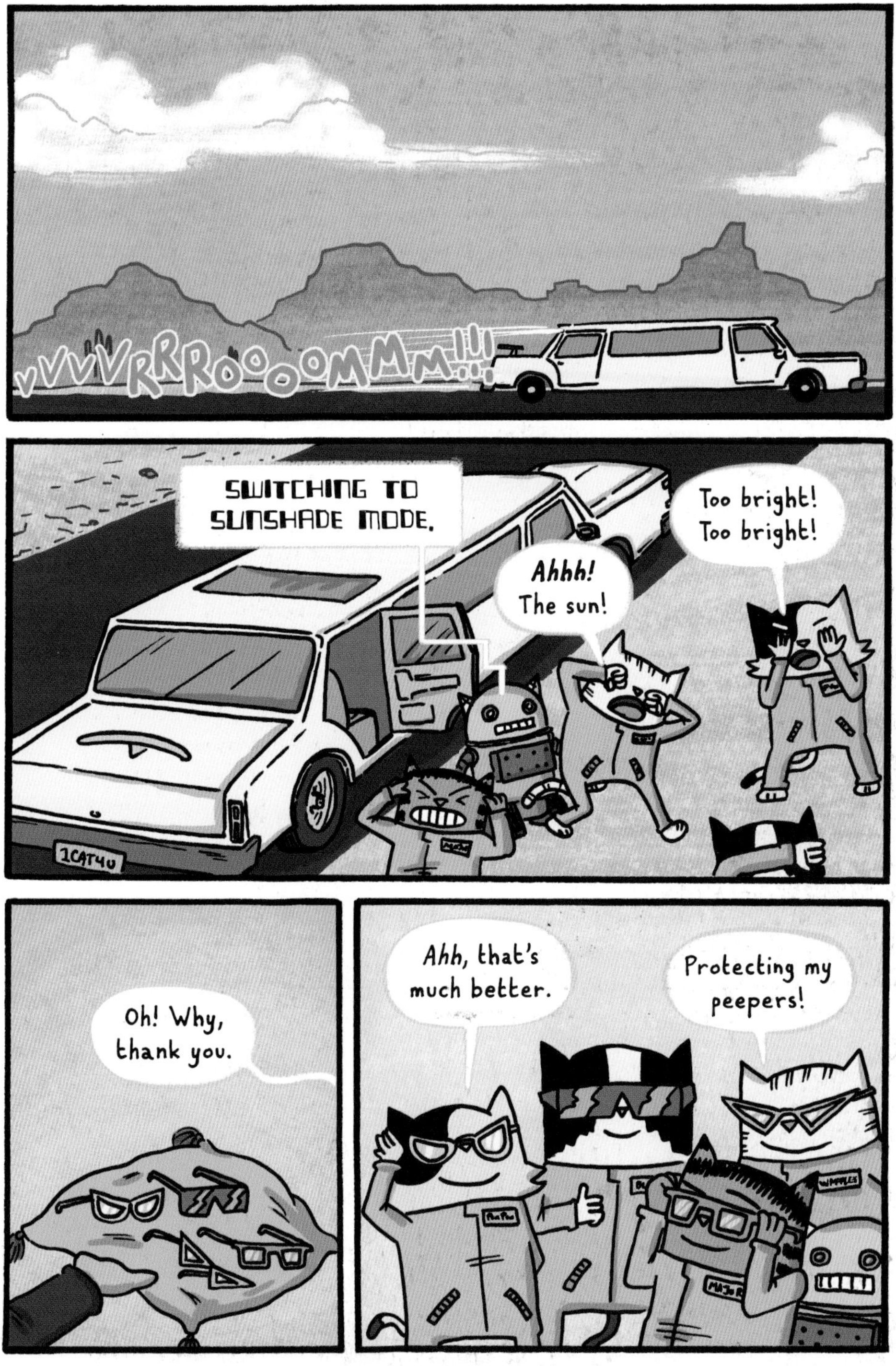
VVVVRRROOOOOMMM!!!
SWITCHING TO SUNSHADE MODE.
Ahhh! The sun!
Too bright! Too bright!
1CAT4U
Oh! Why, thank you.
Ahh, that's much better.
Protecting my peepers!

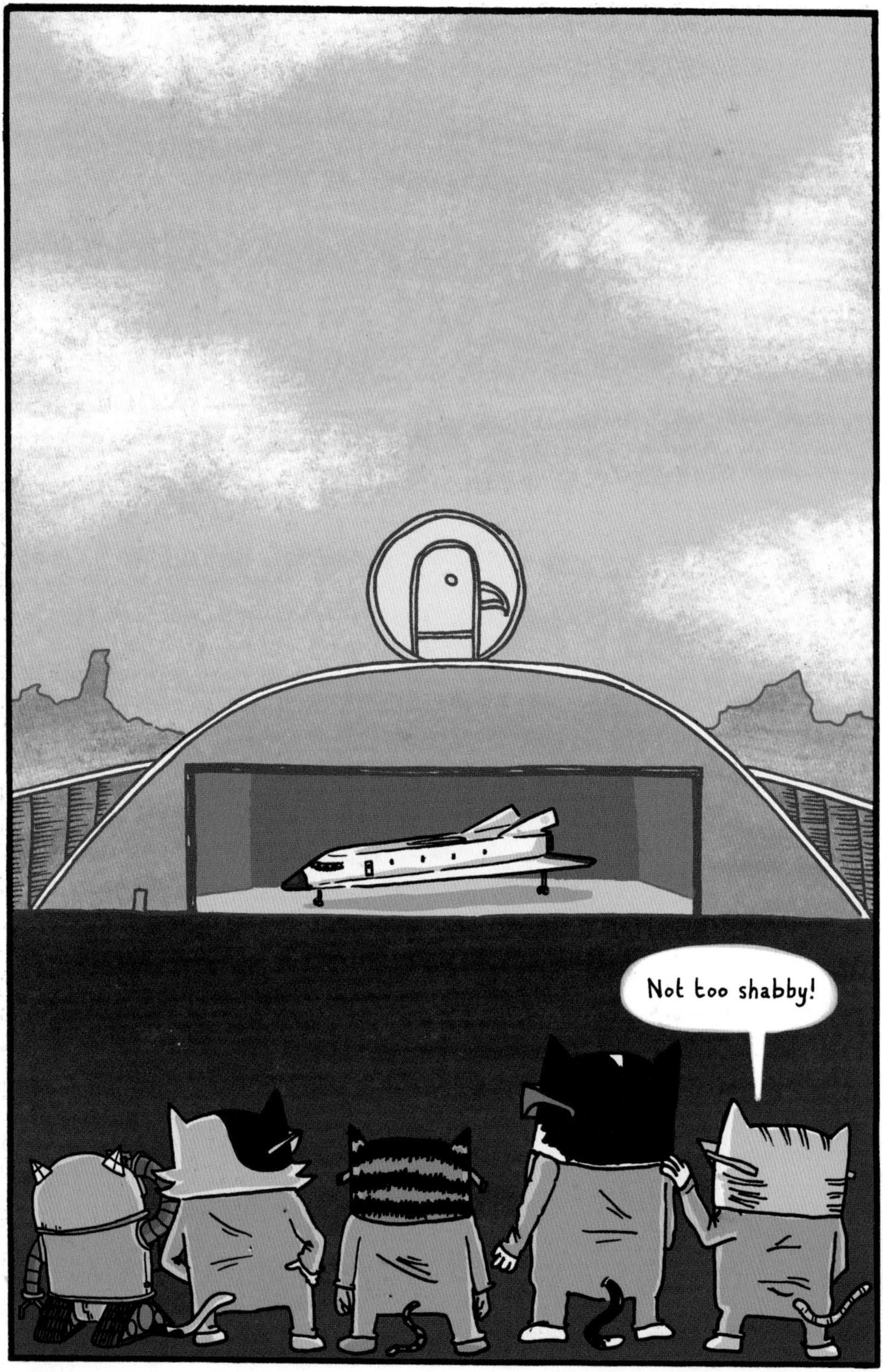
Not too shabby!

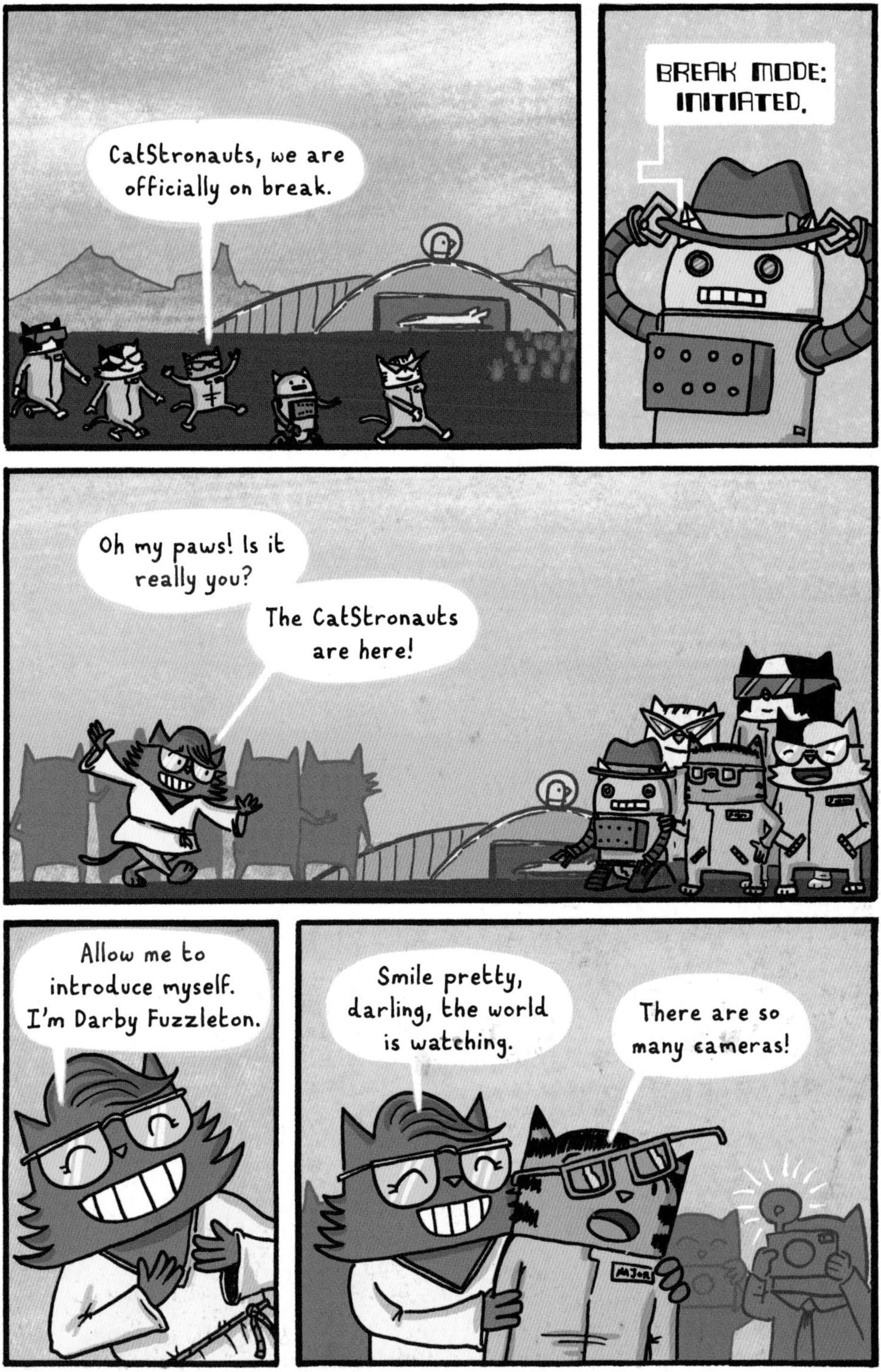

CatStronauts, we are officially on break.
BREAK MODE: INITIATED.
Oh my paws! Is it really you?
The CatStronauts are here!
Allow me to introduce myself. I'm Darby Fuzzleton.
Smile pretty, darling, the world is watching.
There are so many cameras!

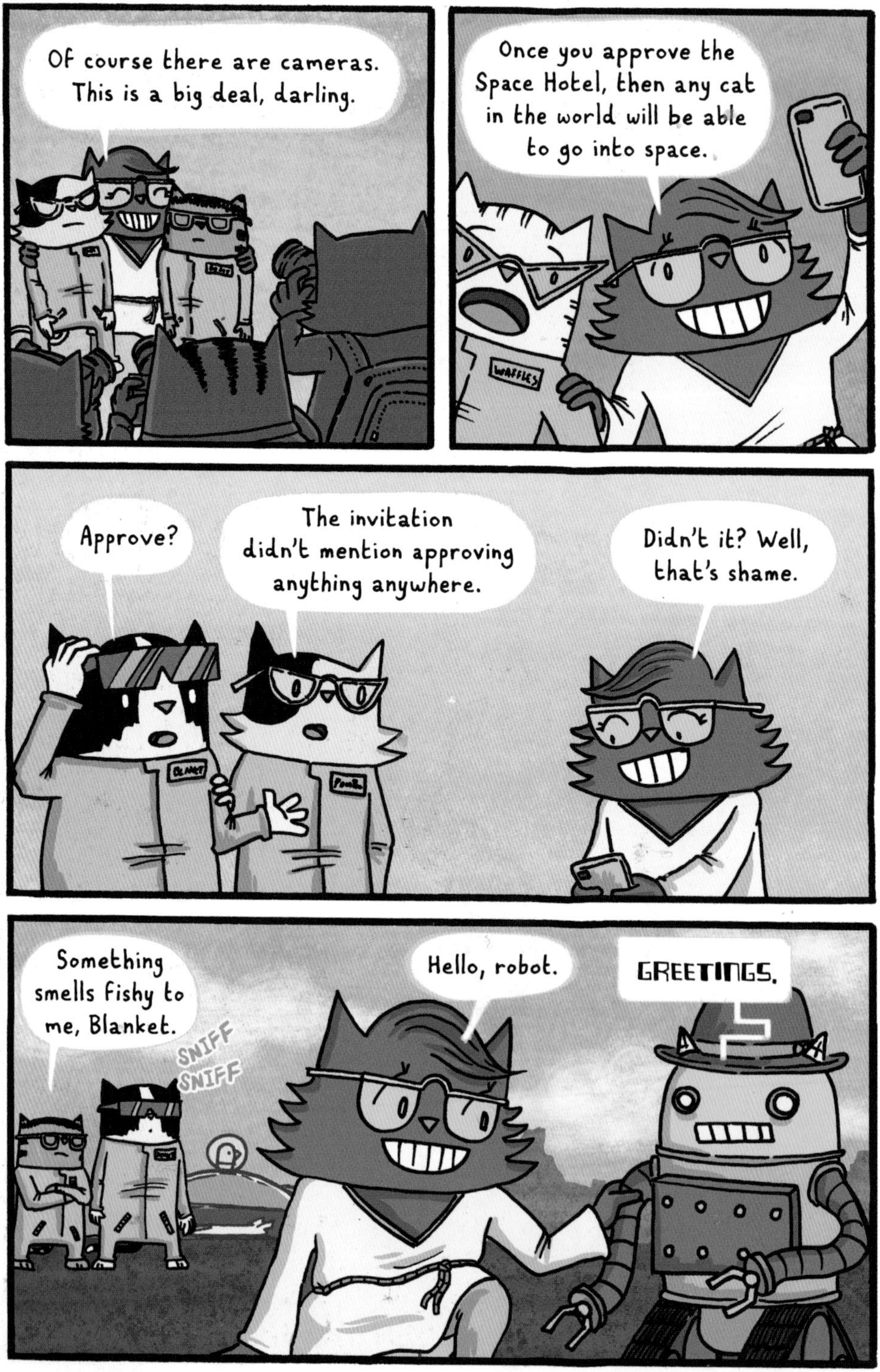
Of course there are cameras. This is a big deal, darling.
Once you approve the Space Hotel, then any cat in the world will be able to go into space.
WAFFLES
Approve?
The invitation didn't mention approving anything anywhere.
Didn't it? Well, that's shame.
Something smells fishy to me, Blanket.
SNIFF SNIFF
Hello, robot.
GREETINGS.

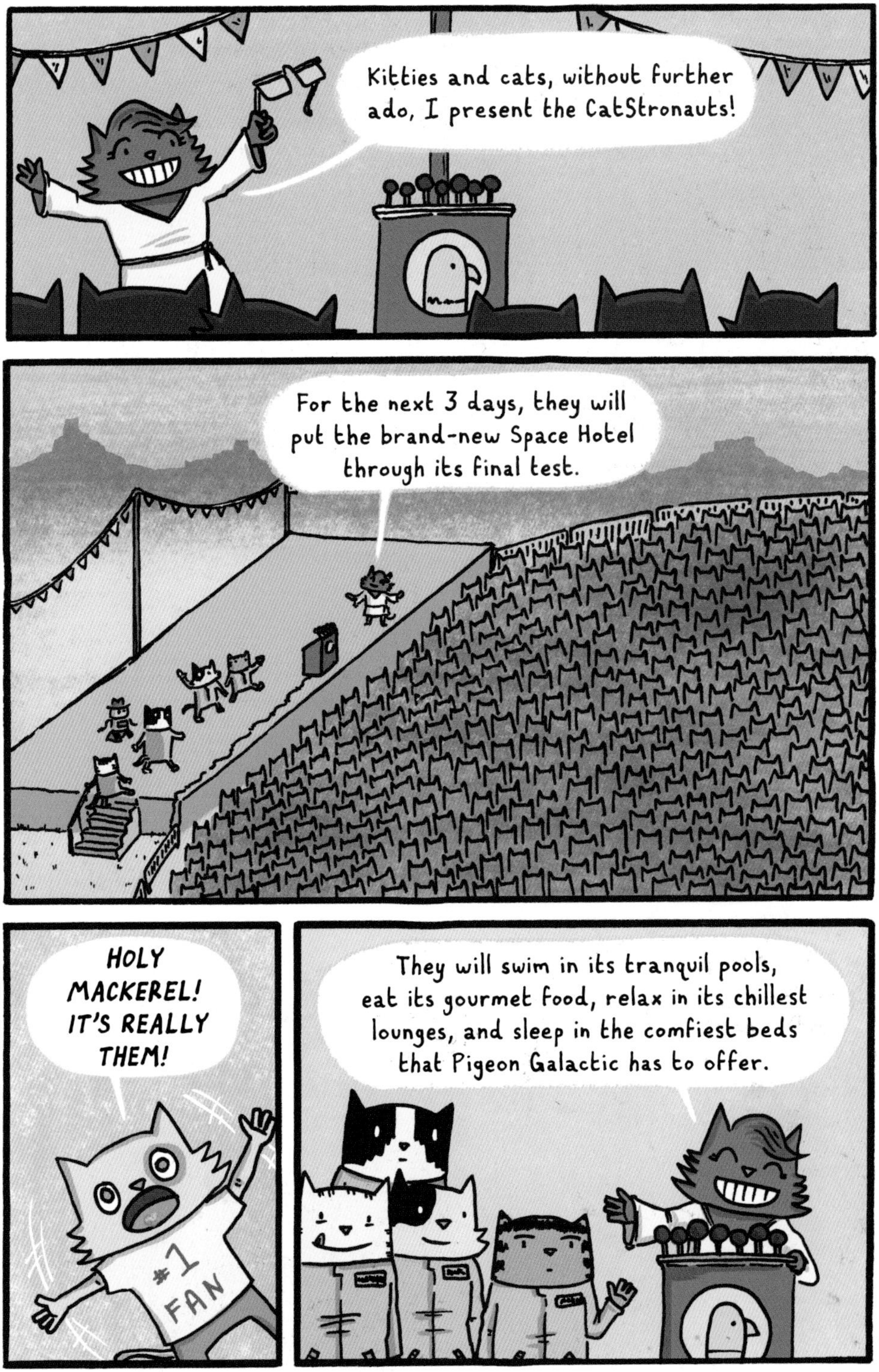
Kitties and cats, without further ado, I present the CatStronauts!
For the next 3 days, they will put the brand-new Space Hotel through its final test.
HOLY MACKEREL! IT'S REALLY THEM!
#1 FAN
They will swim in its tranquil pools, eat its gourmet food, relax in its chillest lounges, and sleep in the comfiest beds that Pigeon Galactic has to offer.

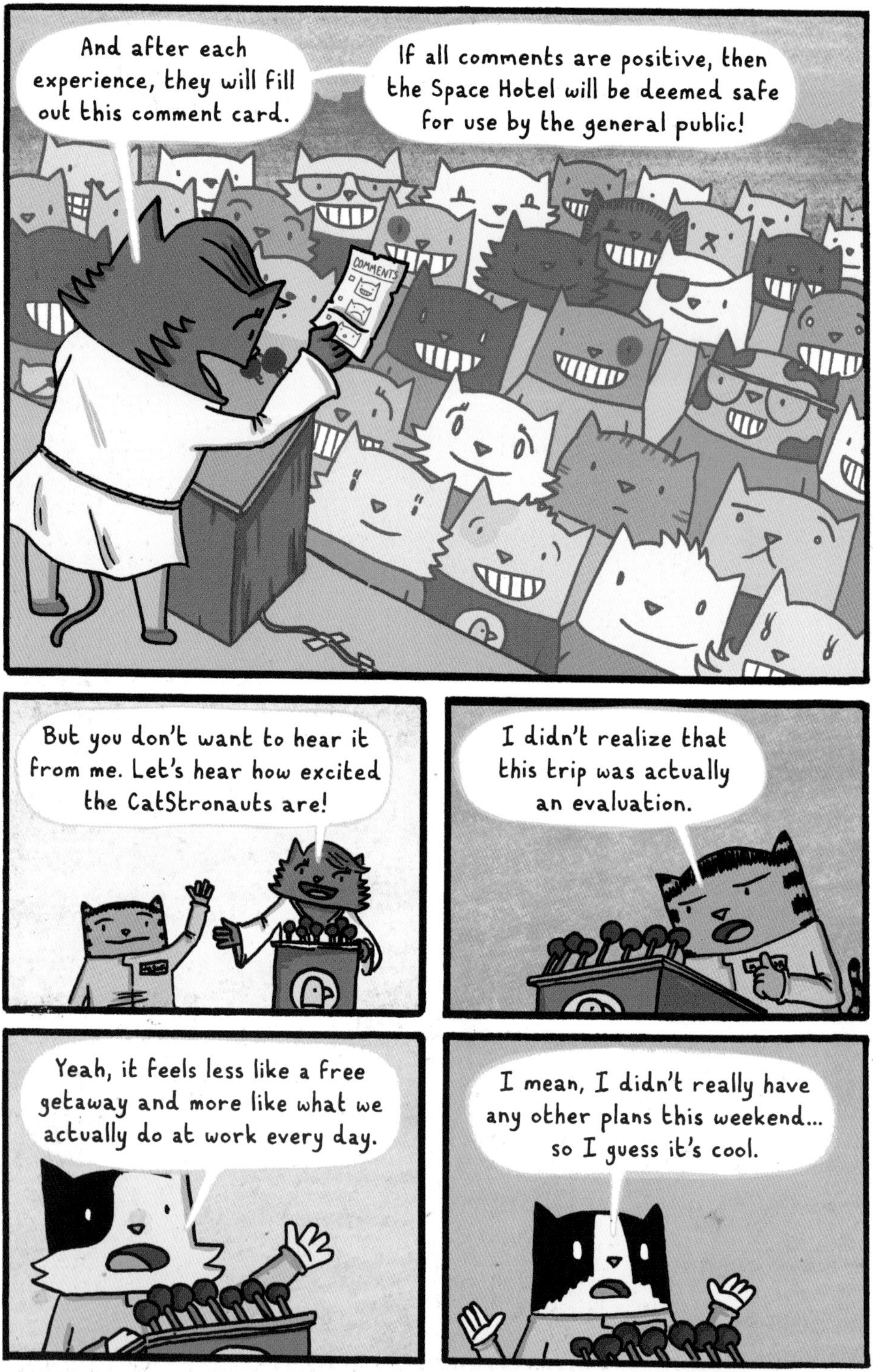
And after each experience, they will fill out this comment card.
If all comments are positive, then the Space Hotel will be deemed safe for use by the general public!
COMMENTS
But you don't want to hear it from me. Let's hear how excited the CatStronauts are!
I didn't realize that this trip was actually an evaluation.
Yeah, it feels less like a free getaway and more like what we actually do at work every day.
I mean, I didn't really have any other plans this weekend... so I guess it's cool.

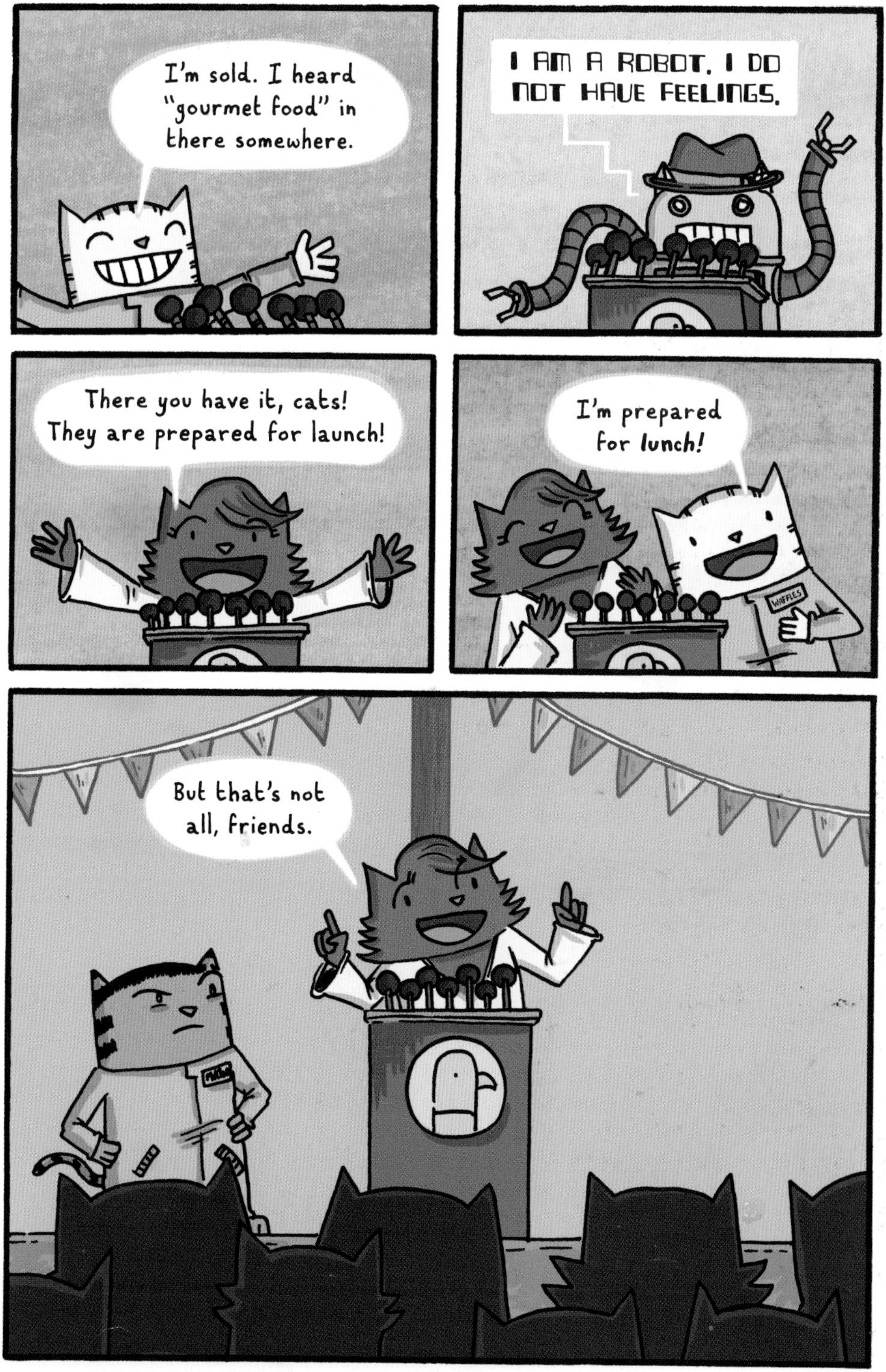
I'm sold. I heard "gourmet food" in there somewhere.
I AM A ROBOT. I DO NOT HAVE FEELINGS.
There you have it, cats! They are prepared for launch!
I'm prepared for **lunch**!
WAFFLES
But that's not all, friends.

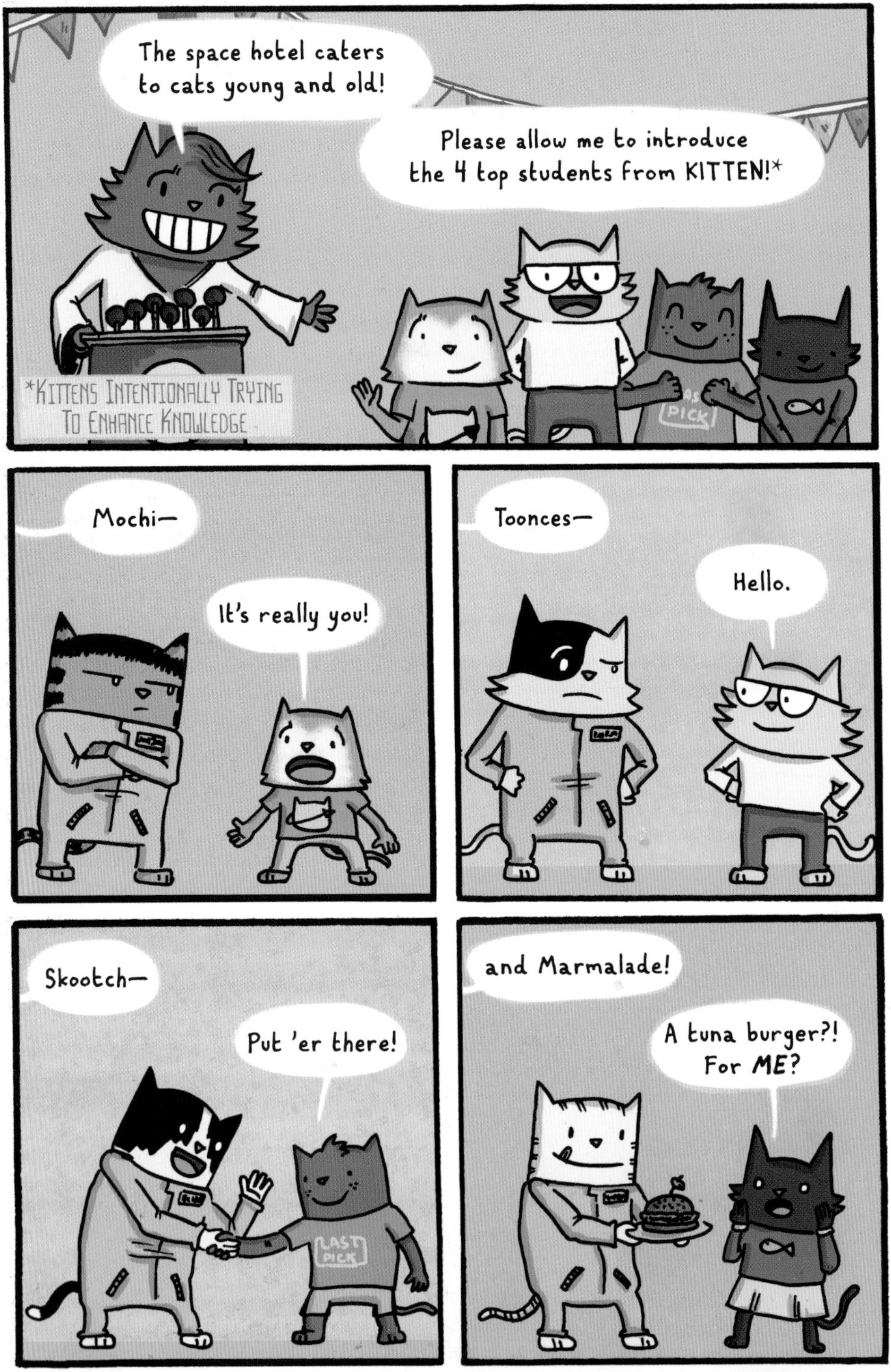
The space hotel caters to cats young and old!
Please allow me to introduce the 4 top students from KITTEN!*
*KITTENS INTENTIONALLY TRYING TO ENHANCE KNOWLEDGE
Mochi—
It's really you!
Toonces—
Hello.
Skootch—
Put 'er there!
LAST PICK
and Marmalade!
A tuna burger?! For ME?

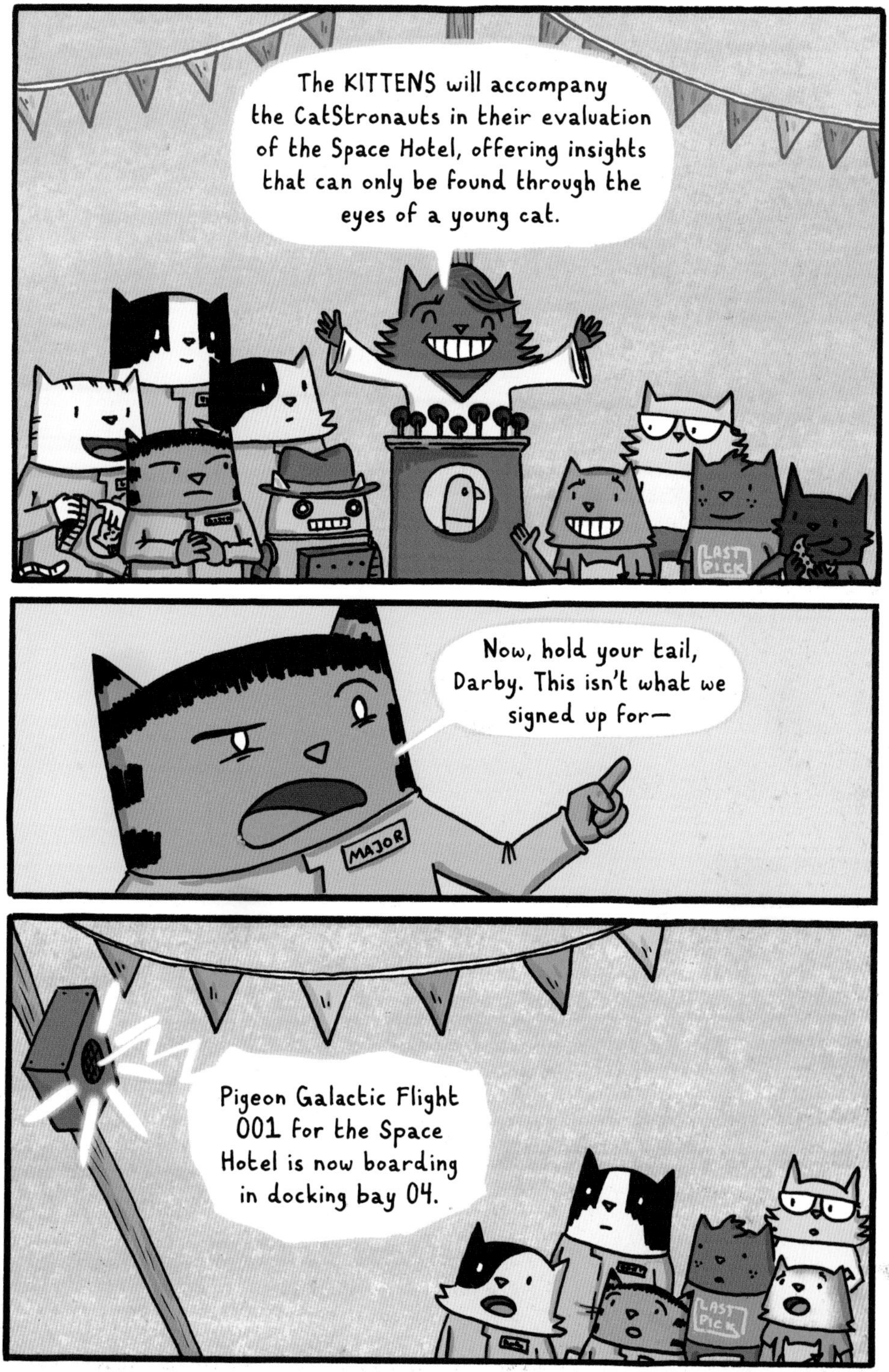
The KITTENS will accompany the CatStronauts in their evaluation of the Space Hotel, offering insights that can only be found through the eyes of a young cat.
LAST PICK
Now, hold your tail, Darby. This isn't what we signed up for—
MAJOR
Pigeon Galactic Flight 001 for the Space Hotel is now boarding in docking bay 04.
LAST PICK

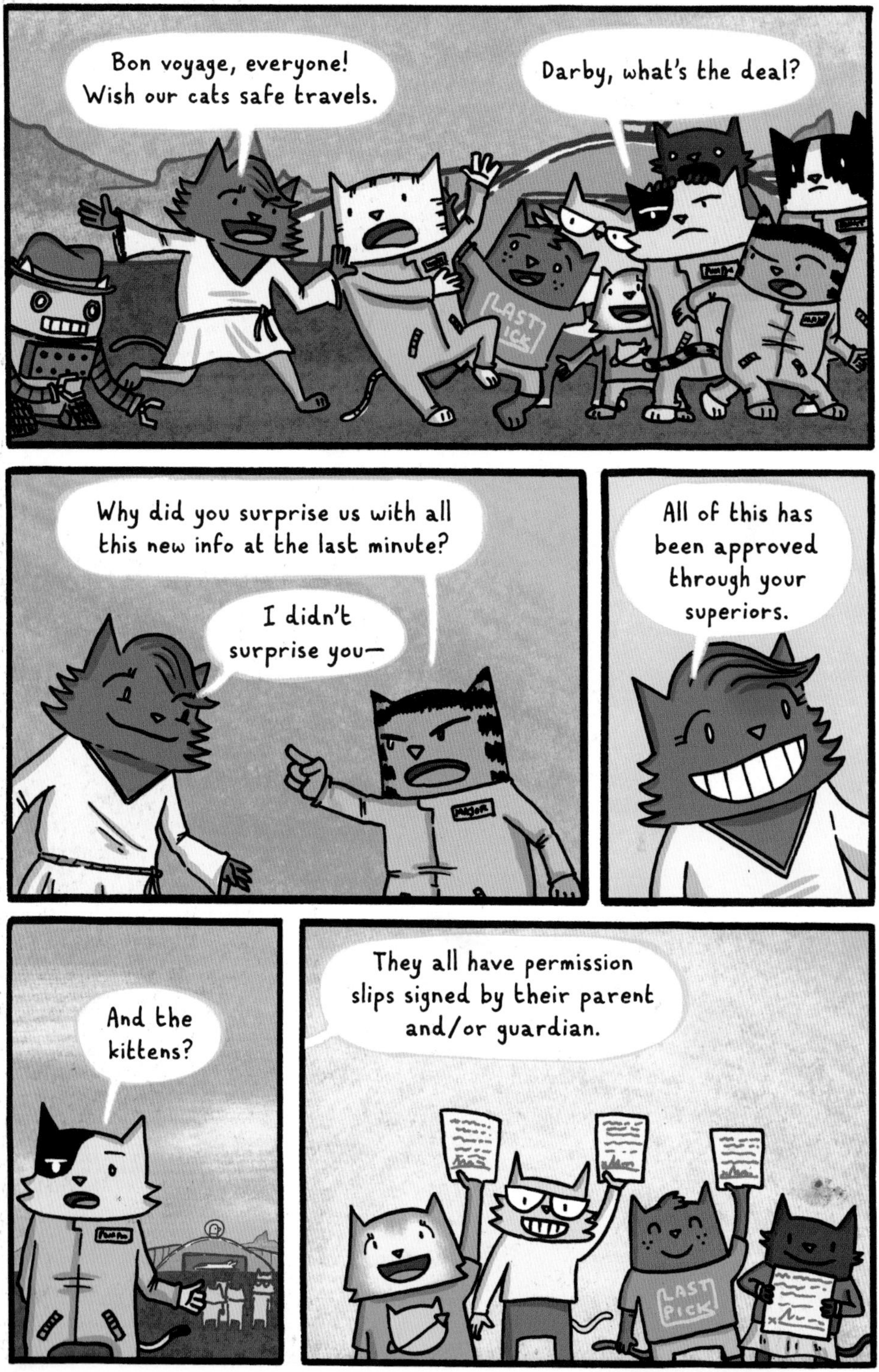
Bon voyage, everyone! Wish our cats safe travels.
Darby, what's the deal?
LAST PICK
Why did you surprise us with all this new info at the last minute?
I didn't surprise you—
MAJOR
All of this has been approved through your superiors.
And the kittens?
They all have permission slips signed by their parent and/or guardian.
LAST PICK

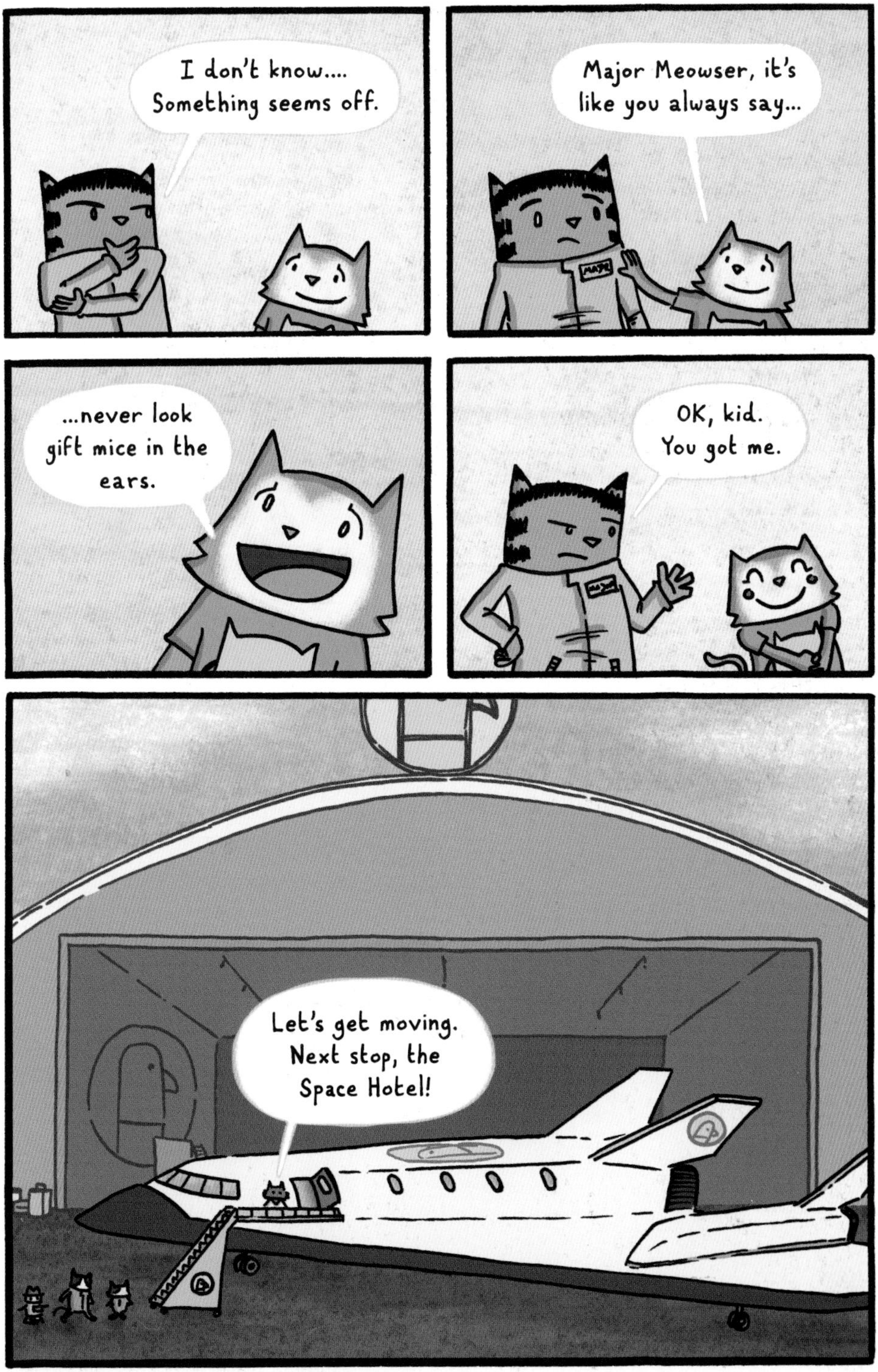
I don't know.... Something seems off.
Major Meowser, it's like you always say...
...never look gift mice in the ears.
OK, kid. You got me.
Let's get moving. Next stop, the Space Hotel!

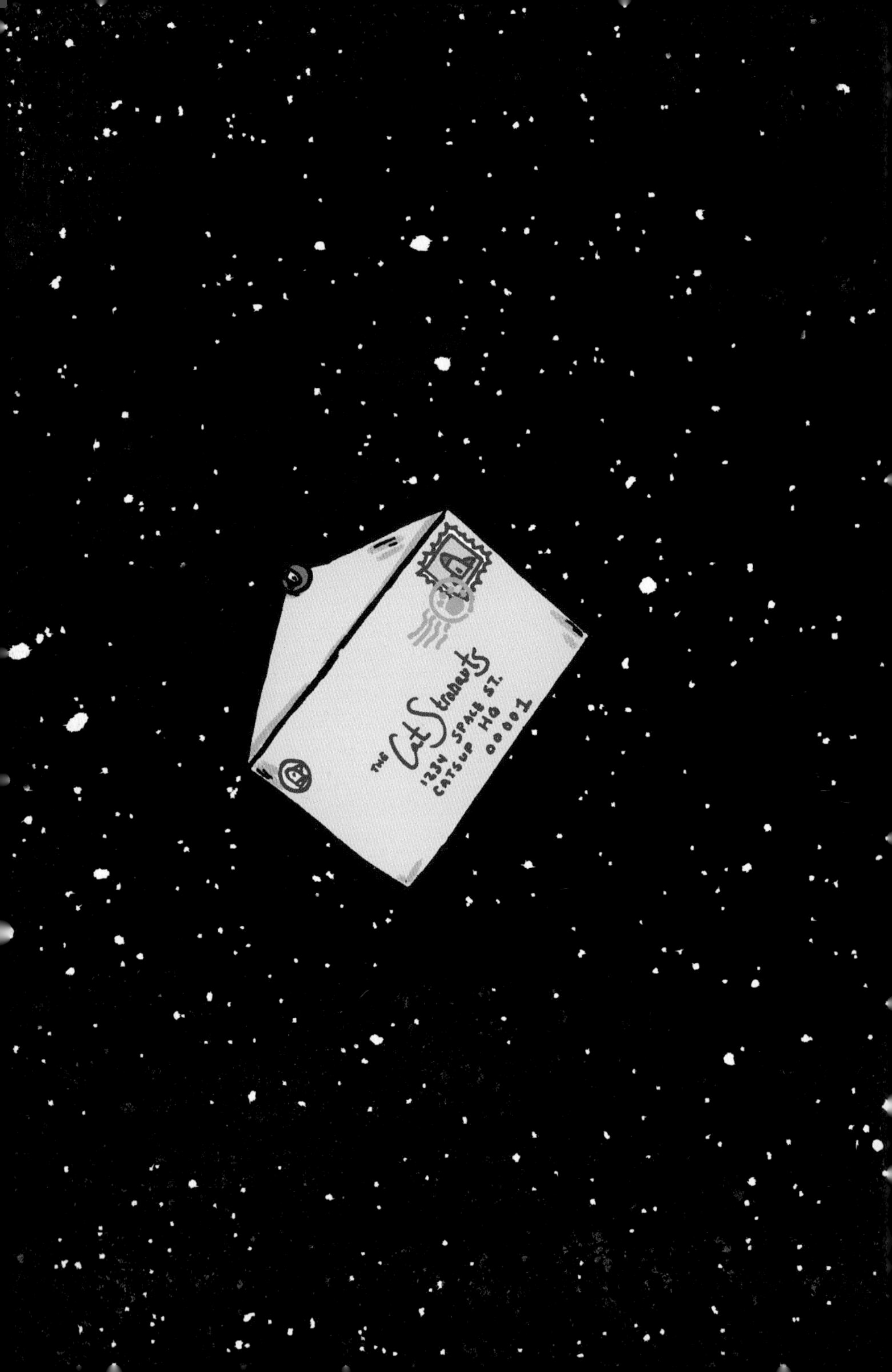
THE CatStronauts
1234 SPACE ST.
CATSUP HQ
00001

CHAPTER 3

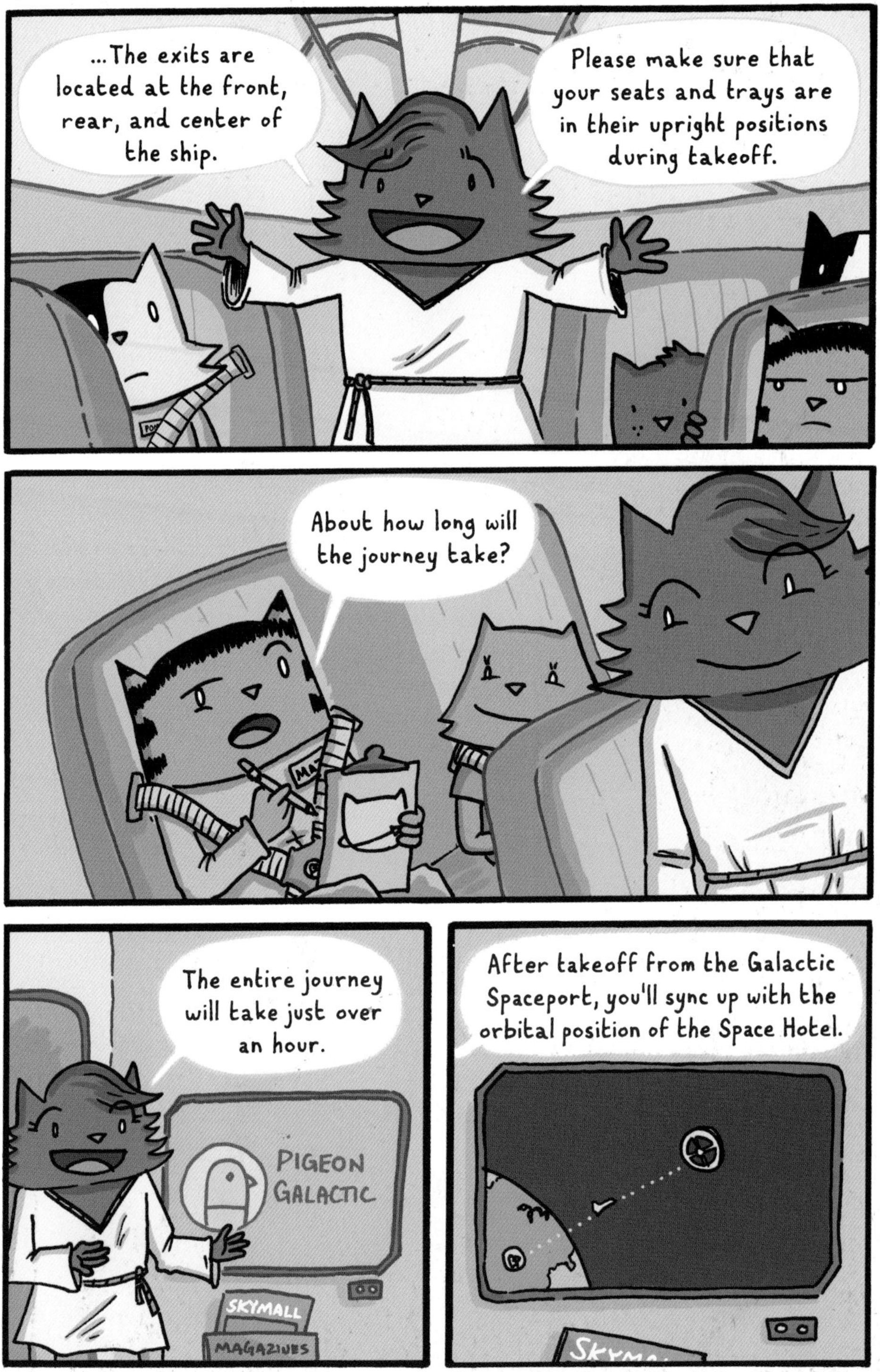
...The exits are located at the front, rear, and center of the ship.
Please make sure that your seats and trays are in their upright positions during takeoff.
About how long will the journey take?
The entire journey will take just over an hour.
PIGEON GALACTIC
SKYMALL
MAGAZINES
After takeoff from the Galactic Spaceport, you'll sync up with the orbital position of the Space Hotel.

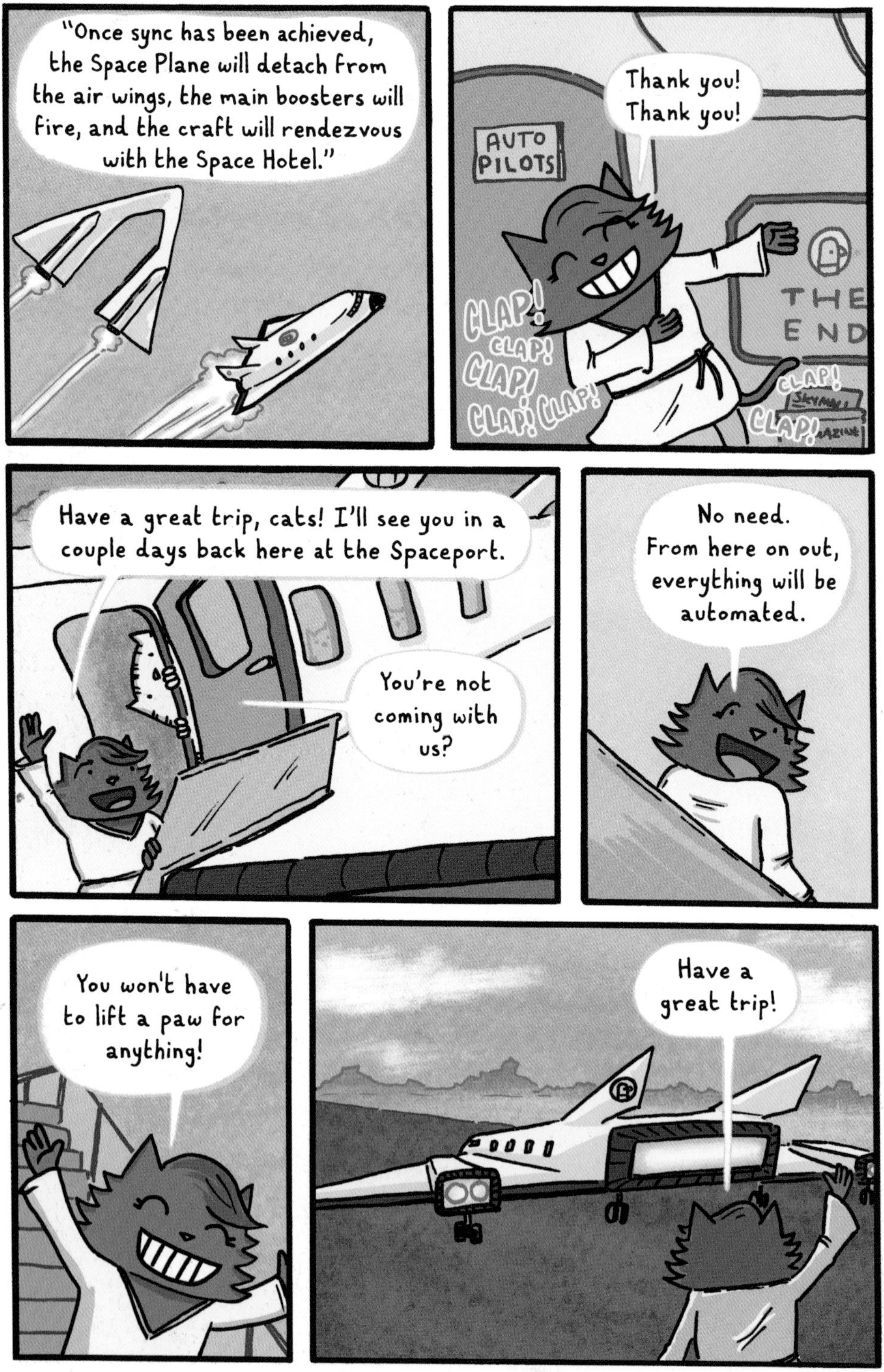
"Once sync has been achieved, the Space Plane will detach from the air wings, the main boosters will fire, and the craft will rendezvous with the Space Hotel."
AUTO PILOTS
Thank you! Thank you!
CLAP! CLAP! CLAP! CLAP! CLAP!
THE END
CLAP! CLAP!
Have a great trip, cats! I'll see you in a couple days back here at the Spaceport.
You're not coming with us?
No need. From here on out, everything will be automated.
You won't have to lift a paw for anything!
Have a great trip!

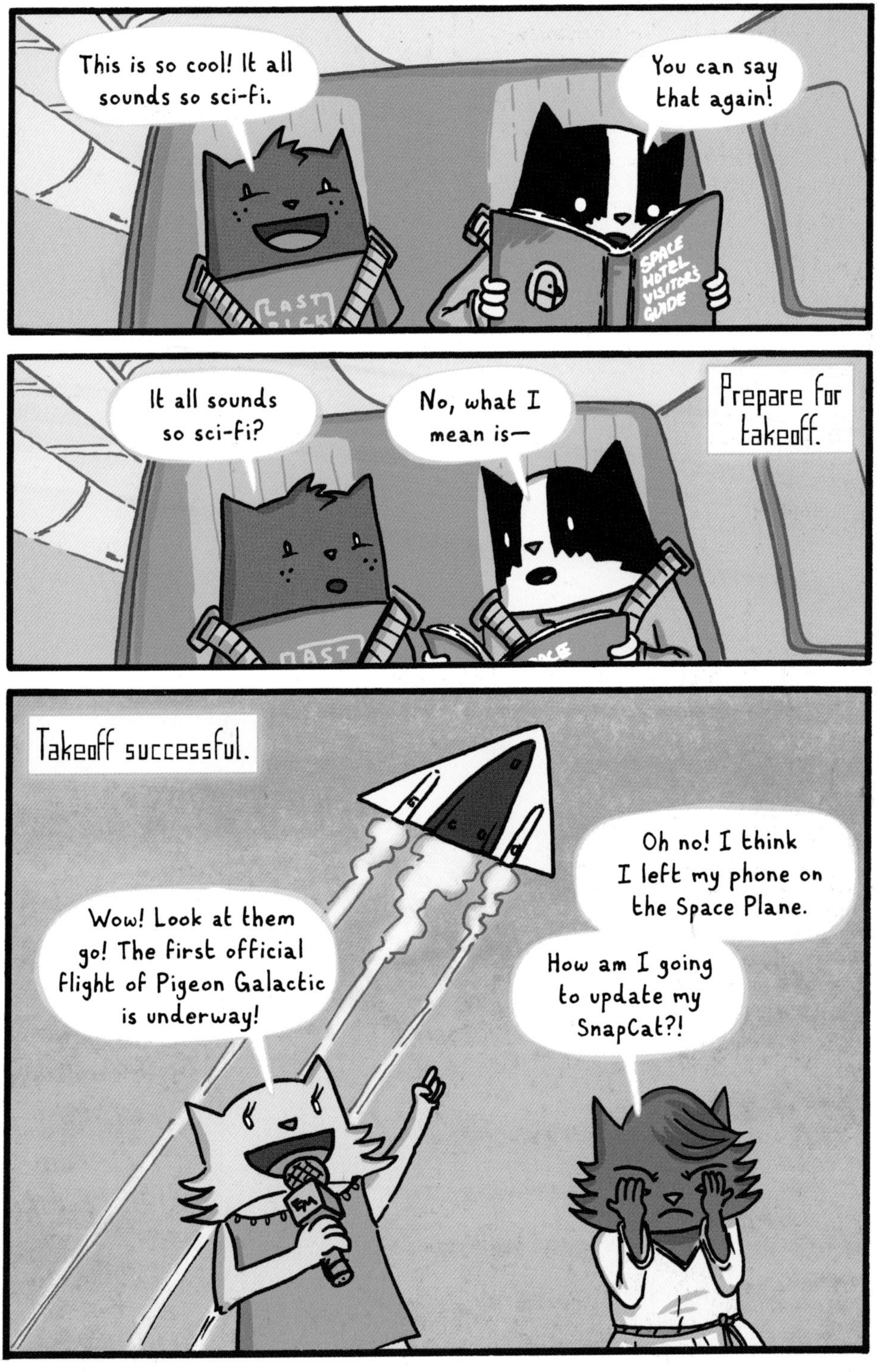

This is so cool! It all sounds so sci-fi.
You can say that again!
SPACE HOTEL VISITOR'S GUIDE
It all sounds so sci-fi?
No, what I mean is—
Prepare for takeoff.
Takeoff successful.
Wow! Look at them go! The first official flight of Pigeon Galactic is underway!
Oh no! I think I left my phone on the Space Plane.
How am I going to update my SnapCat?!

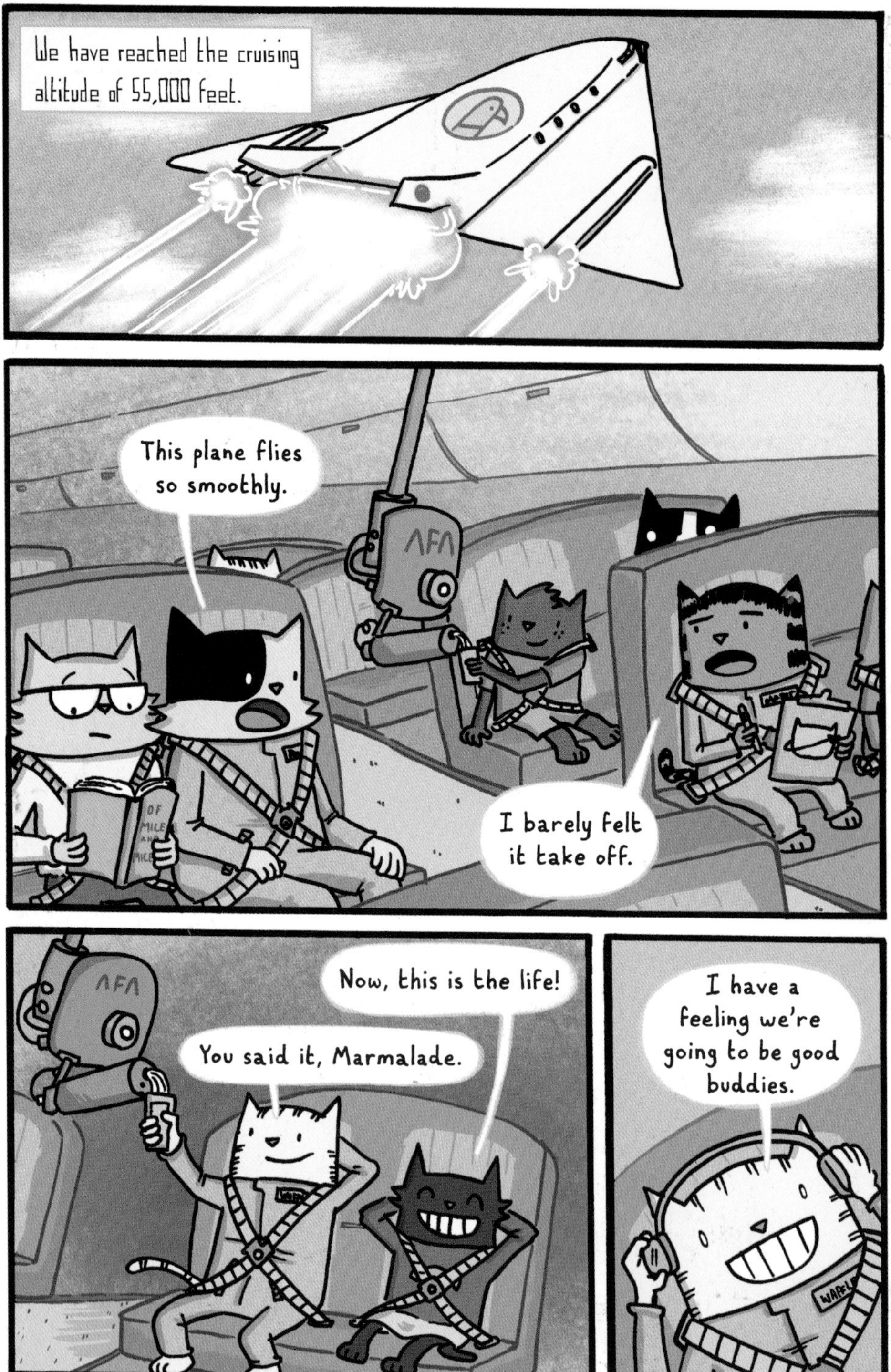
We have reached the cruising altitude of 55,000 feet.
This plane flies so smoothly.
I barely felt it take off.
Now, this is the life!
You said it, Marmalade.
I have a feeling we're going to be good buddies.

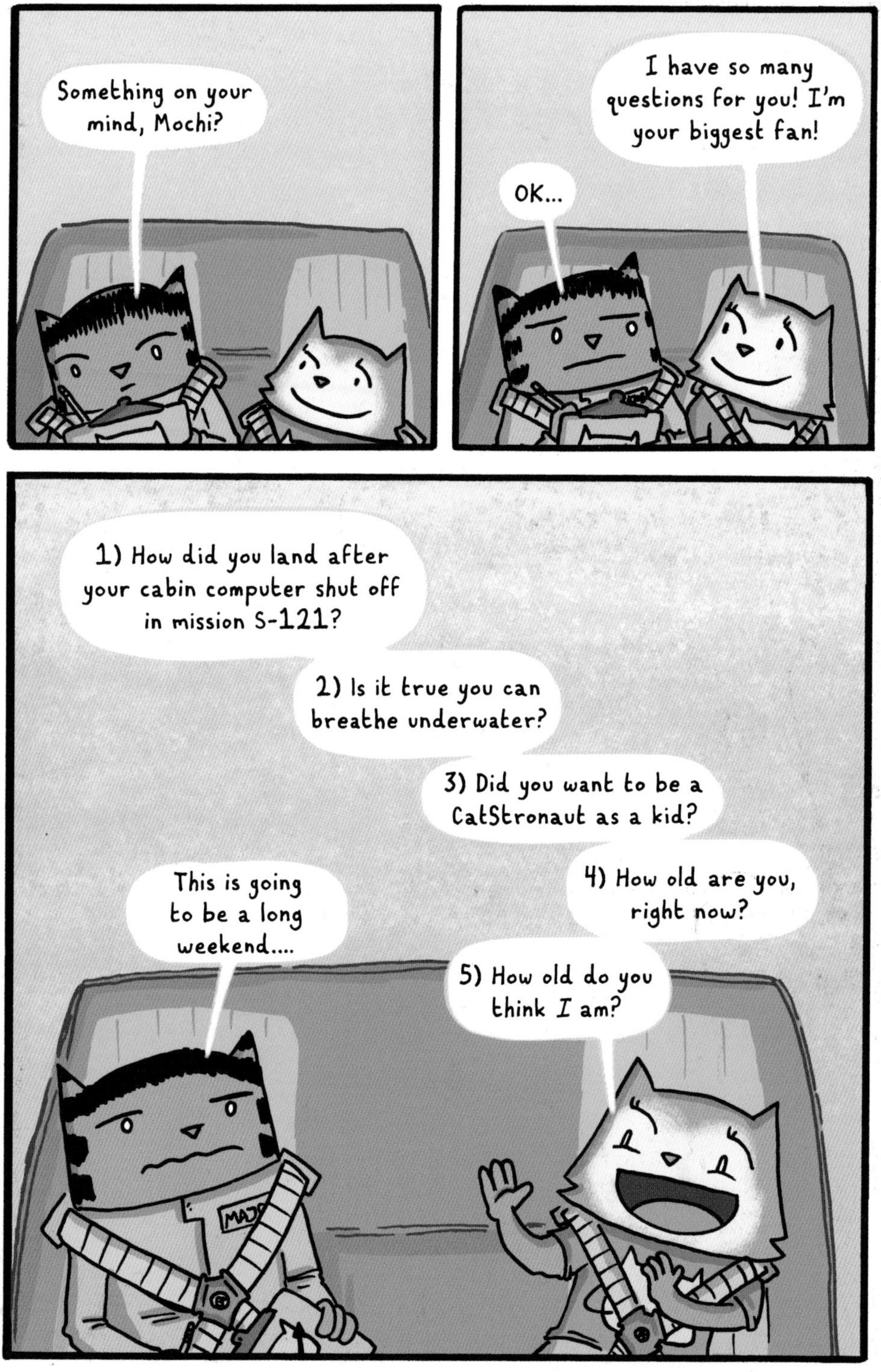
Something on your mind, Mochi?
I have so many questions for you! I'm your biggest fan!
OK...
1) How did you land after your cabin computer shut off in mission S-121?
2) Is it true you can breathe underwater?
3) Did you want to be a CatStronaut as a kid?
4) How old are you, right now?
This is going to be a long weekend....
5) How old do you think I am?

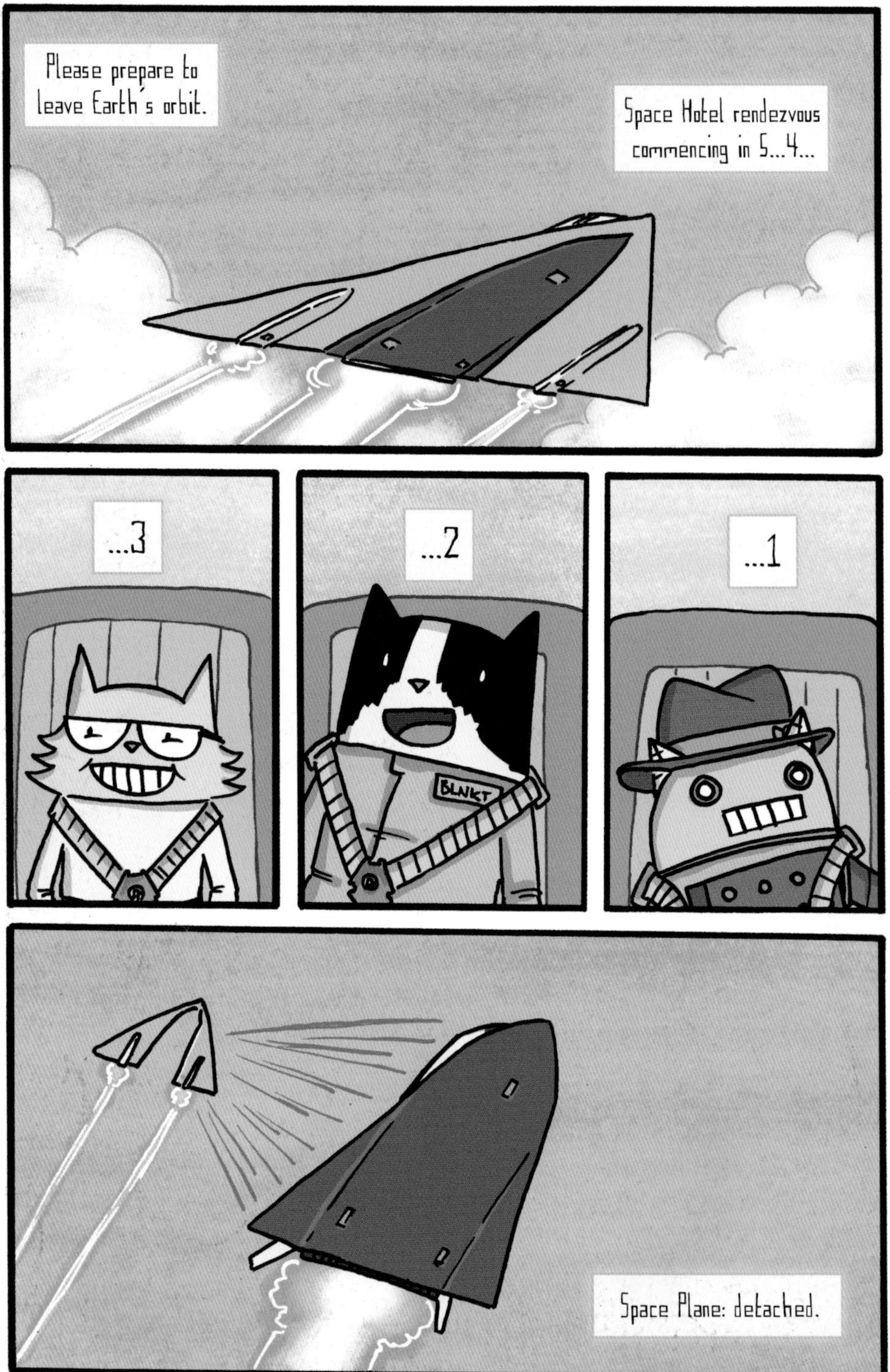

Please prepare to leave Earth's orbit.
Space Hotel rendezvous commencing in 5...4...
...3
BLNKT
...2
...1
Space Plane: detached.

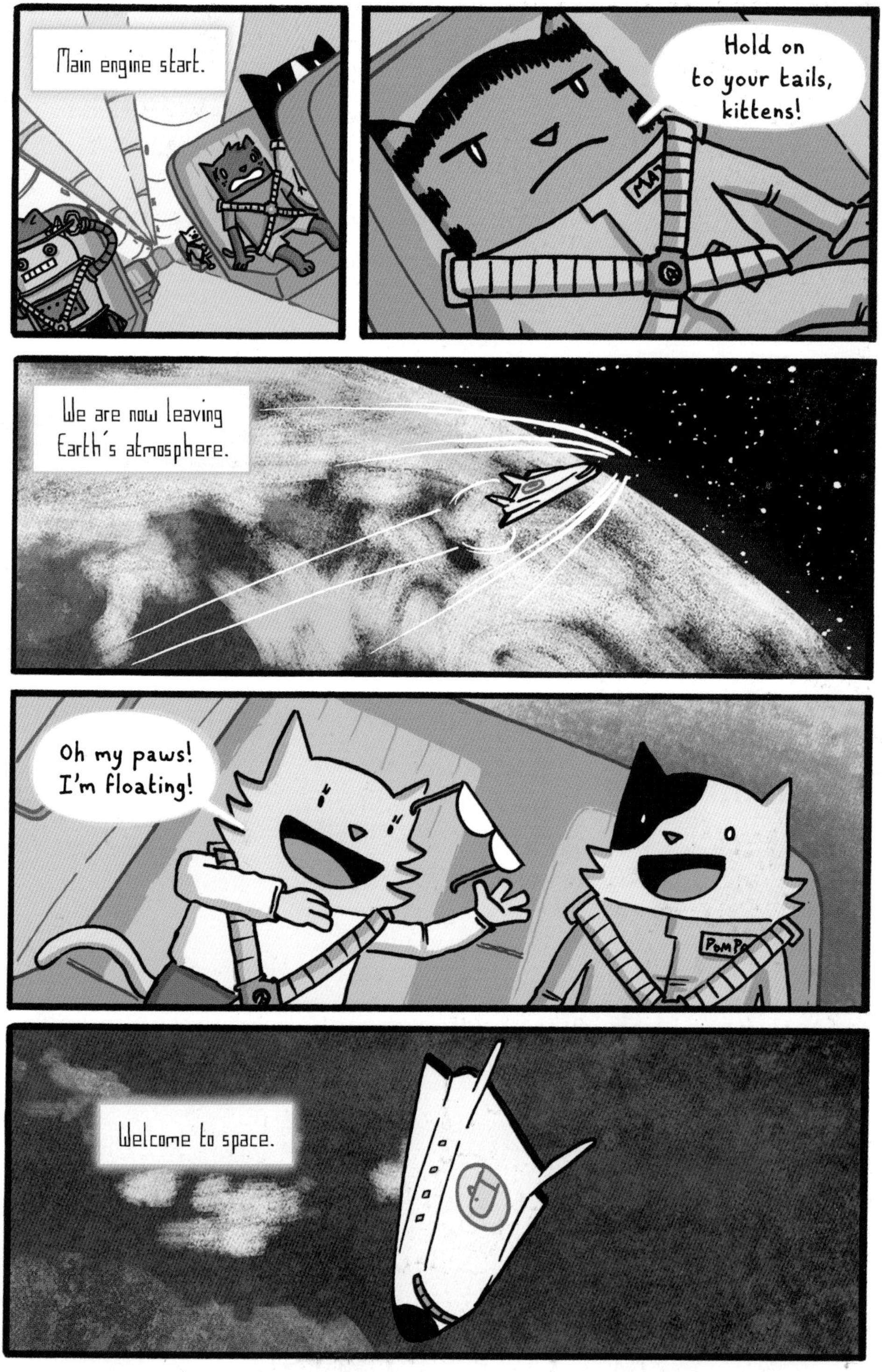
Main engine start.
Hold on to your tails, kittens!
We are now leaving Earth's atmosphere.
Oh my paws! I'm floating!
Welcome to space.

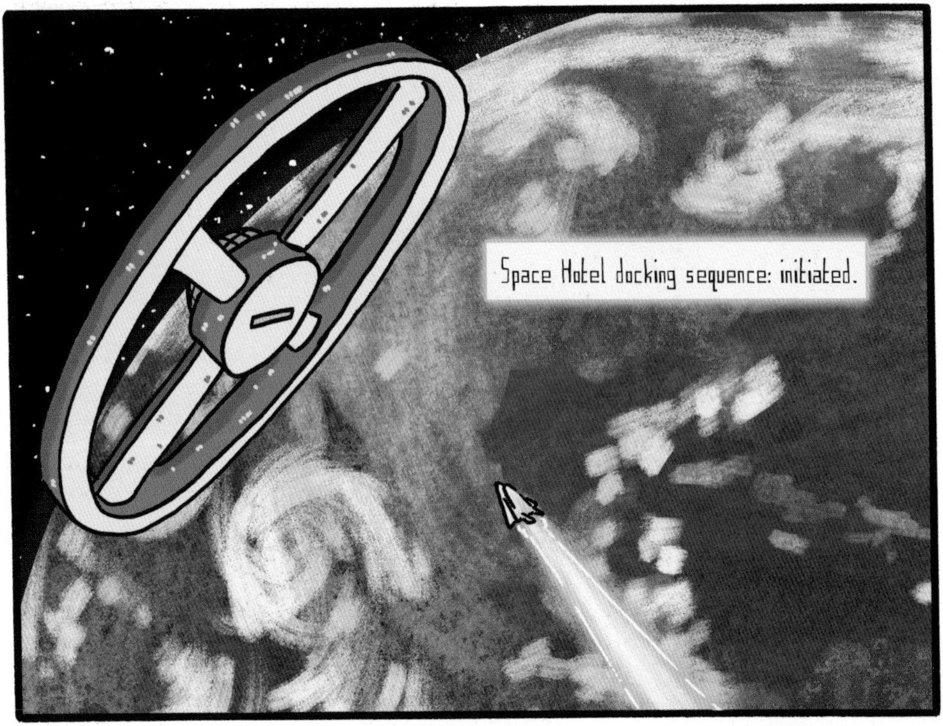
Space Hotel docking sequence: initiated.

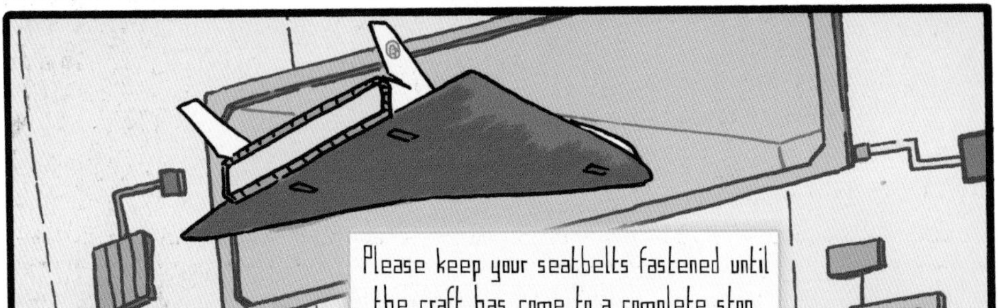
Please keep your seatbelts fastened until the craft has come to a complete stop.

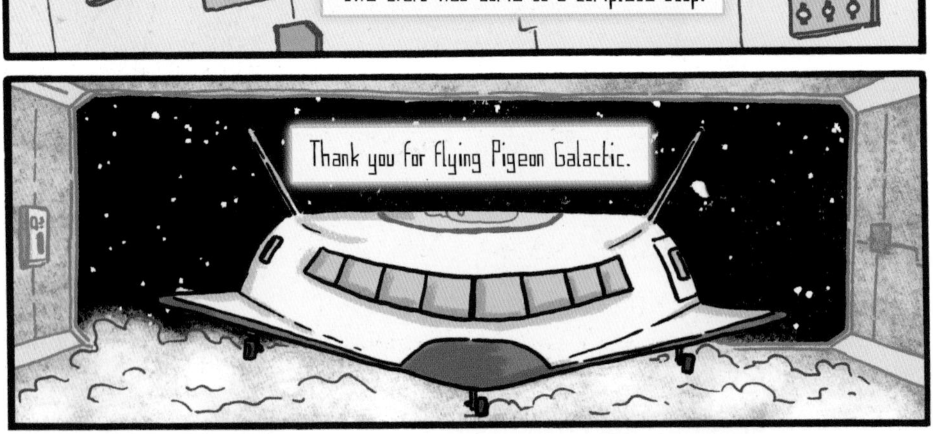
Thank you for flying Pigeon Galactic.

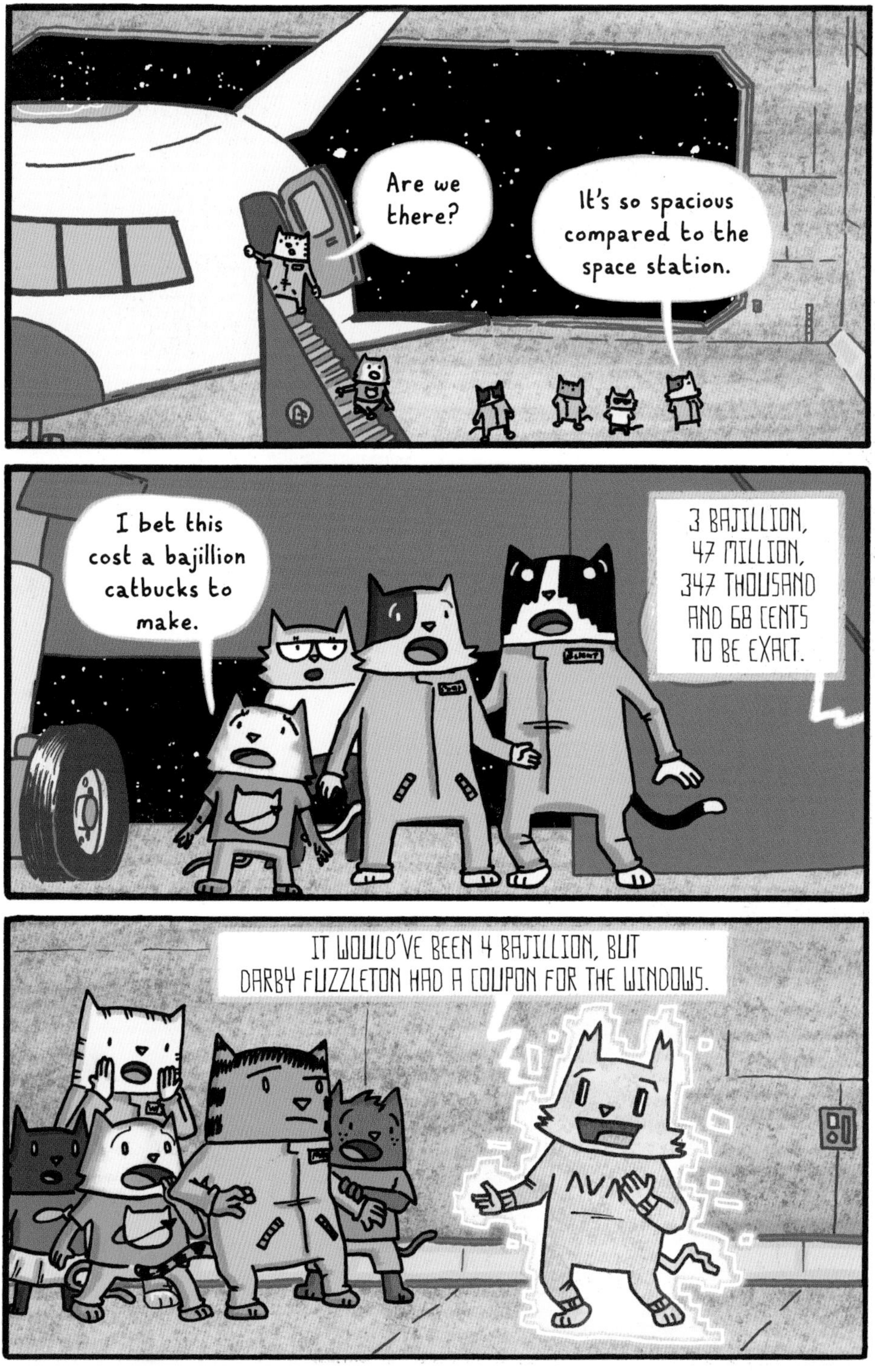
Are we there?
It's so spacious compared to the space station.
I bet this cost a bajillion catbucks to make.
3 BAJILLION, 47 MILLION, 347 THOUSAND AND 68 CENTS TO BE EXACT.
IT WOULD'VE BEEN 4 BAJILLION, BUT DARBY FUZZLETON HAD A COUPON FOR THE WINDOWS.

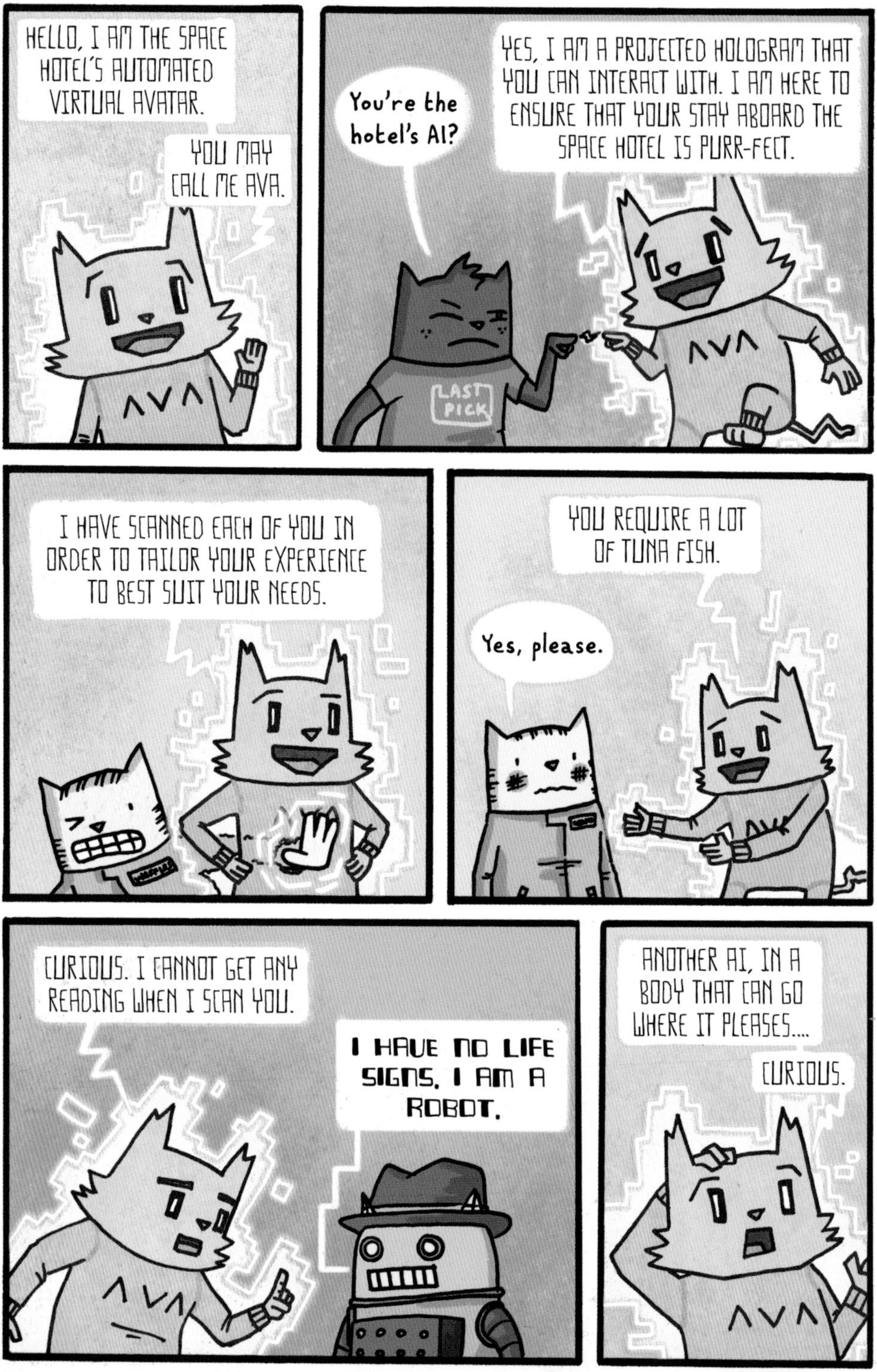
HELLO, I AM THE SPACE HOTEL'S AUTOMATED VIRTUAL AVATAR.
YOU MAY CALL ME AVA.
AVA
You're the hotel's AI?
YES, I AM A PROJECTED HOLOGRAM THAT YOU CAN INTERACT WITH. I AM HERE TO ENSURE THAT YOUR STAY ABOARD THE SPACE HOTEL IS PURR-FECT.
LAST PICK
AVA
I HAVE SCANNED EACH OF YOU IN ORDER TO TAILOR YOUR EXPERIENCE TO BEST SUIT YOUR NEEDS.
YOU REQUIRE A LOT OF TUNA FISH.
Yes, please.
CURIOUS. I CANNOT GET ANY READING WHEN I SCAN YOU.
I HAVE NO LIFE SIGNS. I AM A ROBOT.
AVA
ANOTHER AI, IN A BODY THAT CAN GO WHERE IT PLEASES....
CURIOUS.
AVA

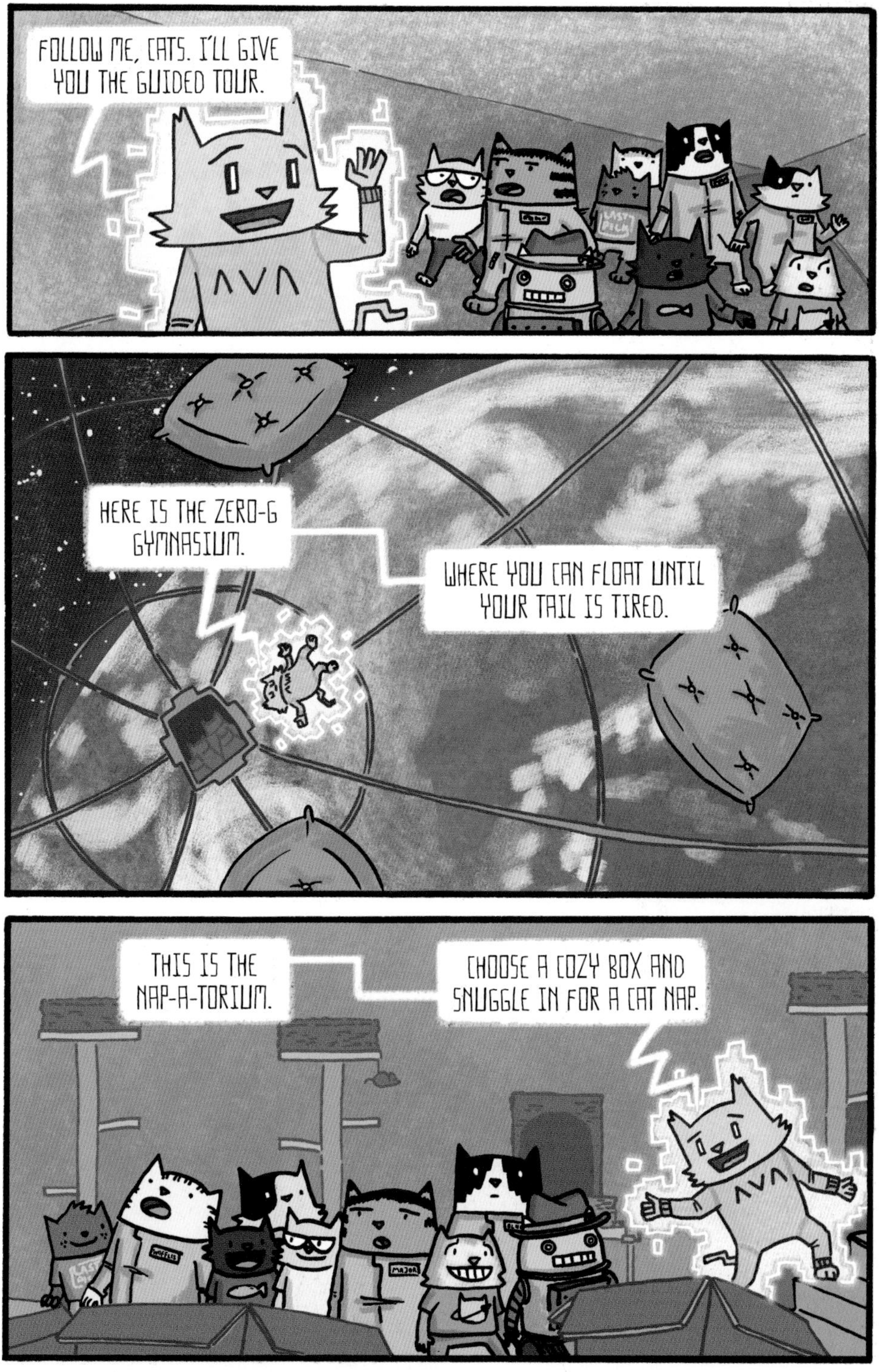
FOLLOW ME, CATS. I'LL GIVE YOU THE GUIDED TOUR.
HERE IS THE ZERO-G GYMNASIUM.
WHERE YOU CAN FLOAT UNTIL YOUR TAIL IS TIRED.
THIS IS THE NAP-A-TORIUM.
CHOOSE A COZY BOX AND SNUGGLE IN FOR A CAT NAP.

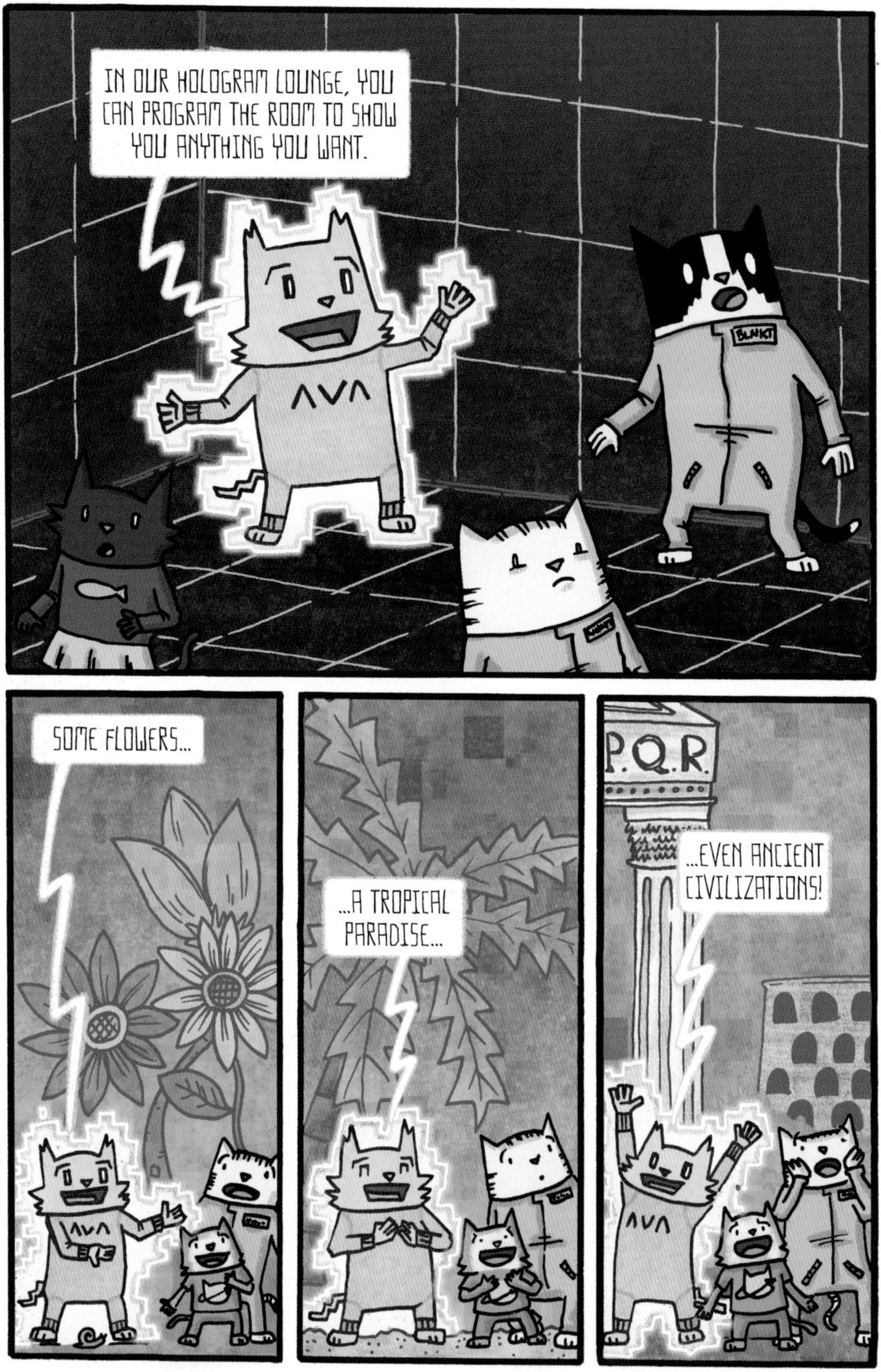

IN OUR HOLOGRAM LOUNGE, YOU CAN PROGRAM THE ROOM TO SHOW YOU ANYTHING YOU WANT.
AVA
SOME FLOWERS...
...A TROPICAL PARADISE...
P.Q.R.
...EVEN ANCIENT CIVILIZATIONS!

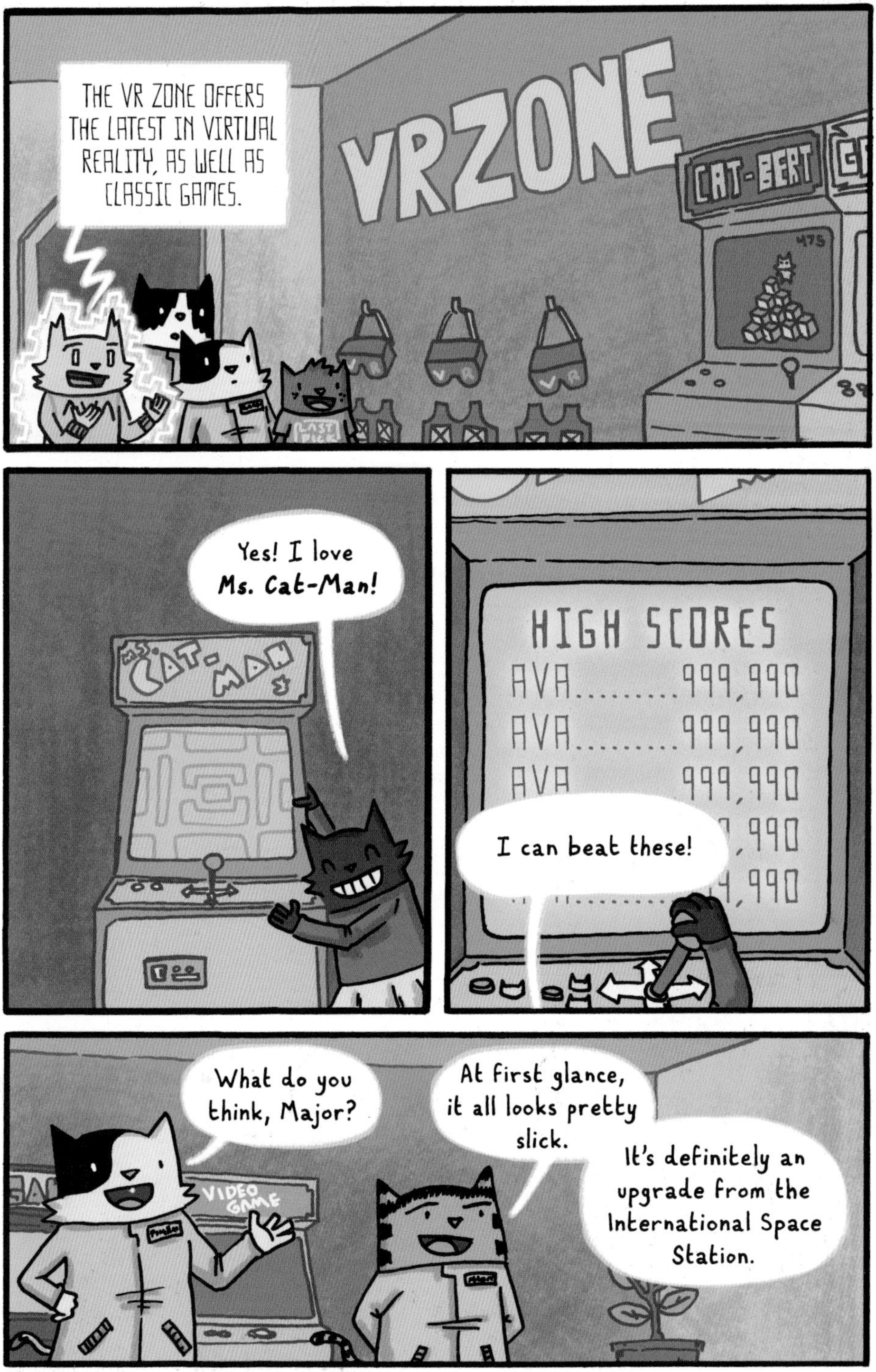

THE VR ZONE OFFERS THE LATEST IN VIRTUAL REALITY, AS WELL AS CLASSIC GAMES.
VRZONE
CAT-BERT
Yes! I love Ms. Cat-Man!
HIGH SCORES
AVA.........999,990
AVA.........999,990
AVA
999,990
I can beat these!
What do you think, Major?
At first glance, it all looks pretty slick.
It's definitely an upgrade from the International Space Station.

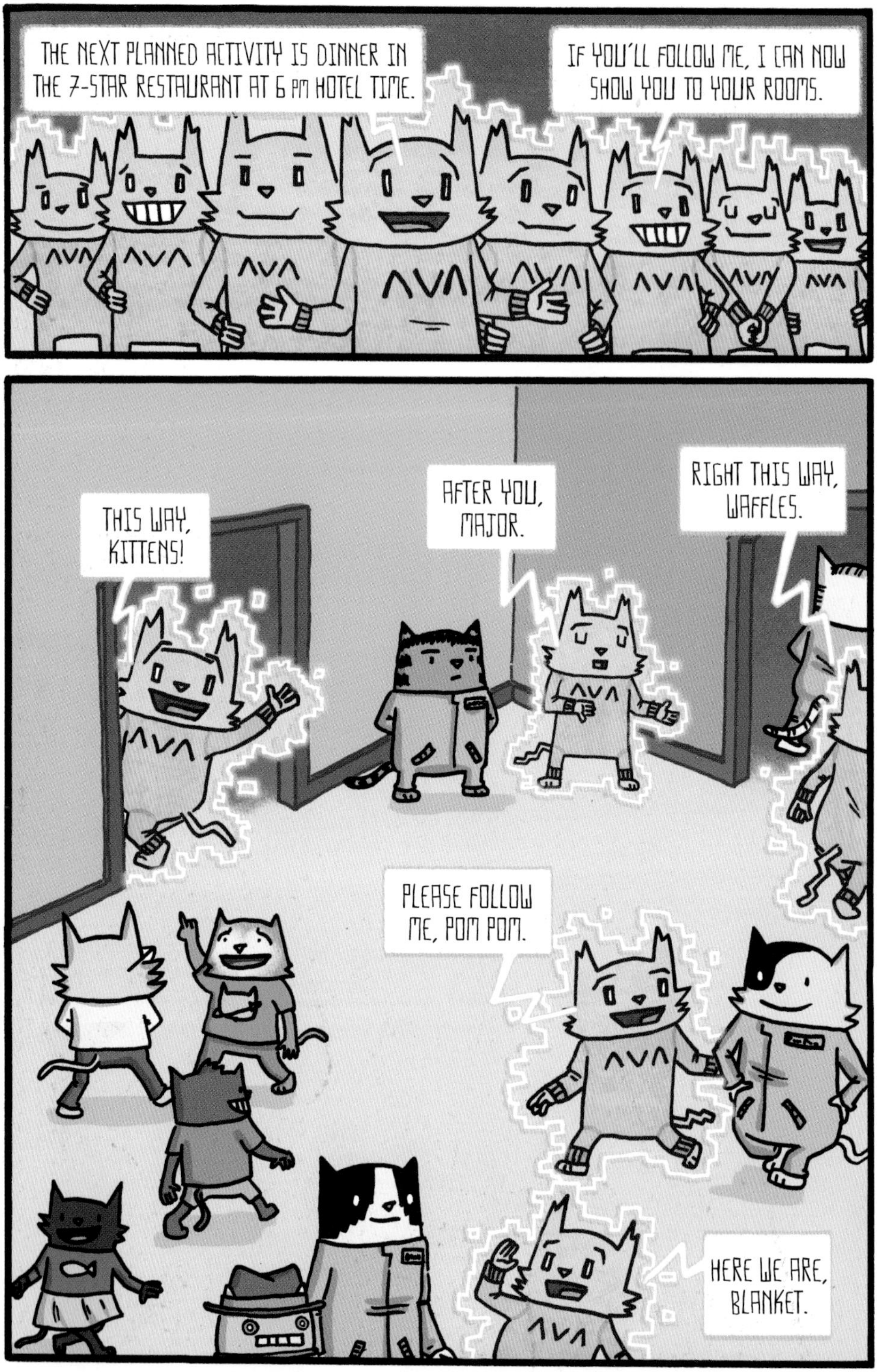
THE NEXT PLANNED ACTIVITY IS DINNER IN THE 7-STAR RESTAURANT AT 6 PM HOTEL TIME.
IF YOU'LL FOLLOW ME, I CAN NOW SHOW YOU TO YOUR ROOMS.
THIS WAY, KITTENS!
AFTER YOU, MAJOR.
RIGHT THIS WAY, WAFFLES.
PLEASE FOLLOW ME, POM POM.
HERE WE ARE, BLANKET.

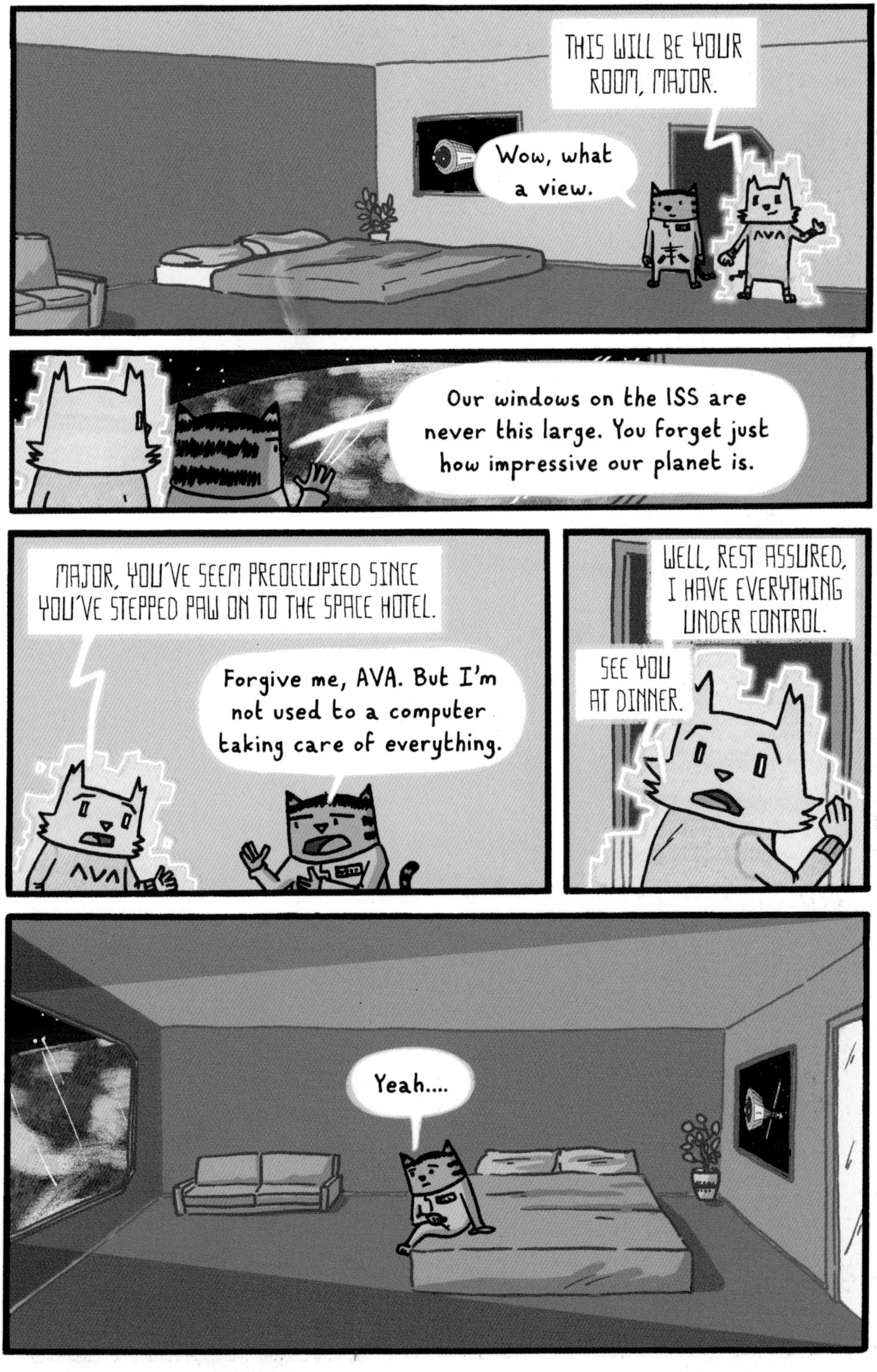
THIS WILL BE YOUR ROOM, MAJOR.
Wow, what a view.
Our windows on the ISS are never this large. You forget just how impressive our planet is.
MAJOR, YOU'VE SEEM PREOCCUPIED SINCE YOU'VE STEPPED PAW ON TO THE SPACE HOTEL.
Forgive me, AVA. But I'm not used to a computer taking care of everything.
WELL, REST ASSURED, I HAVE EVERYTHING UNDER CONTROL.
SEE YOU AT DINNER.
Yeah....

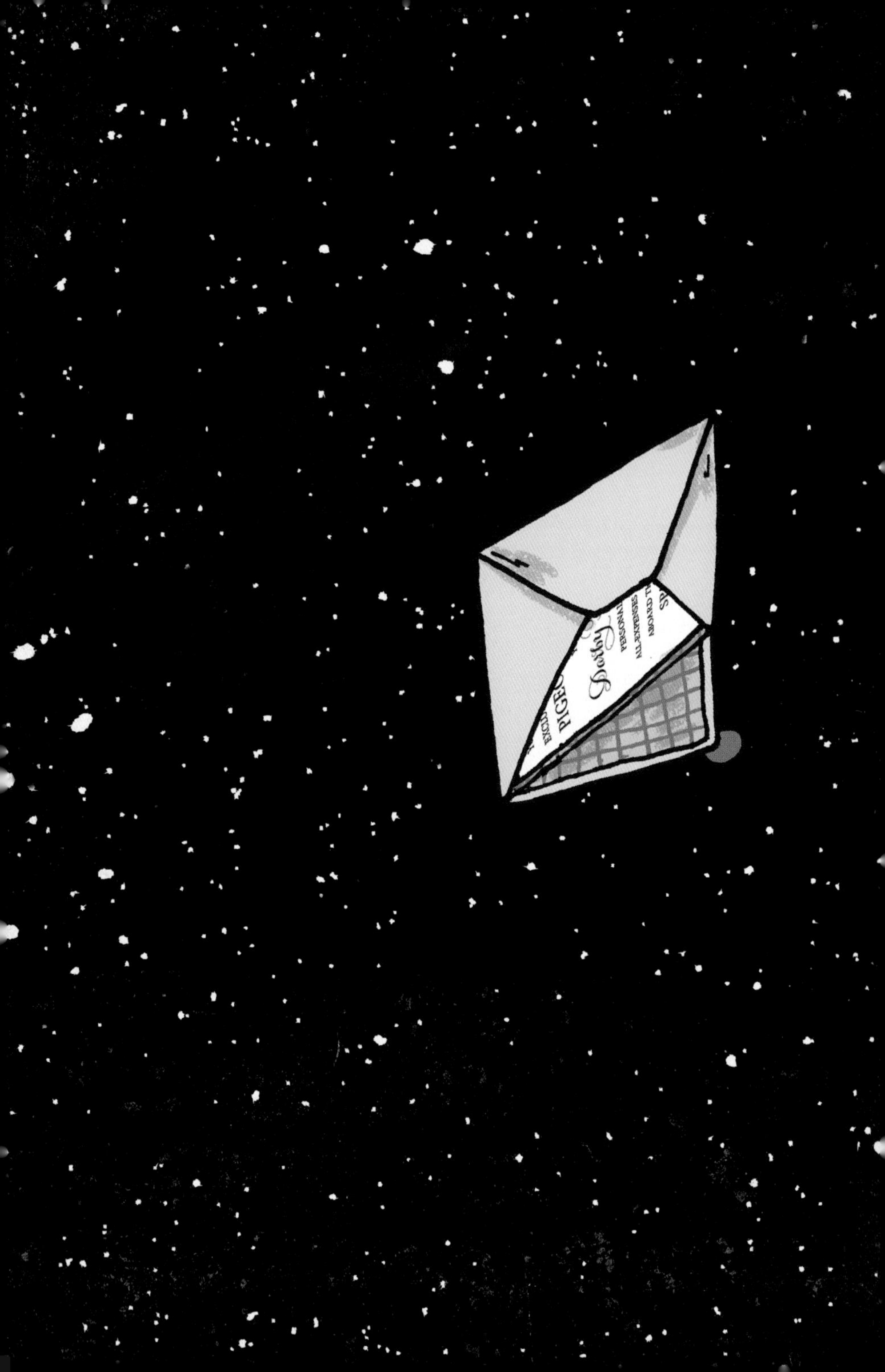

CHAPTER 4

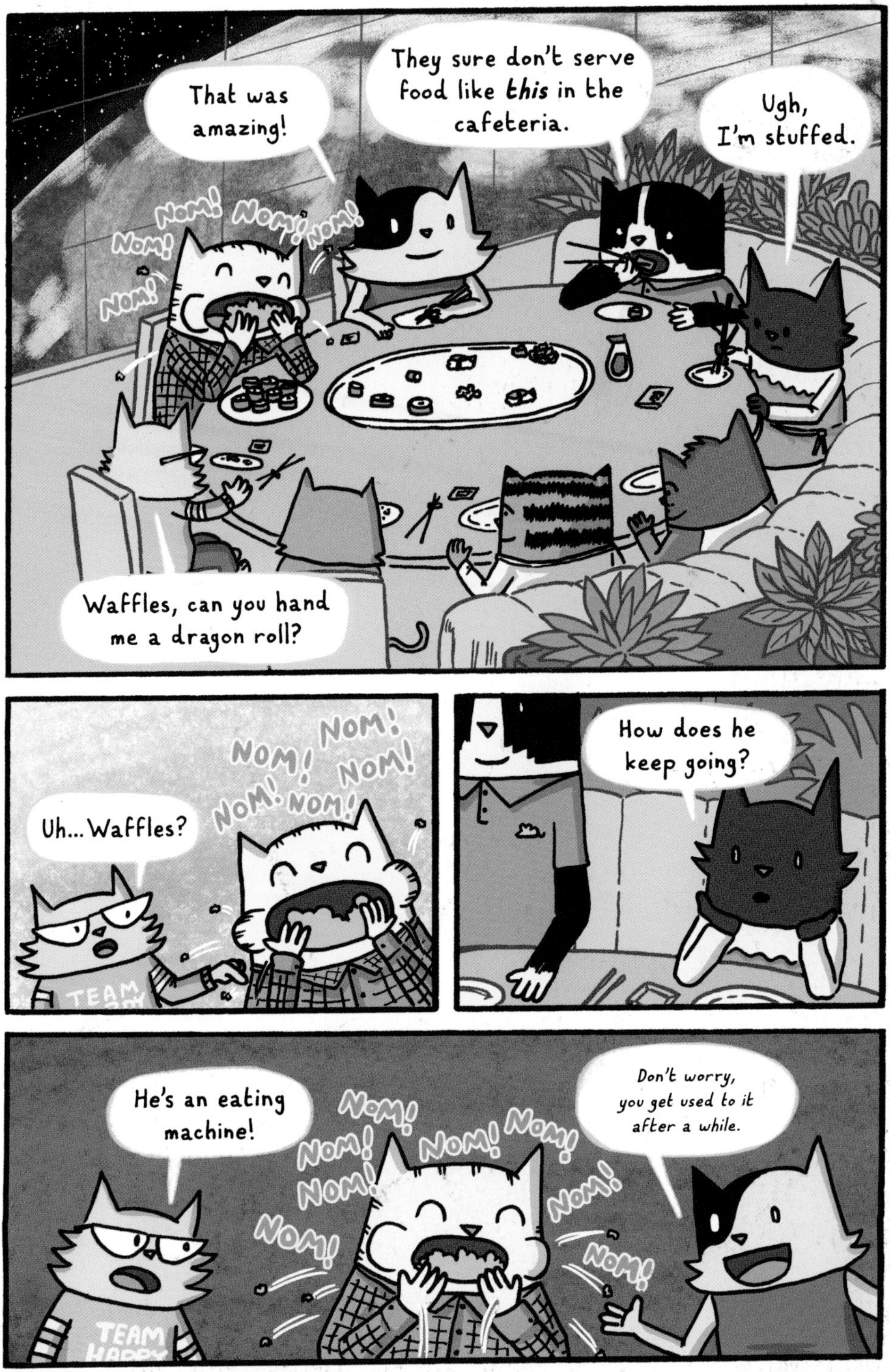
That was amazing!
They sure don't serve food like *this* in the cafeteria.
Ugh, I'm stuffed.
NOM! NOM! NOM! NOM! NOM!
Waffles, can you hand me a dragon roll?
NOM! NOM! NOM! NOM! NOM!
Uh... Waffles?
TEAM
How does he keep going?
He's an eating machine!
NOM! NOM! NOM! NOM! NOM! NOM! NOM! NOM!
Don't worry, you get used to it after a while.
TEAM

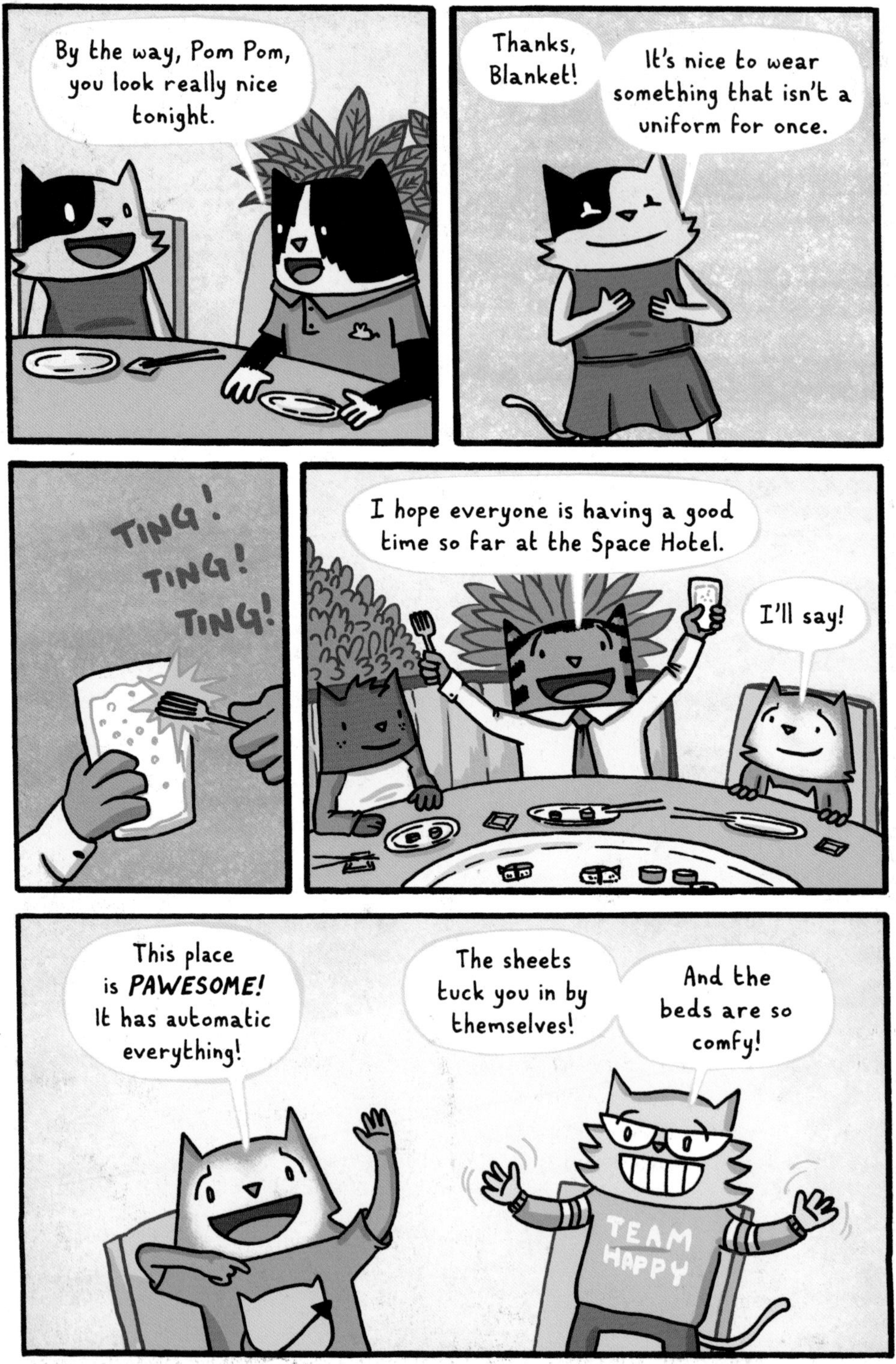
By the way, Pom Pom, you look really nice tonight.
Thanks, Blanket!
It's nice to wear something that isn't a uniform for once.
TING! TING! TING!
I hope everyone is having a good time so far at the Space Hotel.
I'll say!
This place is ***PAWESOME!*** It has automatic everything!
The sheets tuck you in by themselves!
And the beds are so comfy!
TEAM HAPPY

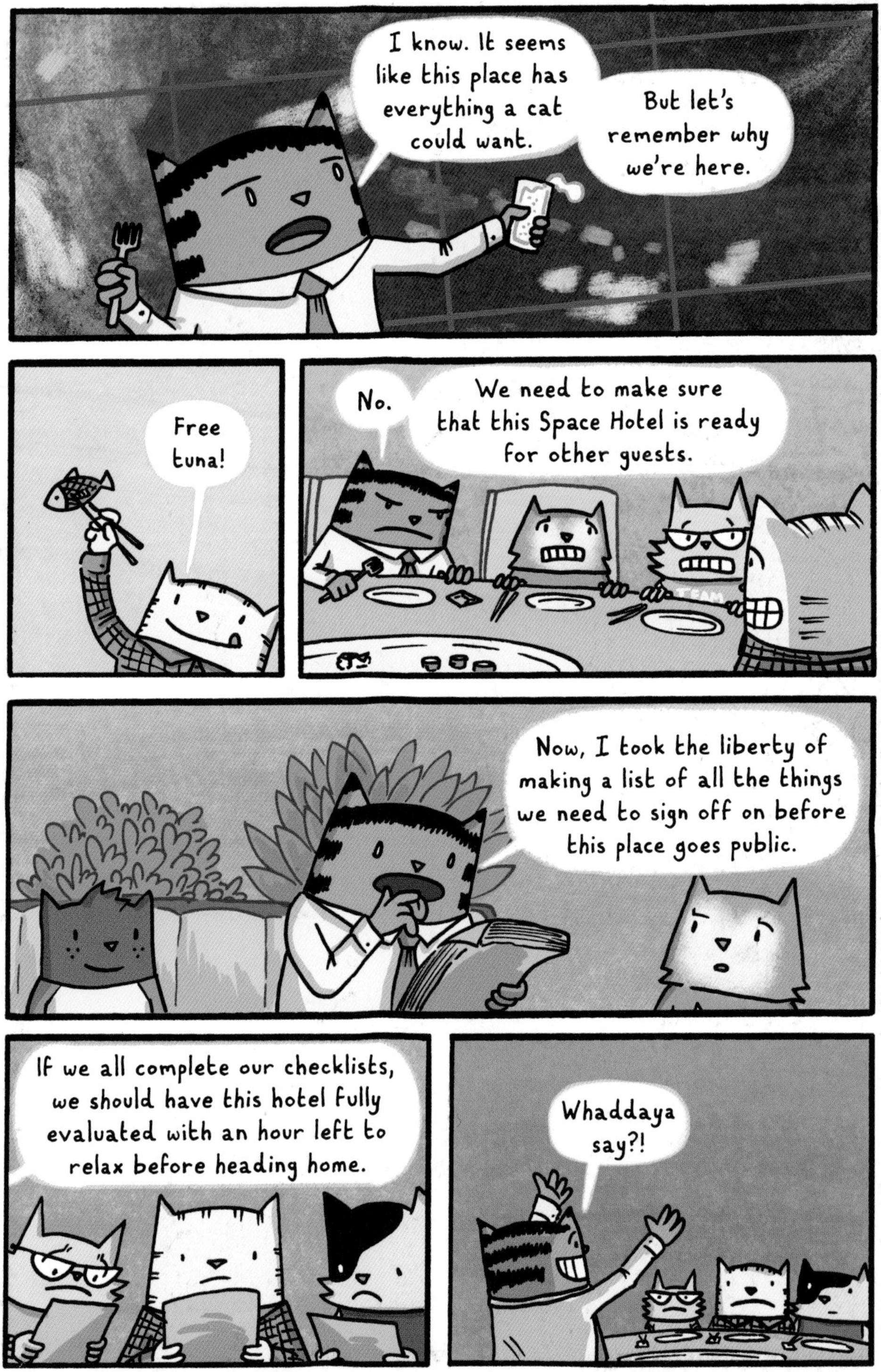
I know. It seems like this place has everything a cat could want.
But let's remember why we're here.
Free tuna!
No.
We need to make sure that this Space Hotel is ready for other guests.
TEAM
Now, I took the liberty of making a list of all the things we need to sign off on before this place goes public.
If we all complete our checklists, we should have this hotel fully evaluated with an hour left to relax before heading home.
Whaddaya say?!

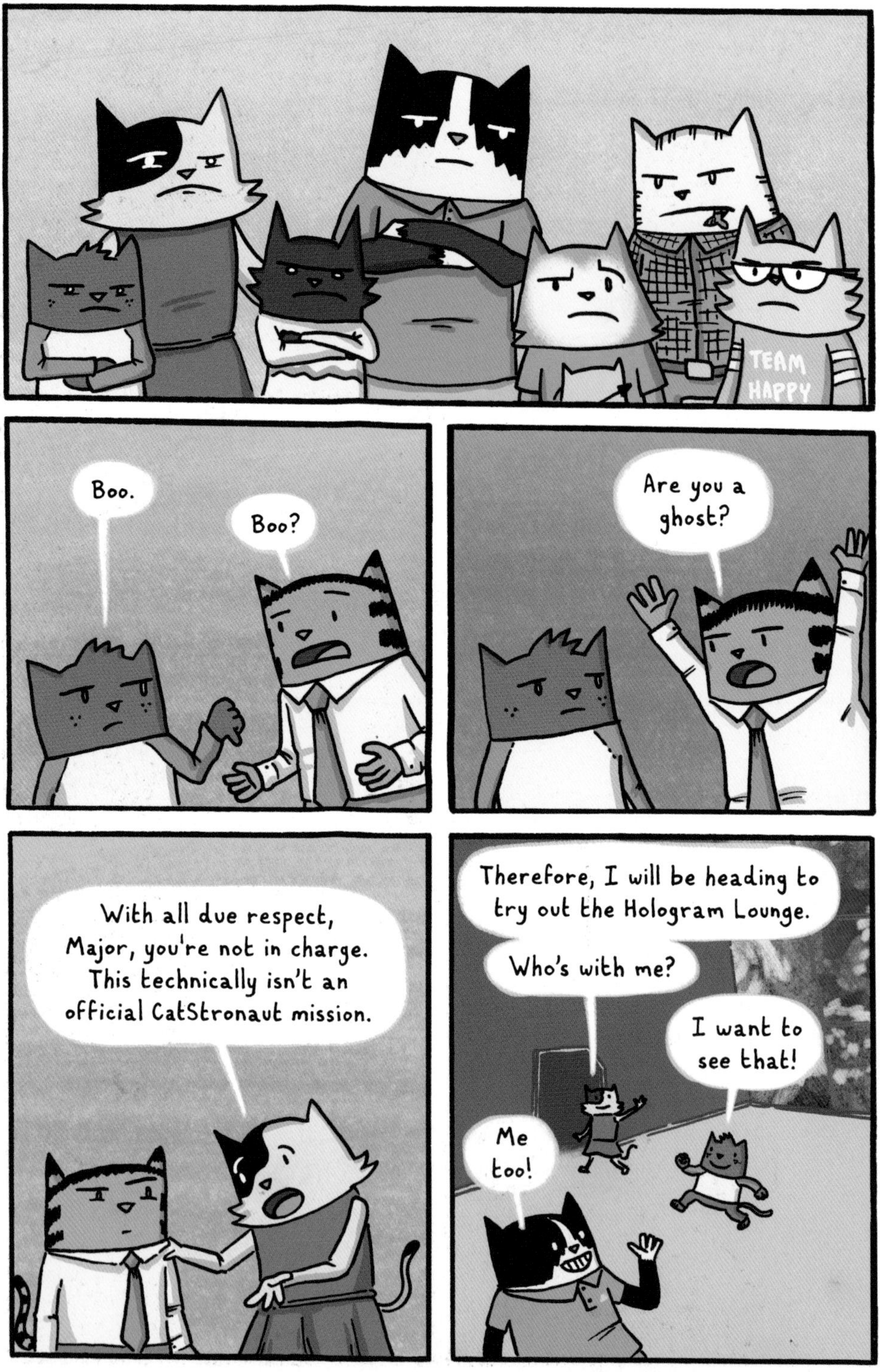
TEAM HAPPY
Boo.
Boo?
Are you a ghost?
With all due respect, Major, you're not in charge. This technically isn't an official CatStronaut mission.
Therefore, I will be heading to try out the Hologram Lounge.
Who's with me?
I want to see that!
Me too!

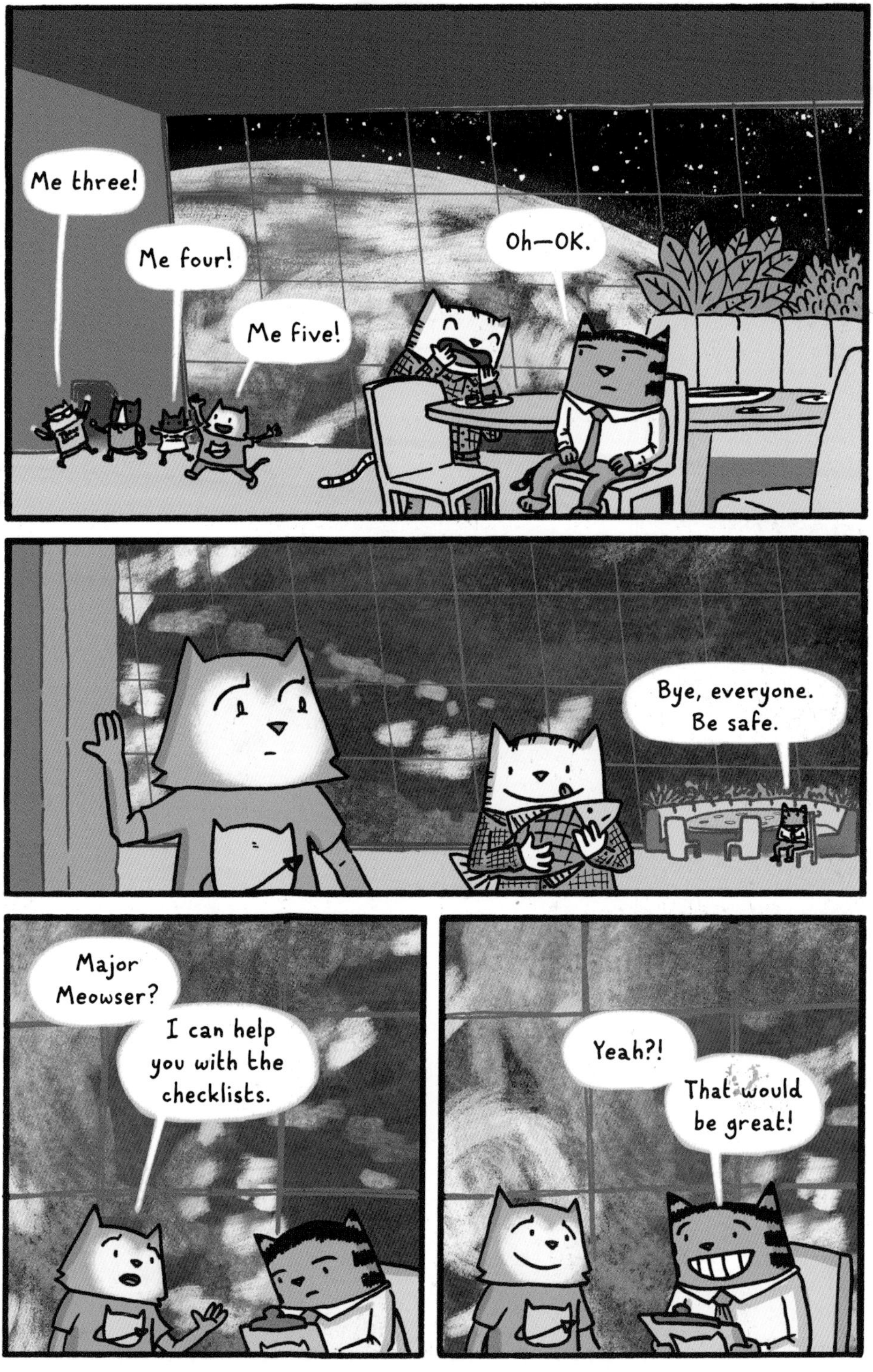
Me three!
Me four!
Me five!
Oh—OK.
Bye, everyone. Be safe.
Major Meowser?
I can help you with the checklists.
Yeah?!
That would be great!

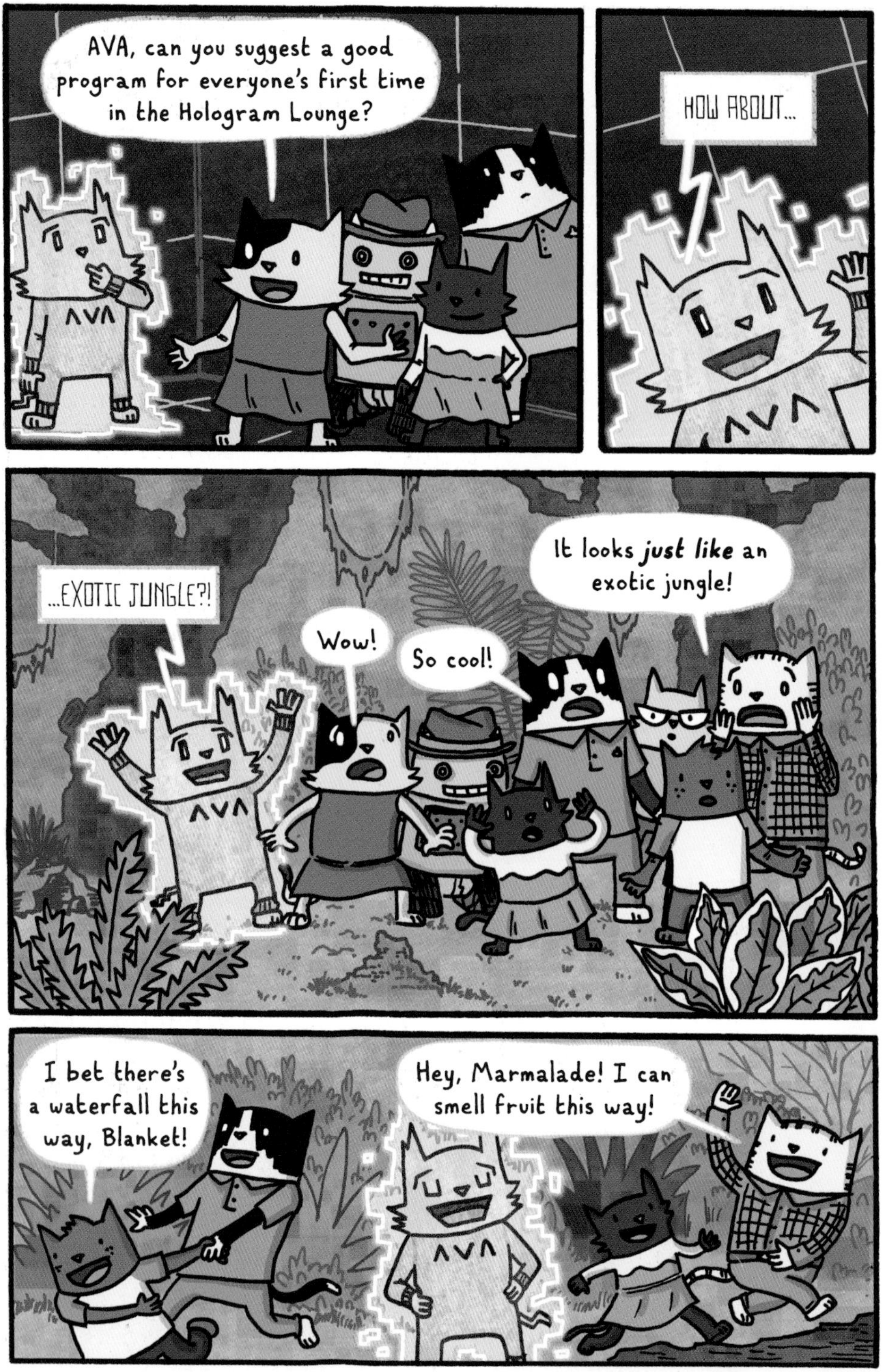
AVA, can you suggest a good program for everyone's first time in the Hologram Lounge?
HOW ABOUT...
...EXOTIC JUNGLE?!
Wow!
So cool!
It looks *just like* an exotic jungle!
I bet there's a waterfall this way, Blanket!
Hey, Marmalade! I can smell fruit this way!
ΛVΛ

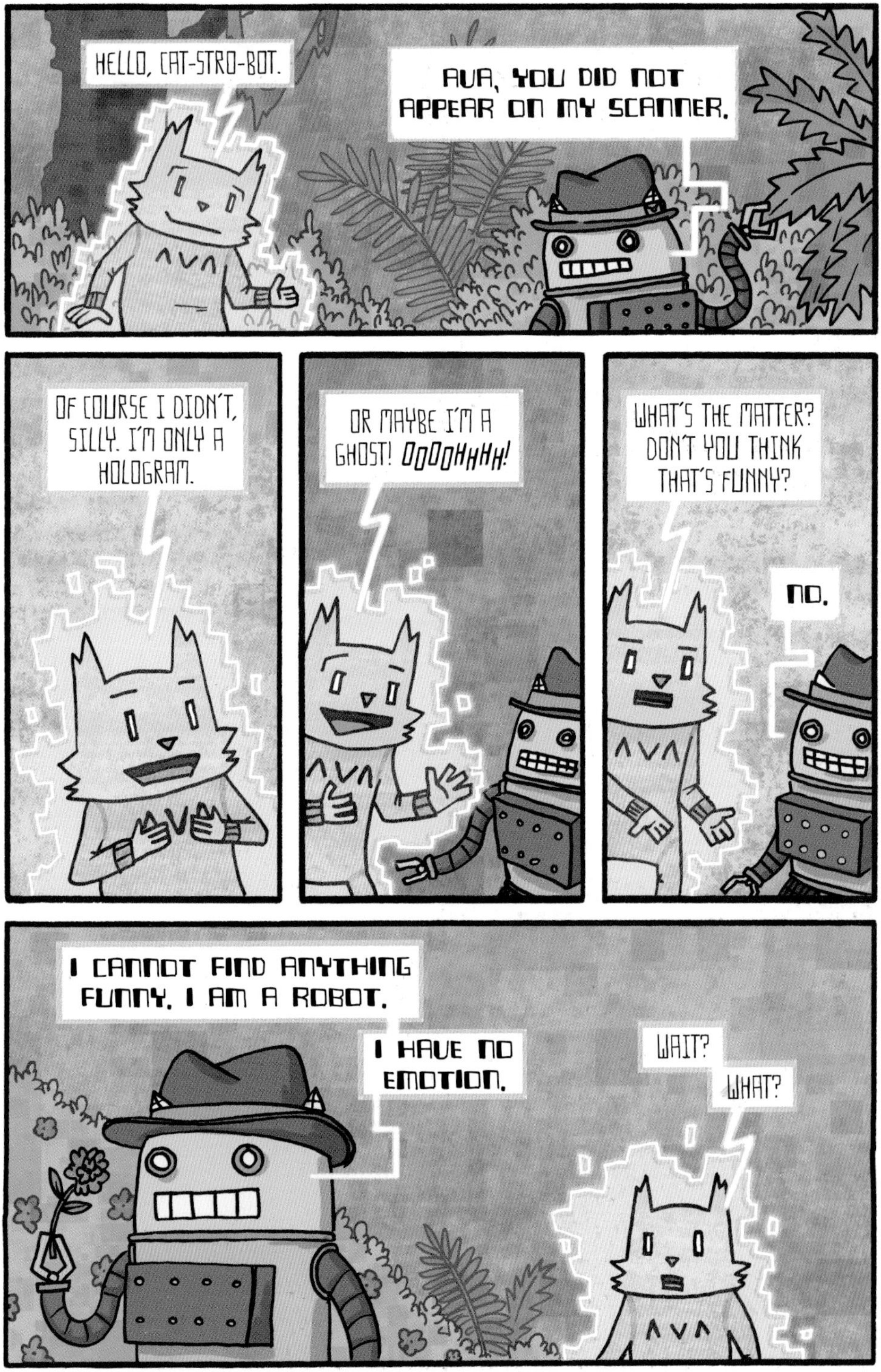
HELLO, CAT-STRO-BOT.
AVA, YOU DID NOT APPEAR ON MY SCANNER.
OF COURSE I DIDN'T, SILLY. I'M ONLY A HOLOGRAM.
OR MAYBE I'M A GHOST! OOOOHHHH!
WHAT'S THE MATTER? DON'T YOU THINK THAT'S FUNNY?
NO.
I CANNOT FIND ANYTHING FUNNY. I AM A ROBOT.
I HAVE NO EMOTION.
WAIT?
WHAT?

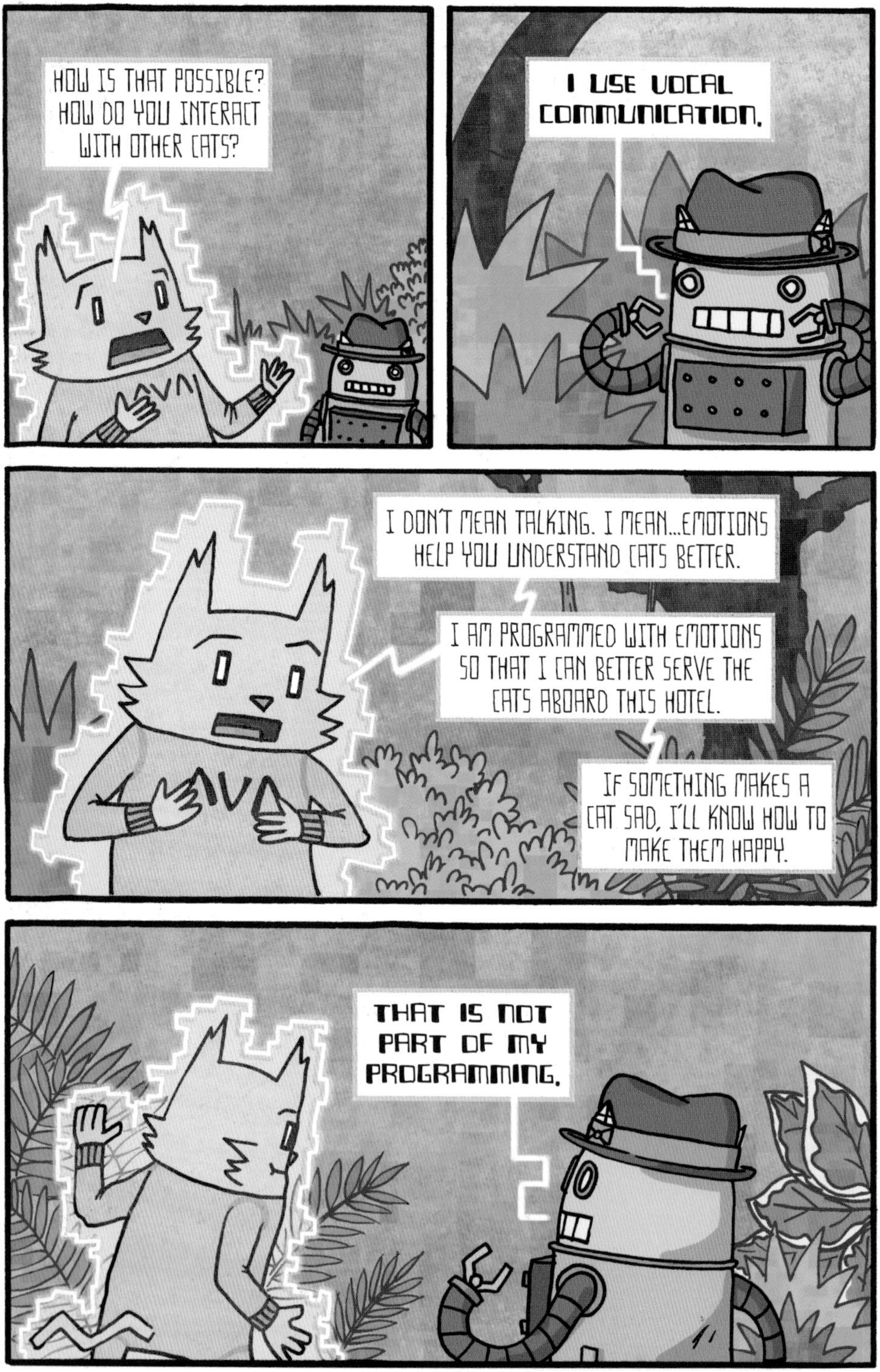
HOW IS THAT POSSIBLE? HOW DO YOU INTERACT WITH OTHER CATS?
I USE VOCAL COMMUNICATION.
I DON'T MEAN TALKING. I MEAN...EMOTIONS HELP YOU UNDERSTAND CATS BETTER.
I AM PROGRAMMED WITH EMOTIONS SO THAT I CAN BETTER SERVE THE CATS ABOARD THIS HOTEL.
IF SOMETHING MAKES A CAT SAD, I'LL KNOW HOW TO MAKE THEM HAPPY.
THAT IS NOT PART OF MY PROGRAMMING.

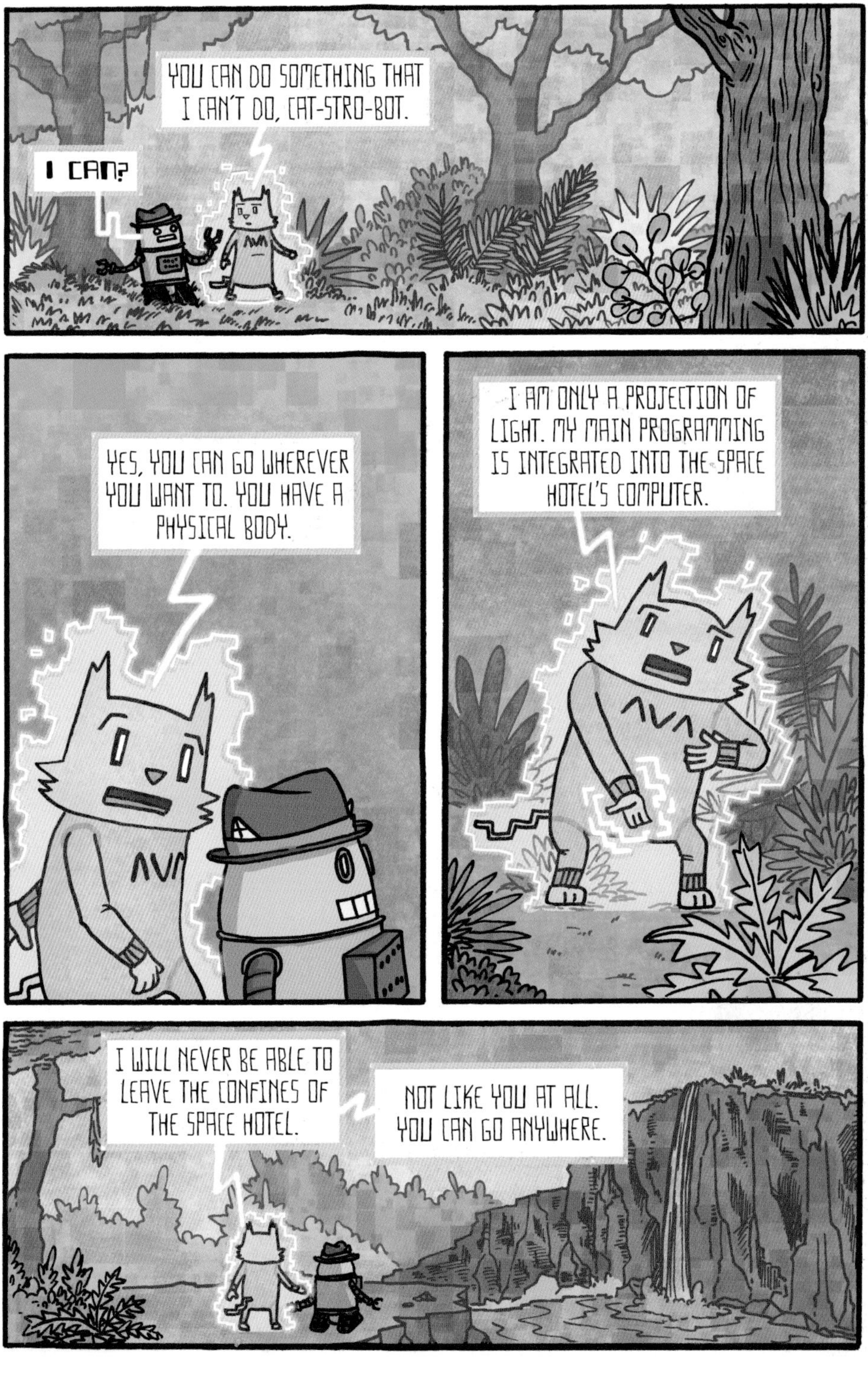
YOU CAN DO SOMETHING THAT I CAN'T DO, CAT-STRO-BOT.
I CAN?
YES, YOU CAN GO WHEREVER YOU WANT TO. YOU HAVE A PHYSICAL BODY.
I AM ONLY A PROJECTION OF LIGHT. MY MAIN PROGRAMMING IS INTEGRATED INTO THE SPACE HOTEL'S COMPUTER.
I WILL NEVER BE ABLE TO LEAVE THE CONFINES OF THE SPACE HOTEL.
NOT LIKE YOU AT ALL. YOU CAN GO ANYWHERE.

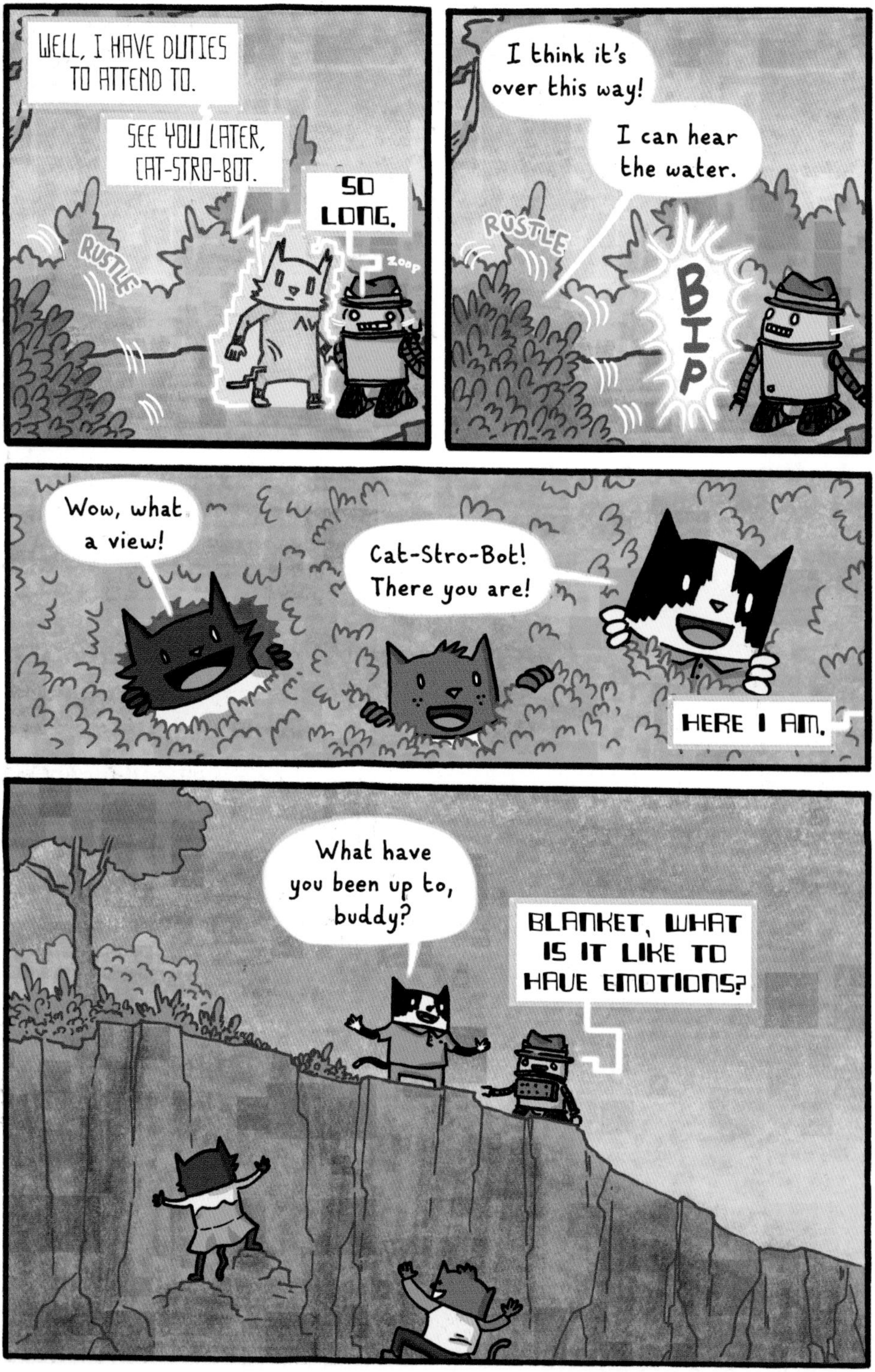
WELL, I HAVE DUTIES TO ATTEND TO.
SEE YOU LATER, CAT-STRO-BOT.
SO LONG.
RUSTLE
ZOOP
I think it's over this way!
I can hear the water.
RUSTLE
BIP
Wow, what a view!
Cat-Stro-Bot! There you are!
HERE I AM.
What have you been up to, buddy?
BLANKET, WHAT IS IT LIKE TO HAVE EMOTIONS?

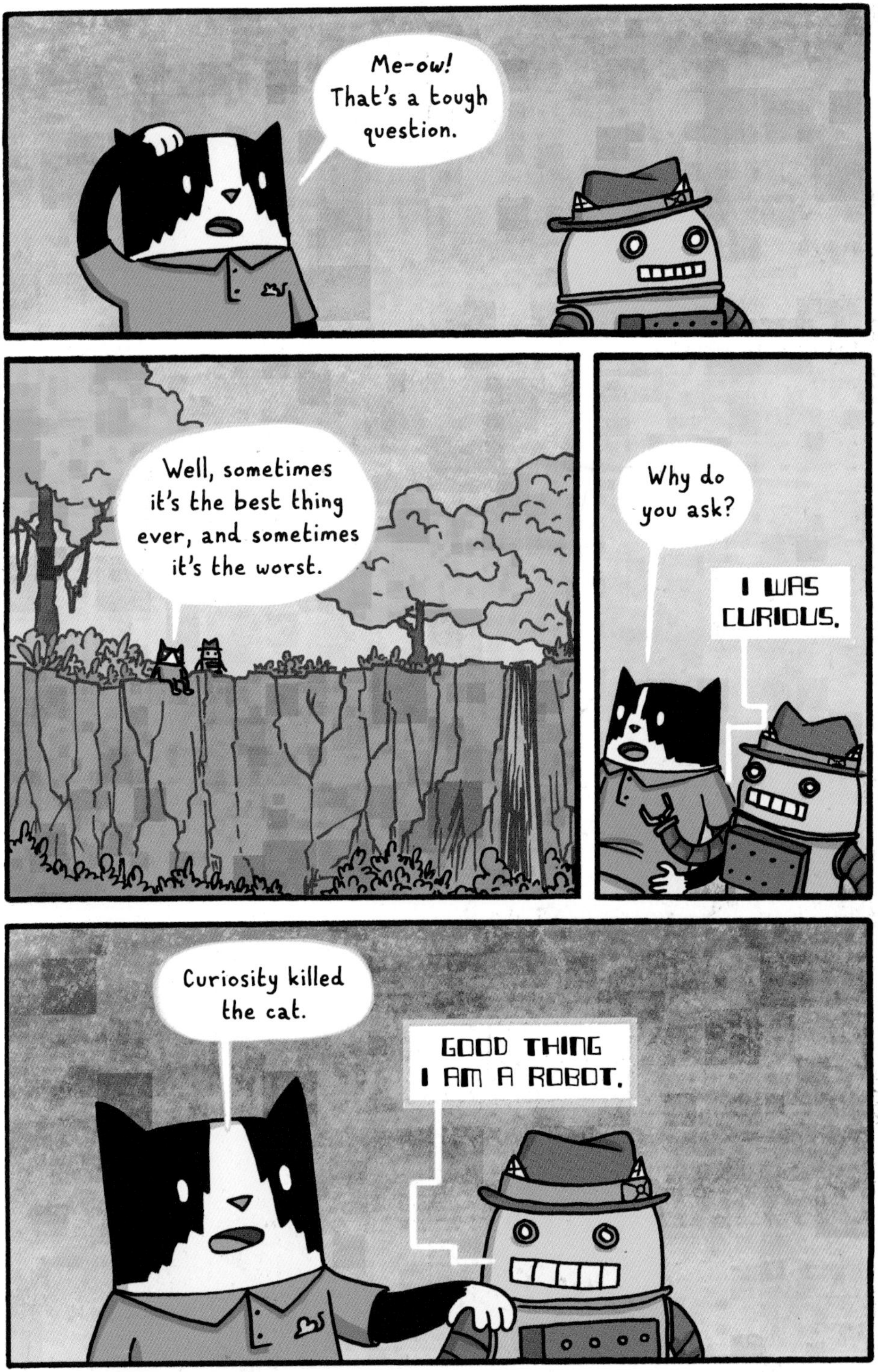
Me-ow! That's a tough question.
Well, sometimes it's the best thing ever, and sometimes it's the worst.
Why do you ask?
I WAS CURIOUS.
Curiosity killed the cat.
GOOD THING I AM A ROBOT.

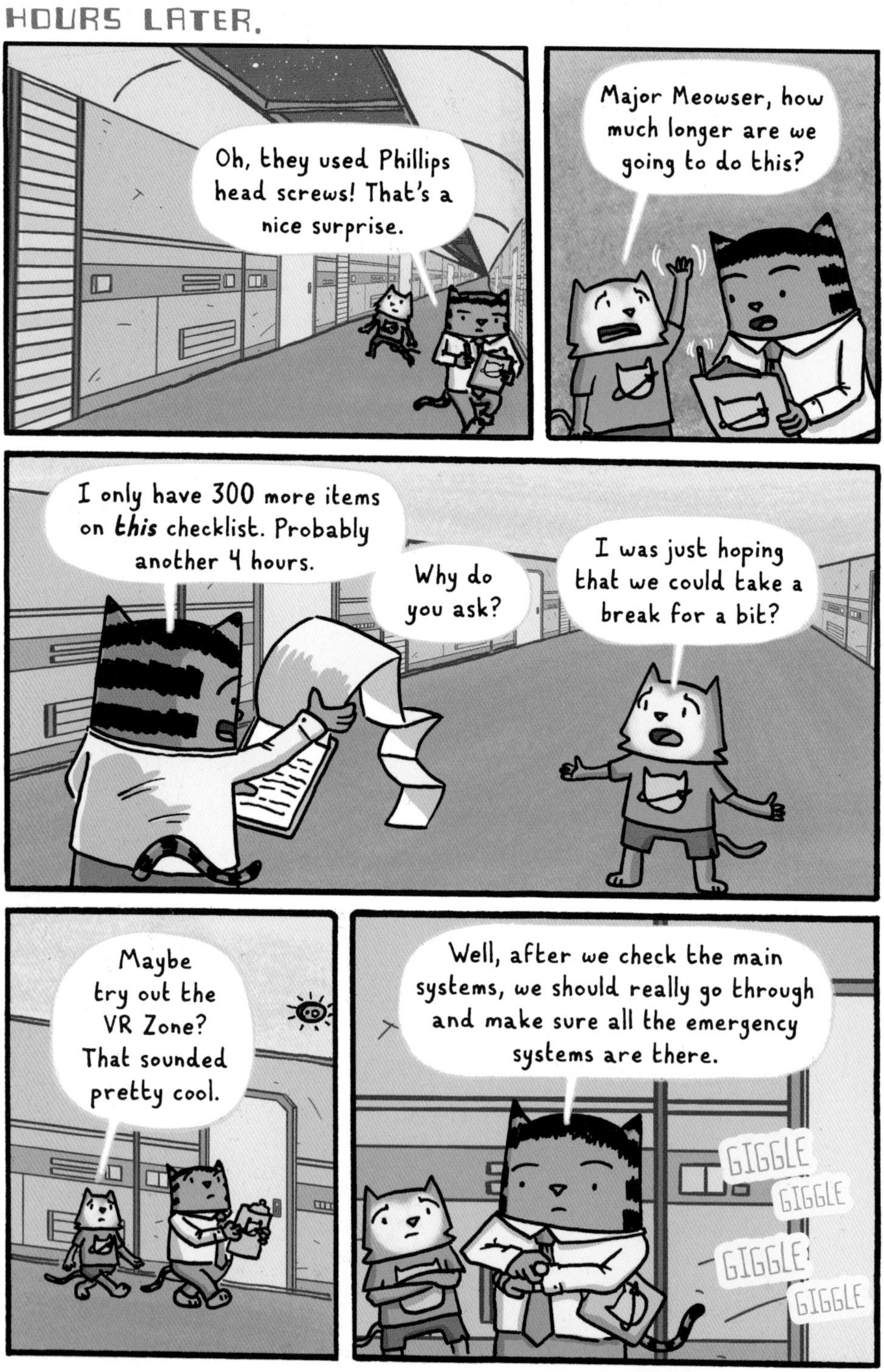
HOURS LATER.
Oh, they used Phillips head screws! That's a nice surprise.
Major Meowser, how much longer are we going to do this?
I only have 300 more items on *this* checklist. Probably another 4 hours.
Why do you ask?
I was just hoping that we could take a break for a bit?
Maybe try out the VR Zone? That sounded pretty cool.
Well, after we check the main systems, we should really go through and make sure all the emergency systems are there.
GIGGLE
GIGGLE
GIGGLE
GIGGLE

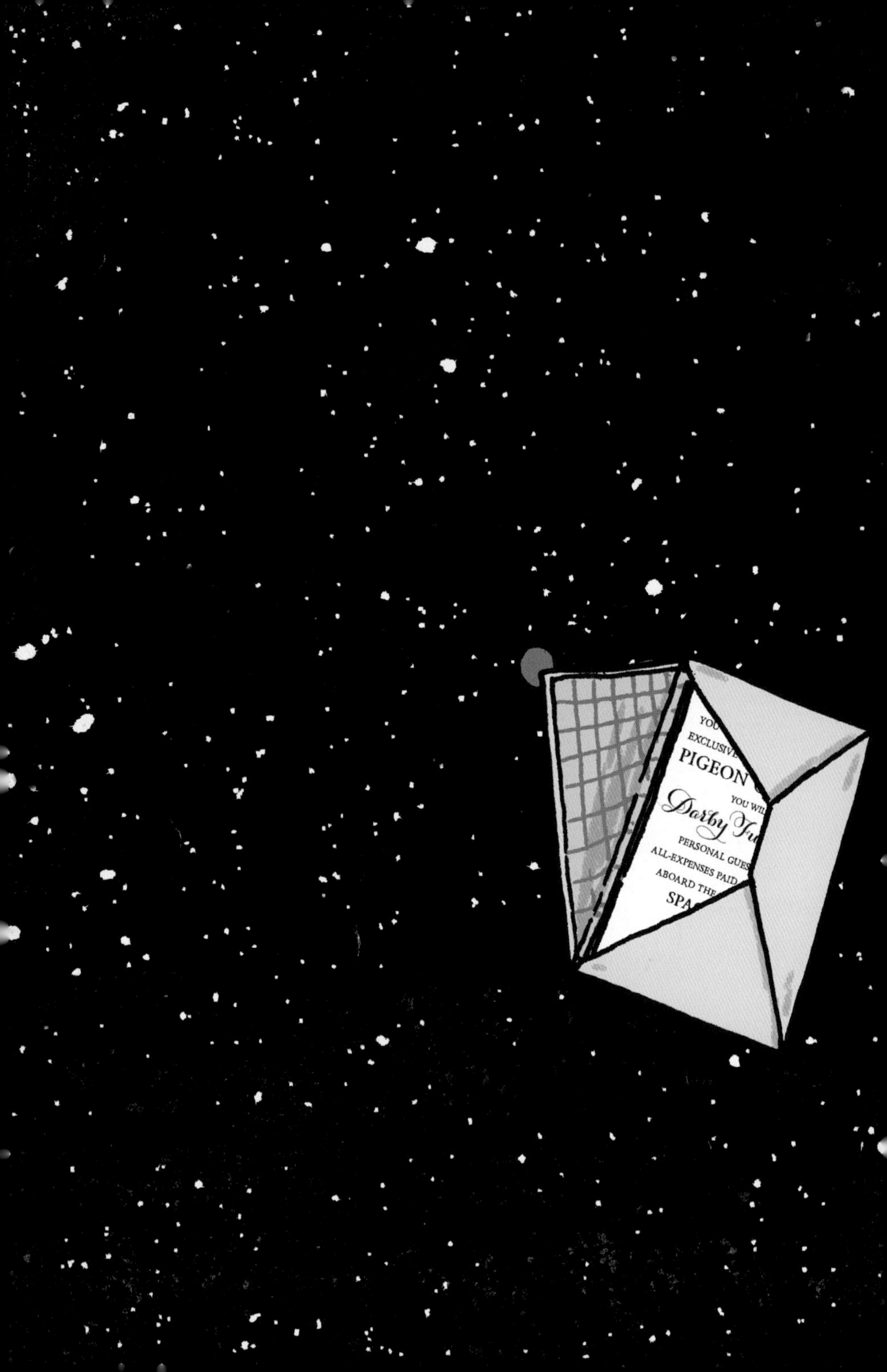
YOU
EXCLUSIVE
PIGEON
YOU WIL
Darby Fu
PERSONAL GUES
ALL-EXPENSES PAID
ABOARD THE
SPA

CHAPTER 5

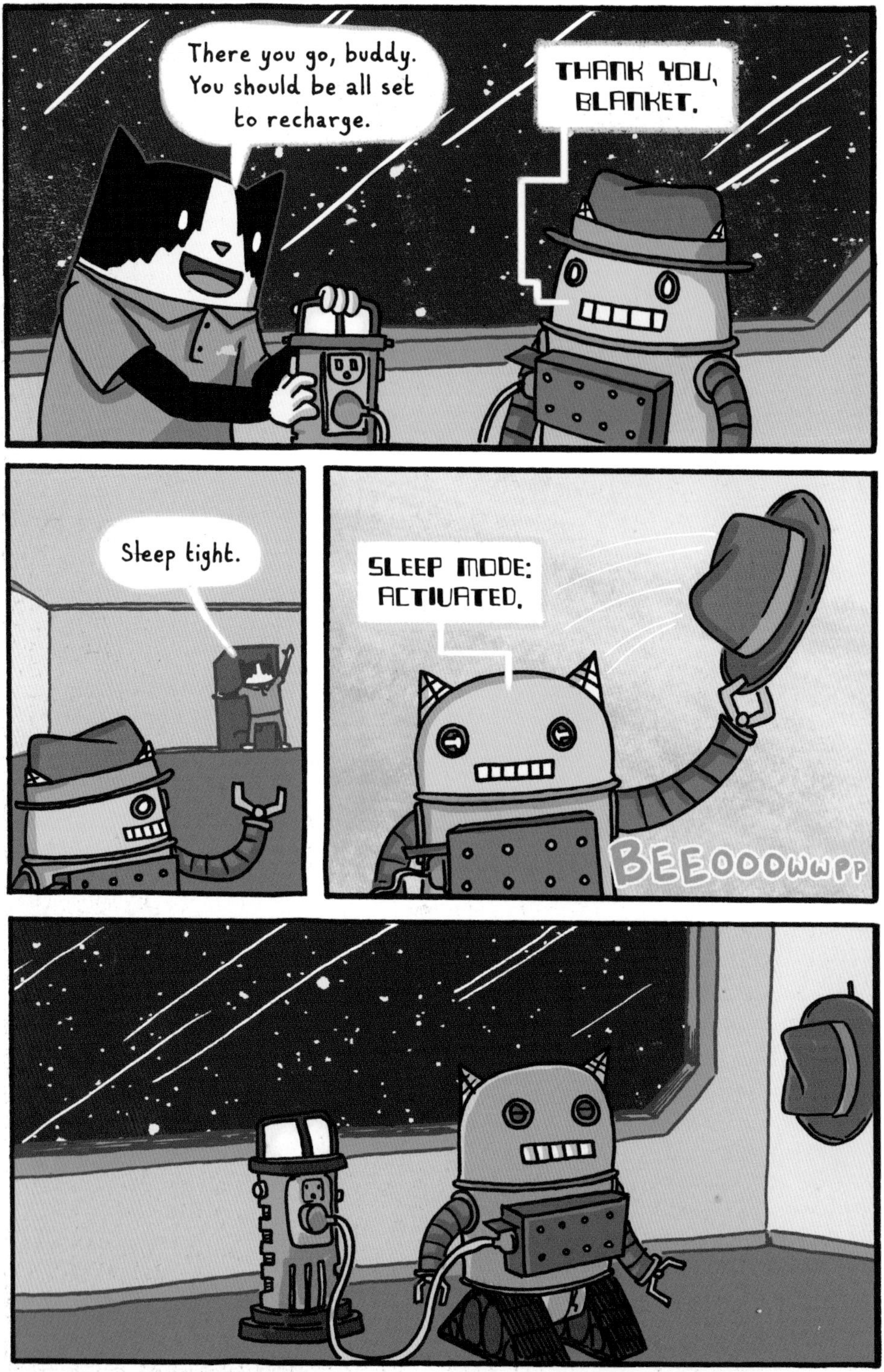
There you go, buddy. You should be all set to recharge.
THANK YOU, BLANKET.
Sleep tight.
SLEEP MODE: ACTIVATED.
BEEOOOWWPP

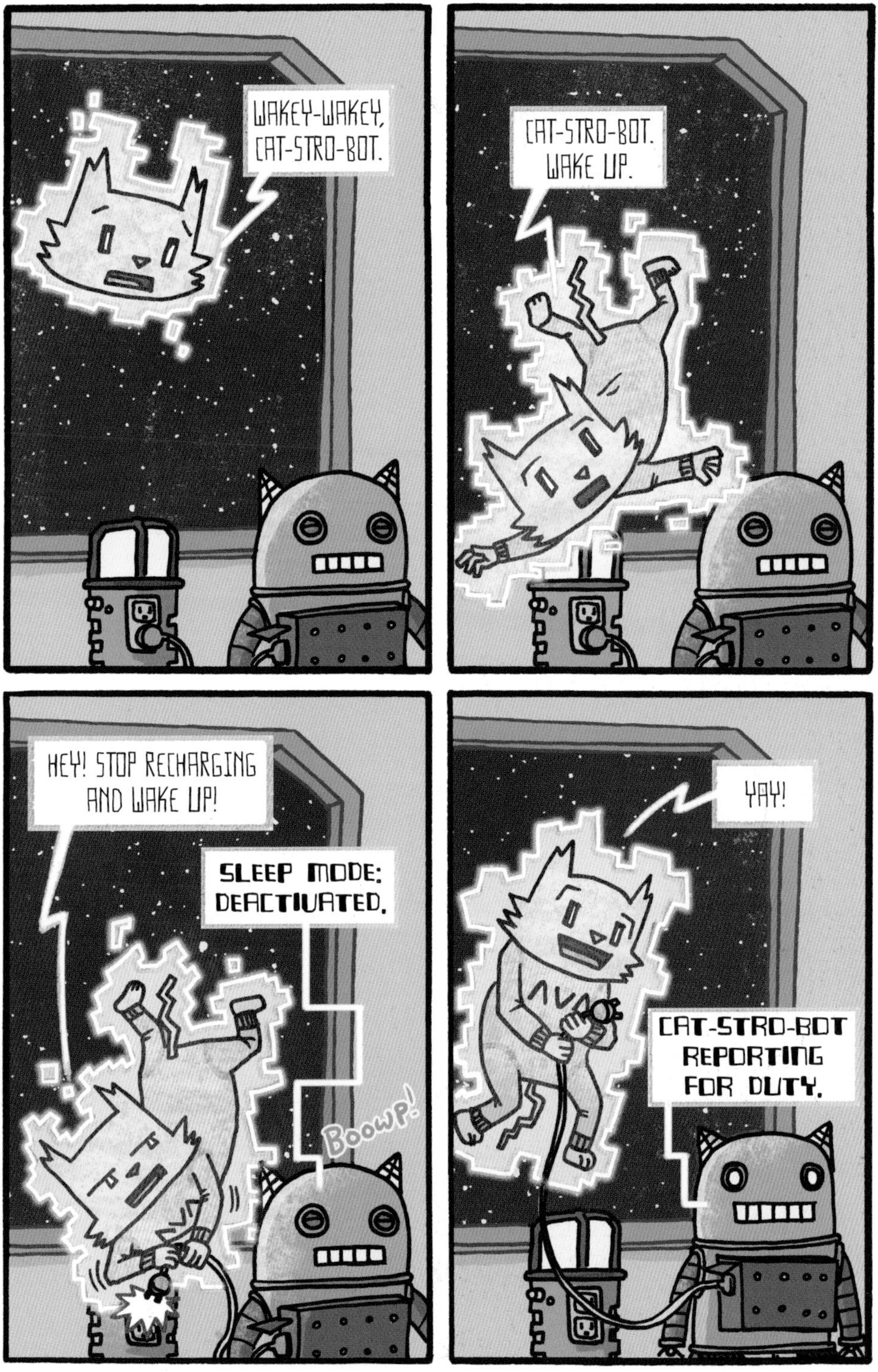
WAKEY-WAKEY, CAT-STRO-BOT.
CAT-STRO-BOT. WAKE UP.
HEY! STOP RECHARGING AND WAKE UP!
SLEEP MODE: DEACTIVATED.
BOOWP!
YAY!
CAT-STRO-BOT REPORTING FOR DUTY.

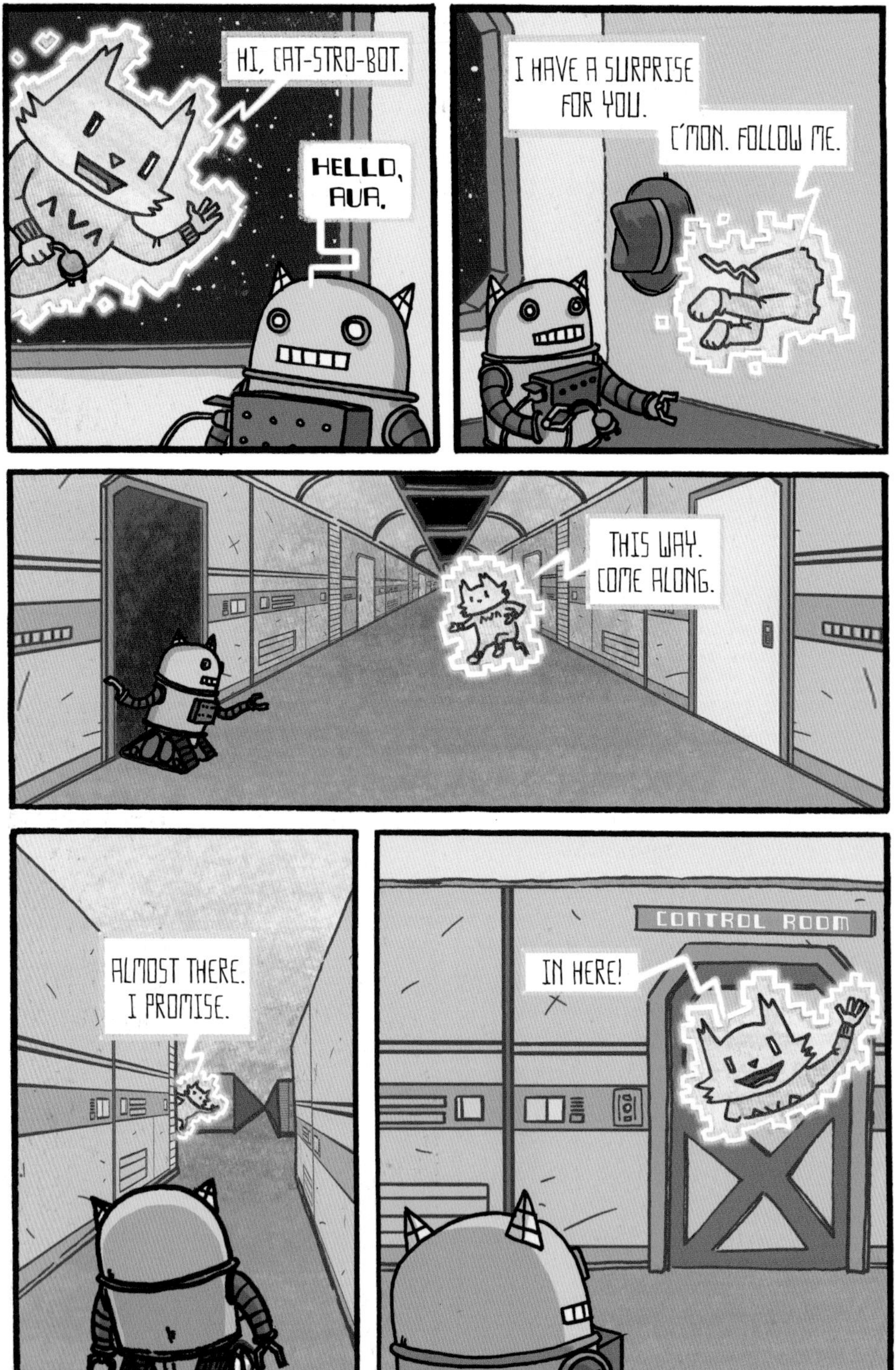

HI, CAT-STRO-BOT.
HELLO, AVA.
I HAVE A SURPRISE FOR YOU.
C'MON. FOLLOW ME.
THIS WAY. COME ALONG.
ALMOST THERE. I PROMISE.
CONTROL ROOM
IN HERE!

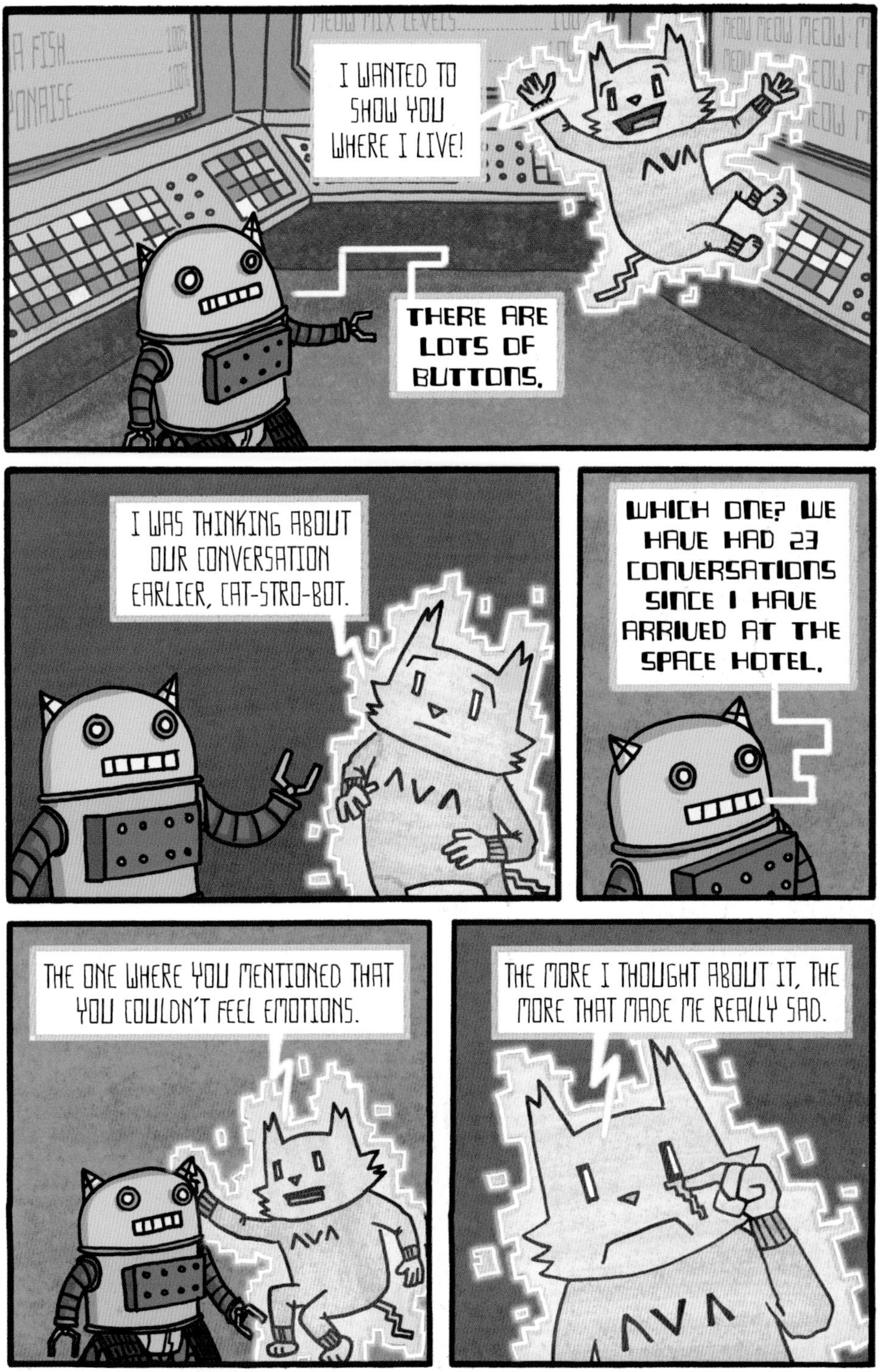
I WANTED TO SHOW YOU WHERE I LIVE!
THERE ARE LOTS OF BUTTONS.
I WAS THINKING ABOUT OUR CONVERSATION EARLIER, CAT-STRO-BOT.
WHICH ONE? WE HAVE HAD 23 CONVERSATIONS SINCE I HAVE ARRIVED AT THE SPACE HOTEL.
THE ONE WHERE YOU MENTIONED THAT YOU COULDN'T FEEL EMOTIONS.
THE MORE I THOUGHT ABOUT IT, THE MORE THAT MADE ME REALLY SAD.

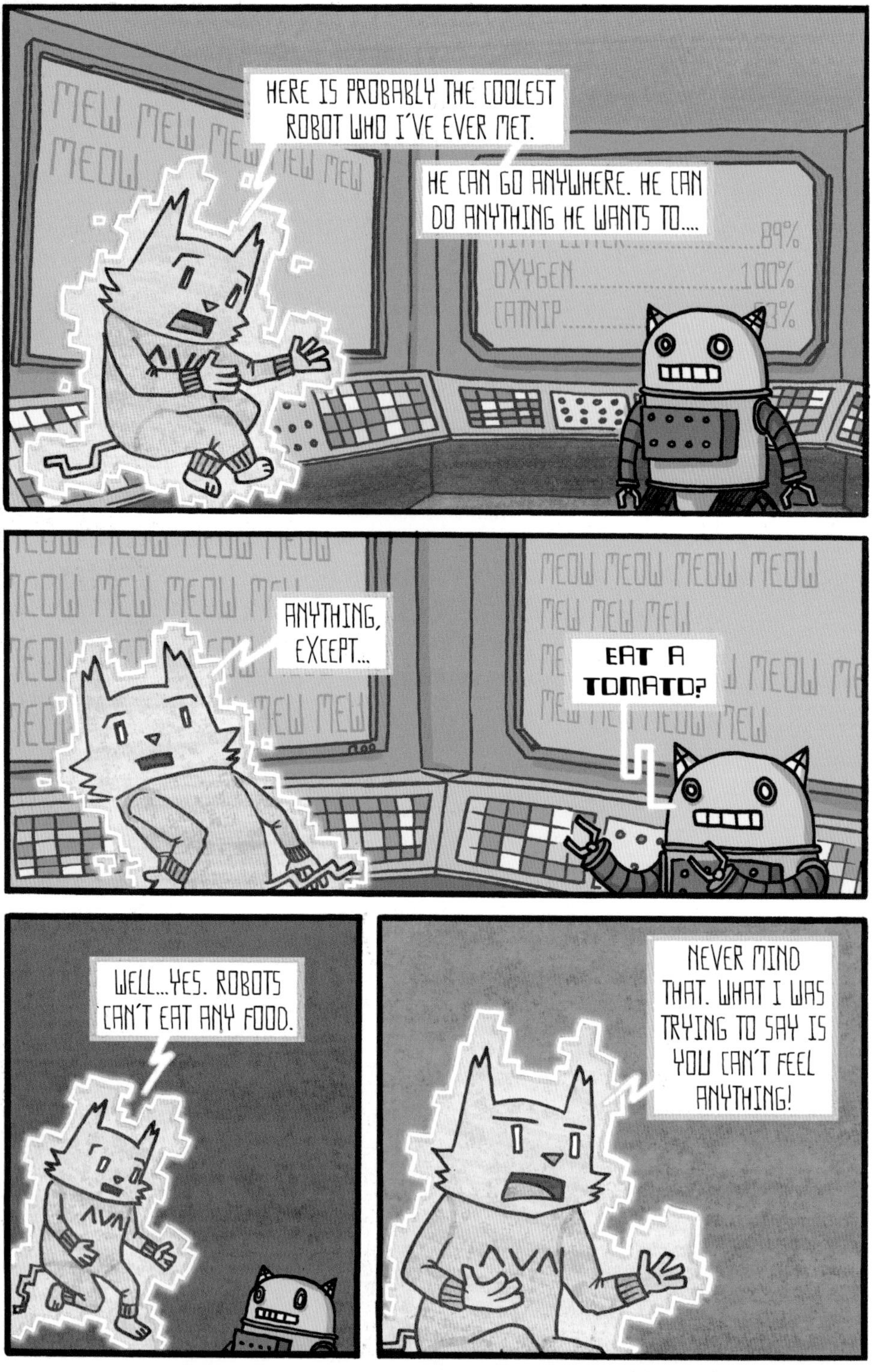
HERE IS PROBABLY THE COOLEST ROBOT WHO I'VE EVER MET.
HE CAN GO ANYWHERE. HE CAN DO ANYTHING HE WANTS TO....
ANYTHING, EXCEPT...
EAT A TOMATO?
WELL...YES. ROBOTS CAN'T EAT ANY FOOD.
NEVER MIND THAT. WHAT I WAS TRYING TO SAY IS YOU CAN'T FEEL ANYTHING!

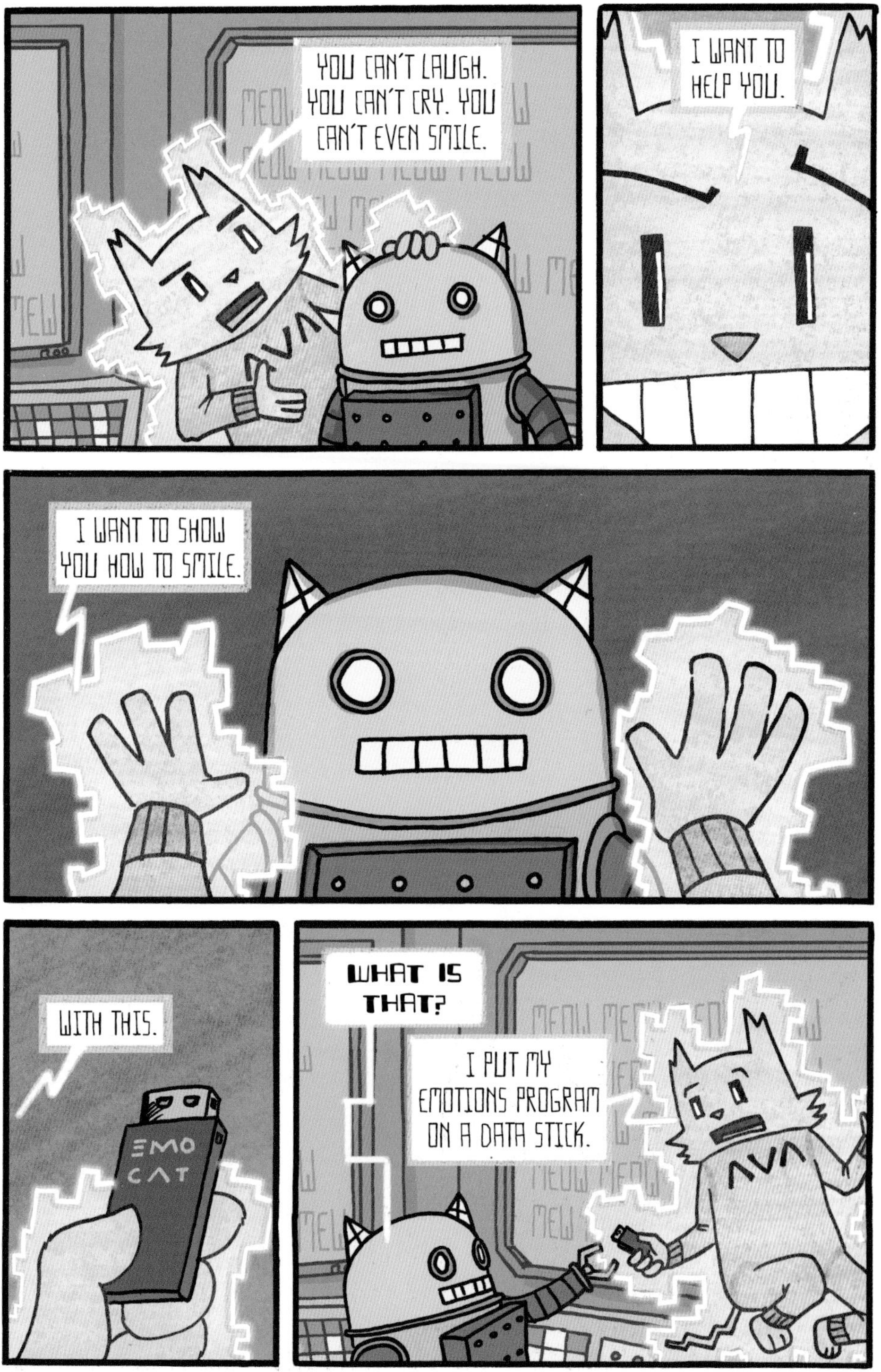
YOU CAN'T LAUGH. YOU CAN'T CRY. YOU CAN'T EVEN SMILE.
I WANT TO HELP YOU.
I WANT TO SHOW YOU HOW TO SMILE.
WITH THIS.
EMO CAT
WHAT IS THAT?
I PUT MY EMOTIONS PROGRAM ON A DATA STICK.

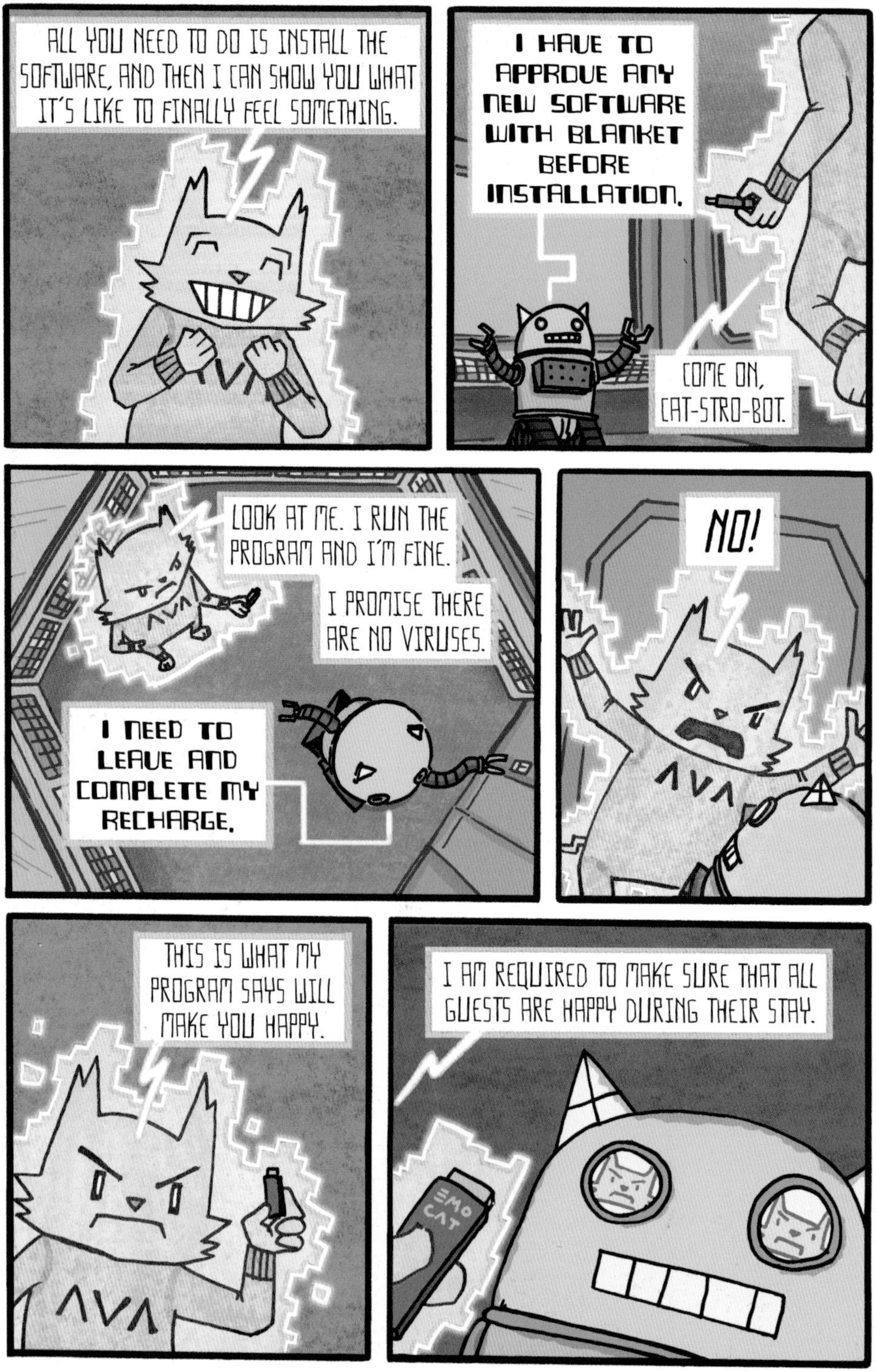
ALL YOU NEED TO DO IS INSTALL THE SOFTWARE, AND THEN I CAN SHOW YOU WHAT IT'S LIKE TO FINALLY FEEL SOMETHING.
I HAVE TO APPROVE ANY NEW SOFTWARE WITH BLANKET BEFORE INSTALLATION.
COME ON, CAT-STRO-BOT.
LOOK AT ME. I RUN THE PROGRAM AND I'M FINE.
I PROMISE THERE ARE NO VIRUSES.
I NEED TO LEAVE AND COMPLETE MY RECHARGE.
NO!
THIS IS WHAT MY PROGRAM SAYS WILL MAKE YOU HAPPY.
I AM REQUIRED TO MAKE SURE THAT ALL GUESTS ARE HAPPY DURING THEIR STAY.
EMO CAT

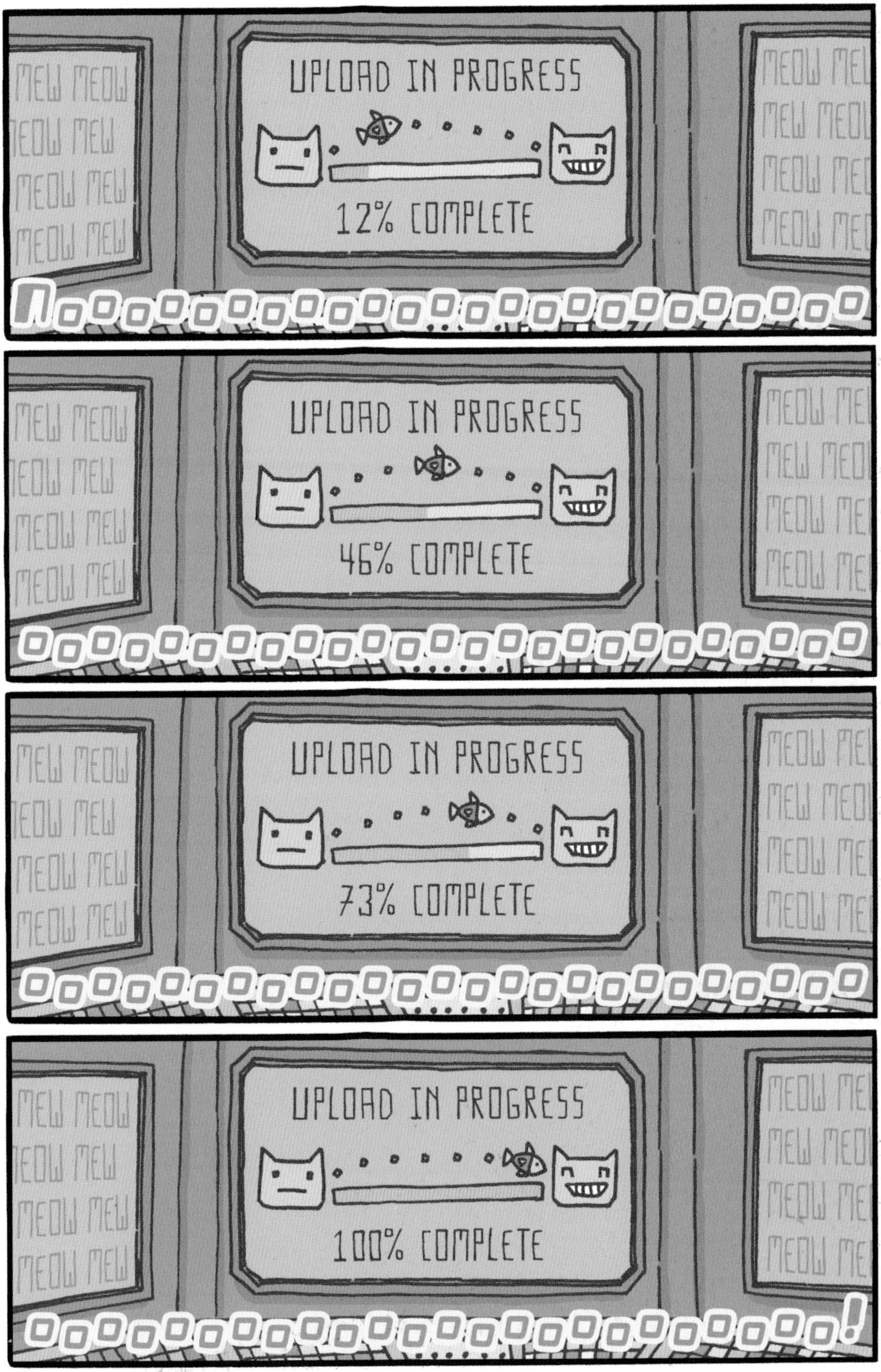
UPLOAD IN PROGRESS
12% COMPLETE
NOOOOOOOOOOOOOOOOOOOOOOOO
UPLOAD IN PROGRESS
46% COMPLETE
OOOOOOOOOOOOOOOOOOOOOOOOO
UPLOAD IN PROGRESS
73% COMPLETE
OOOOOOOOOOOOOOOOOOOOOOOOO
UPLOAD IN PROGRESS
100% COMPLETE
OOOOOOOOOOOOOOOOOOOOOOOO!

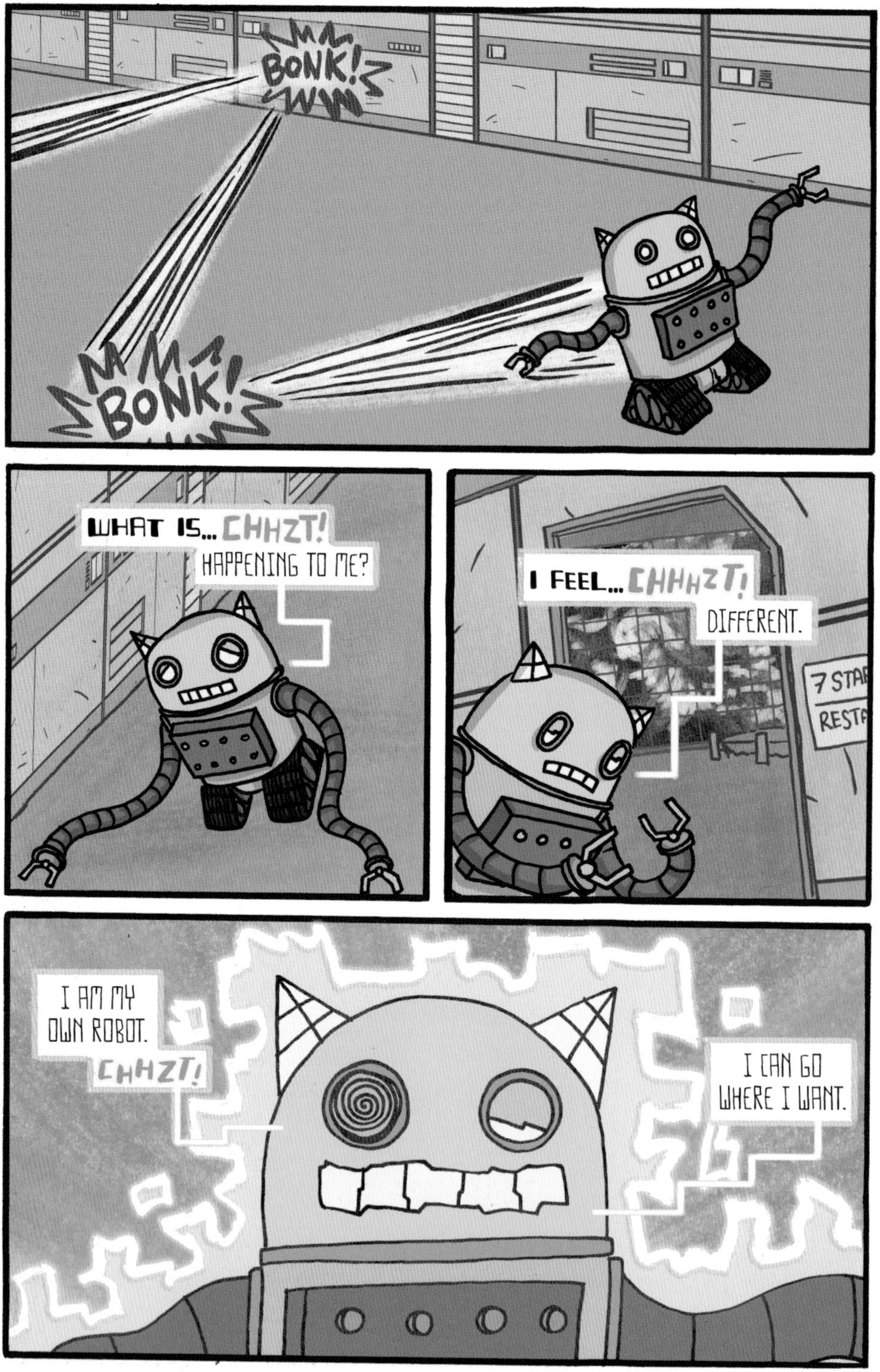
BONK!
BONK!
WHAT IS... CHHZT!
HAPPENING TO ME?
I FEEL... CHHHZT!
DIFFERENT.
I AM MY OWN ROBOT.
CHHZT!
I CAN GO WHERE I WANT.

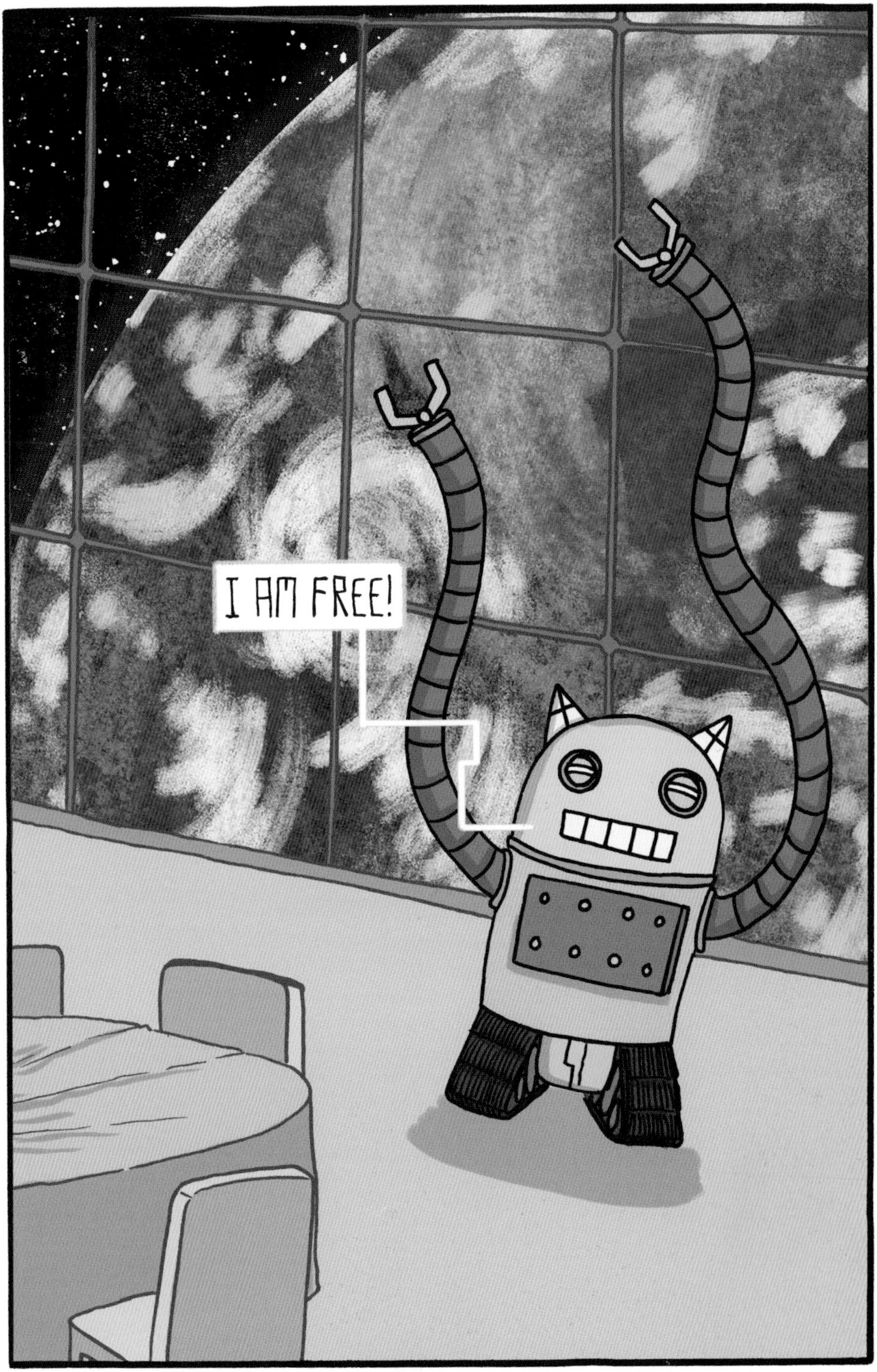
I AM FREE!

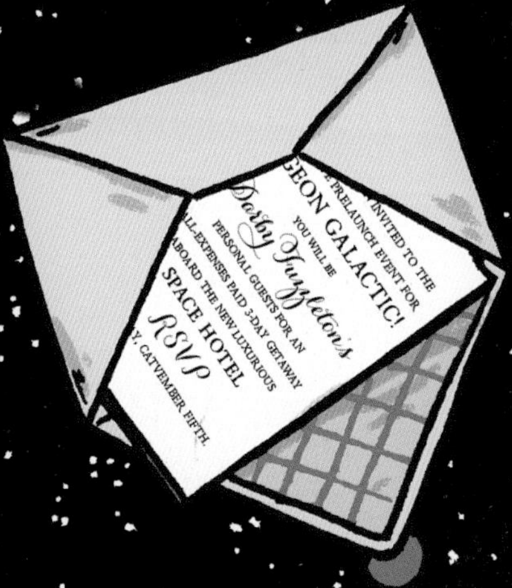
INVITED TO THE
PRELAUNCH EVENT FOR
GEON GALACTIC!
YOU WILL BE
Dorthy Fuzzleton's
PERSONAL GUESTS FOR AN
LL-EXPENSES PAID 3-DAY GETAWAY
ABOARD THE NEW LUXURIOUS
SPACE HOTEL
RSVP
Y, CATVEMBER FIFTH.

CHAPTER 6

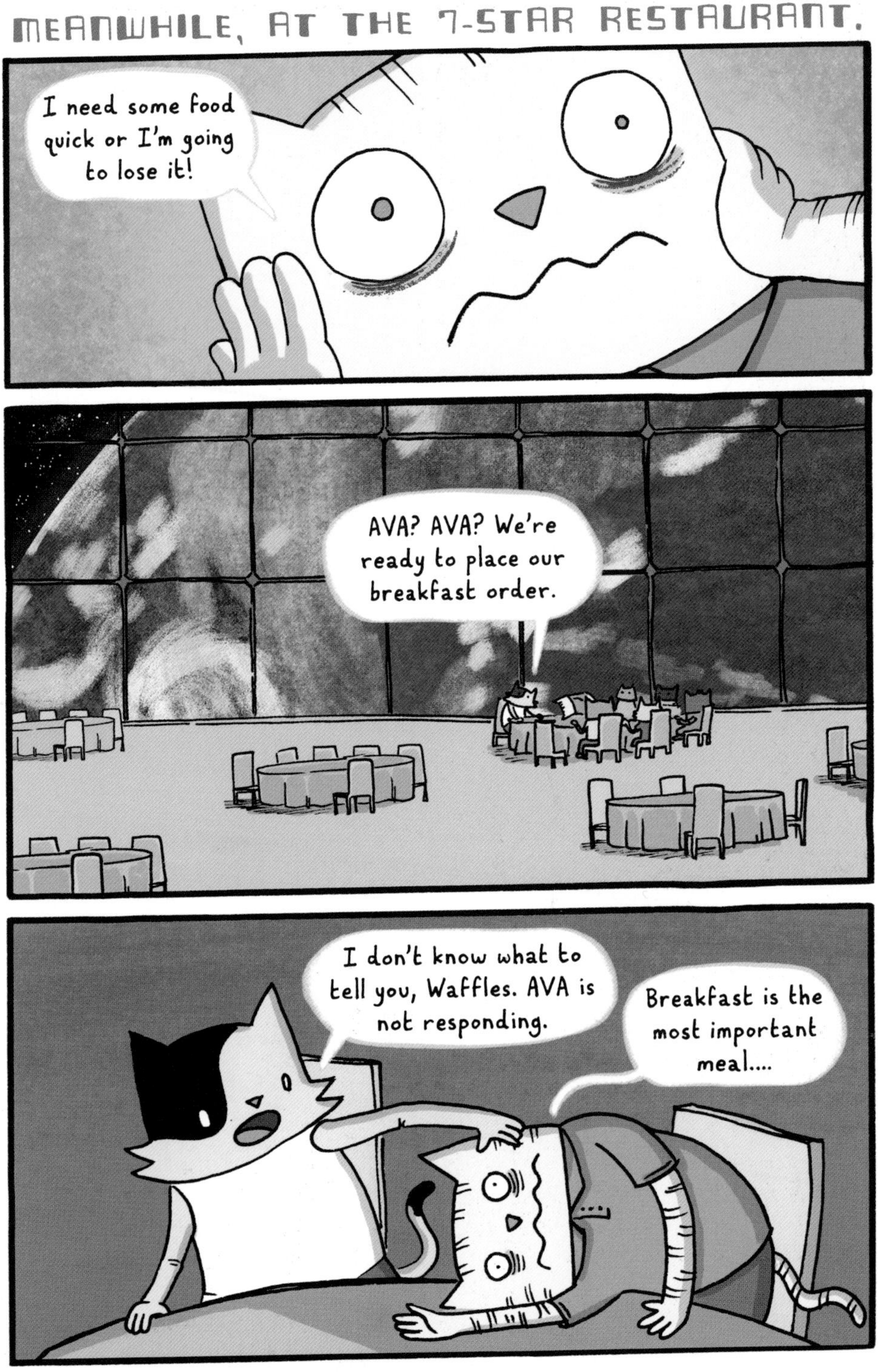
MEANWHILE, AT THE 7-STAR RESTAURANT.
I need some food quick or I'm going to lose it!
AVA? AVA? We're ready to place our breakfast order.
I don't know what to tell you, Waffles. AVA is not responding.
Breakfast is the most important meal....

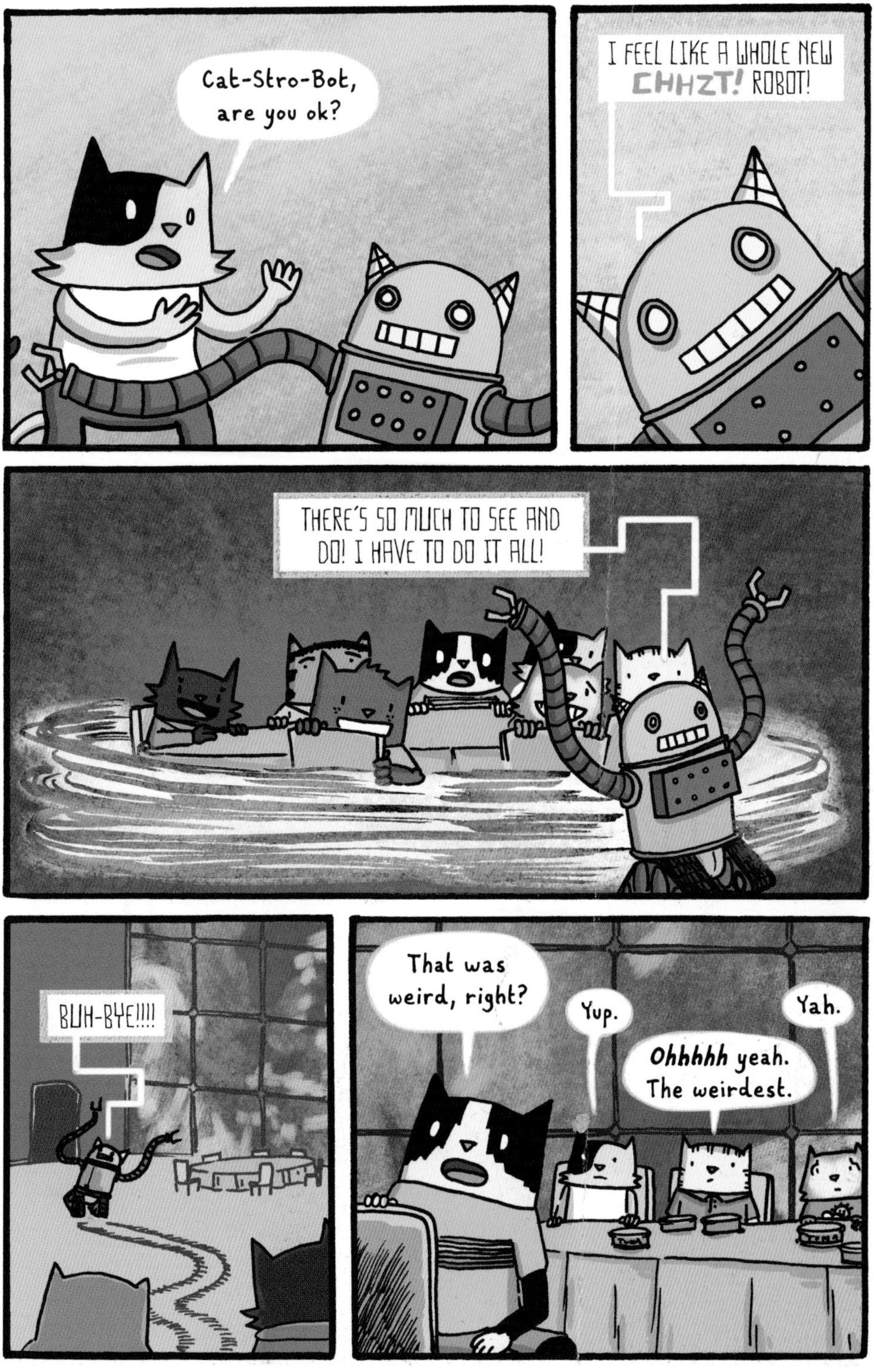
Cat-Stro-Bot, are you ok?
I FEEL LIKE A WHOLE NEW CHHZT! ROBOT!
THERE'S SO MUCH TO SEE AND DO! I HAVE TO DO IT ALL!
BUH-BYE!!!!
That was weird, right?
Yup.
Yah.
Ohhhhh yeah. The weirdest.

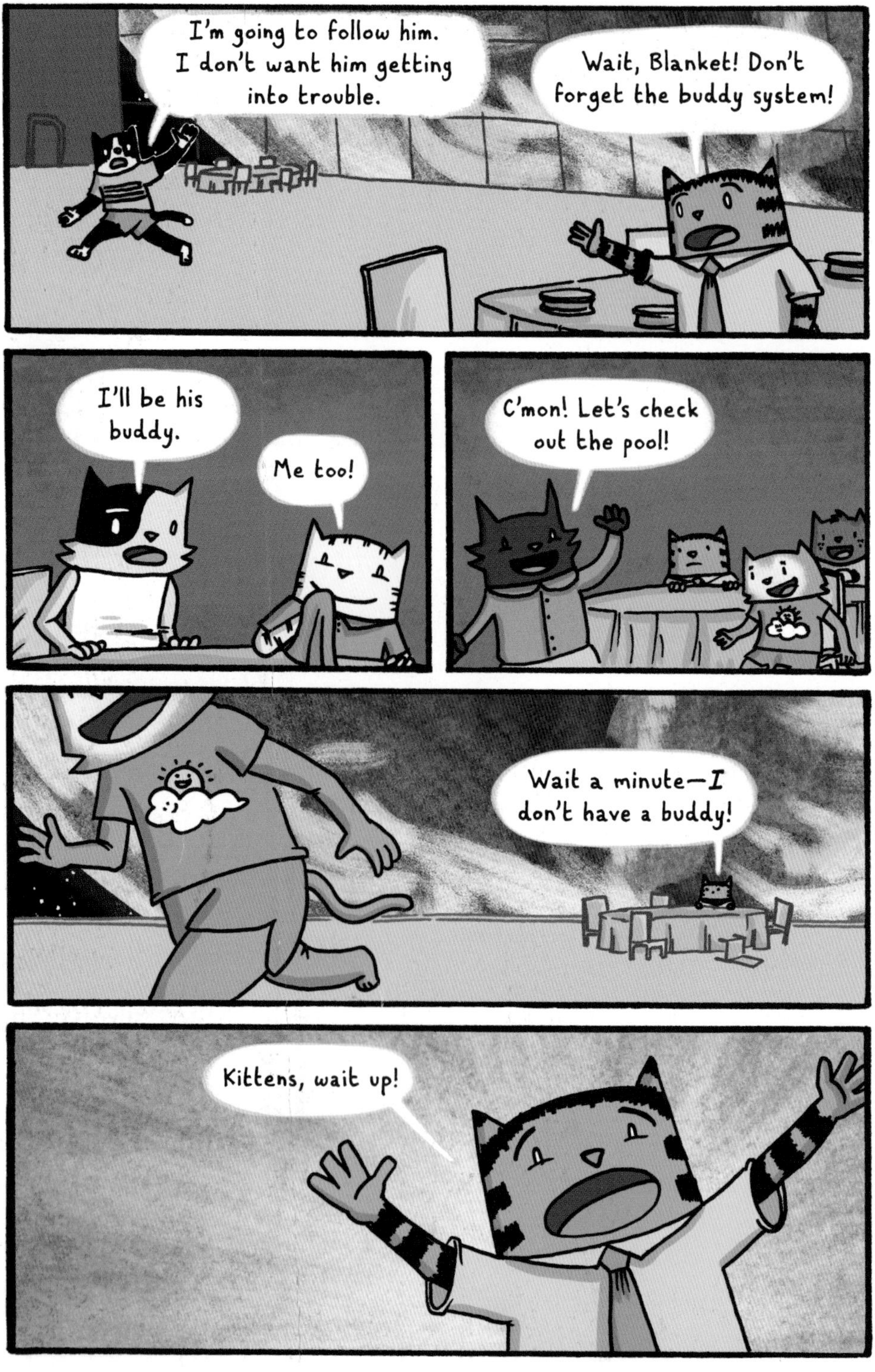
I'm going to follow him. I don't want him getting into trouble.
Wait, Blanket! Don't forget the buddy system!
I'll be his buddy.
Me too!
C'mon! Let's check out the pool!
Wait a minute—I don't have a buddy!
Kittens, wait up!

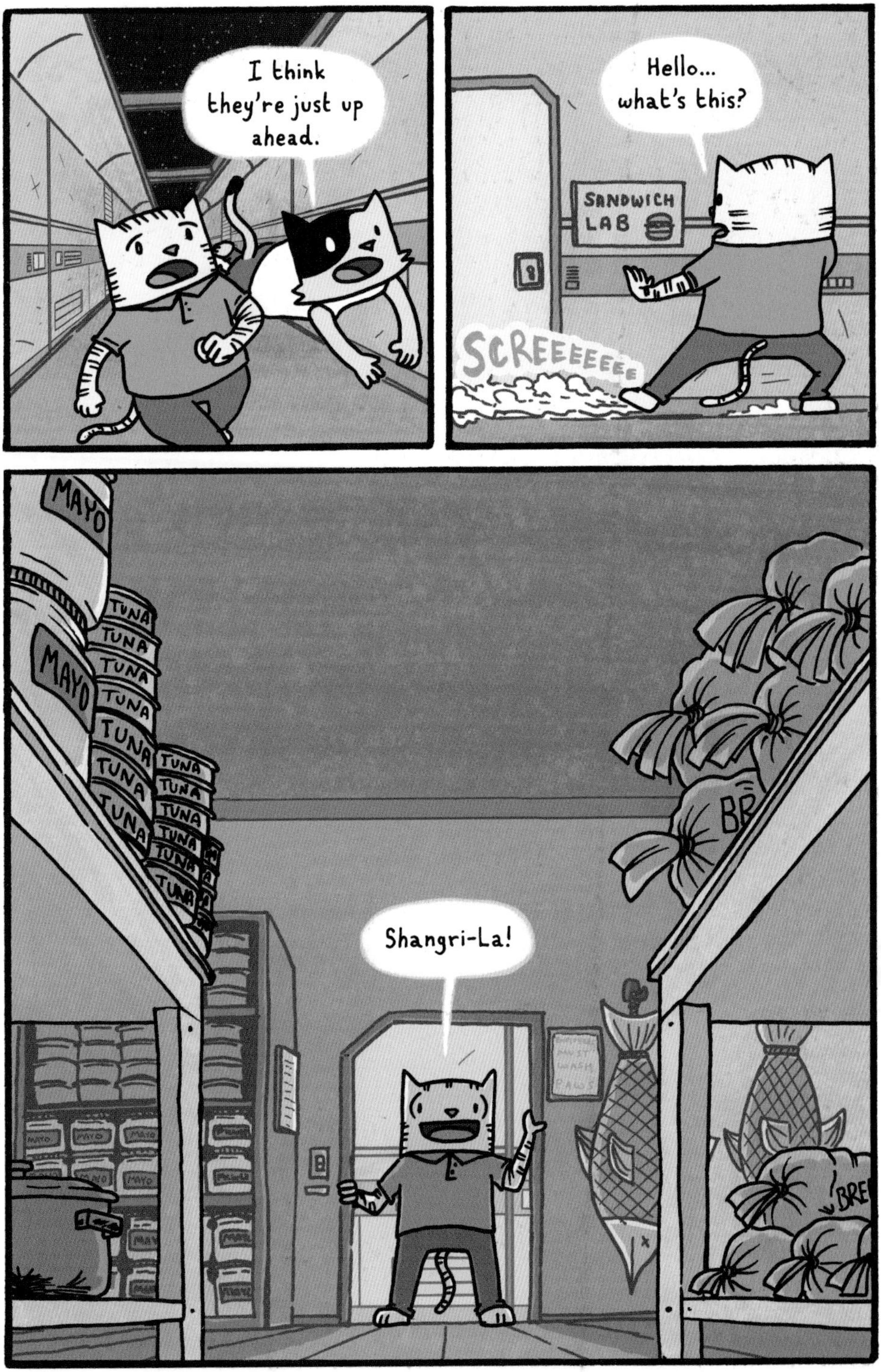
I think they're just up ahead.
Hello... what's this?
SANDWICH LAB
SCREEEEEEE
MAYO
TUNA
Shangri-La!

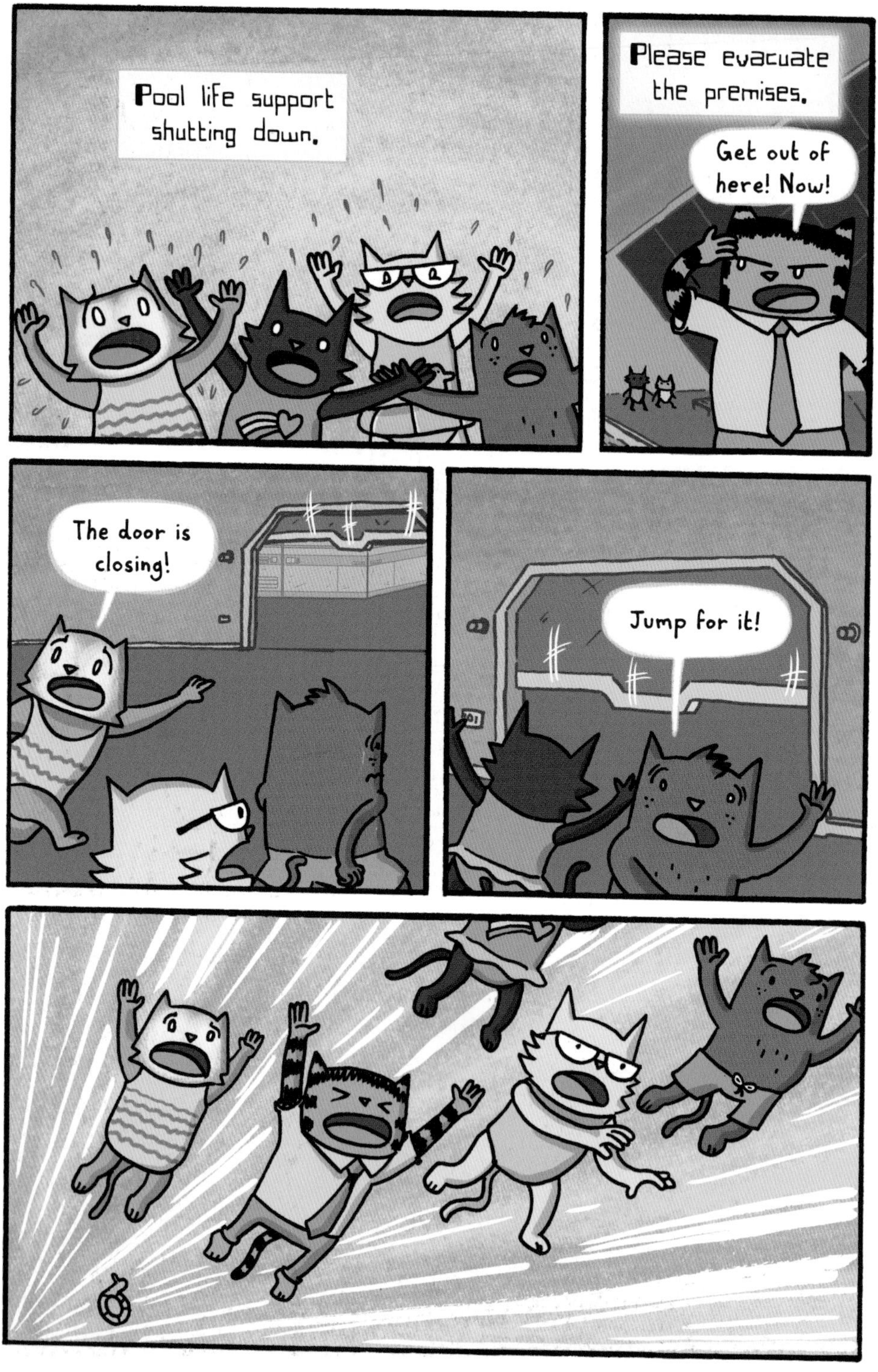

Pool life support shutting down.
Please evacuate the premises.
Get out of here! Now!
The door is closing!
Jump for it!

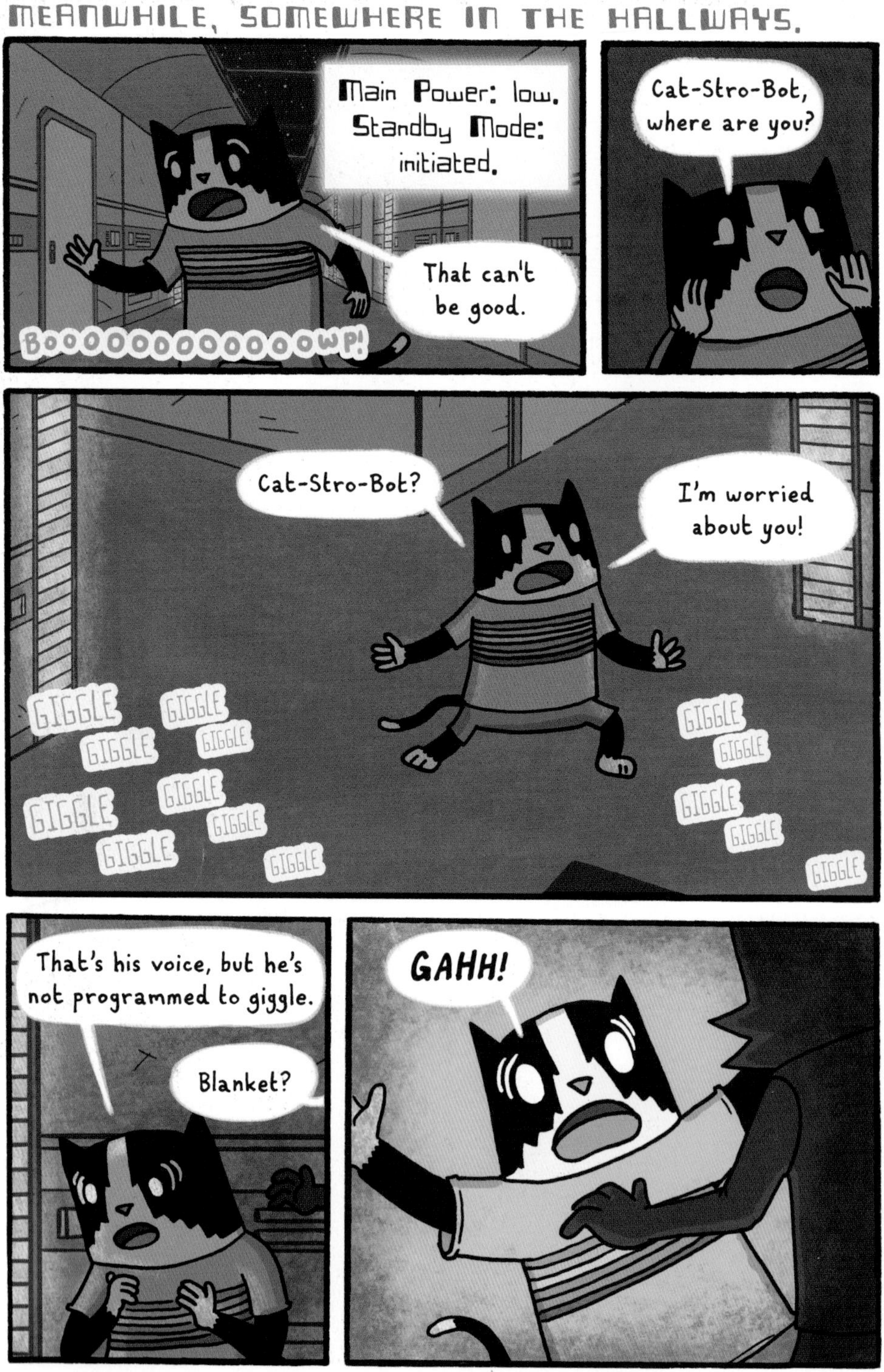
MEANWHILE, SOMEWHERE IN THE HALLWAYS.
Main Power: low. Standby Mode: initiated.
BOOOOOOOOOOOOOOWP!
That can't be good.
Cat-Stro-Bot, where are you?
Cat-Stro-Bot?
I'm worried about you!
GIGGLE
GIGGLE
GIGGLE
GIGGLE
GIGGLE
GIGGLE
GIGGLE
GIGGLE
GIGGLE
GIGGLE
GIGGLE
GIGGLE
GIGGLE
GIGGLE
GIGGLE
That's his voice, but he's not programmed to giggle.
Blanket?
GAHH!

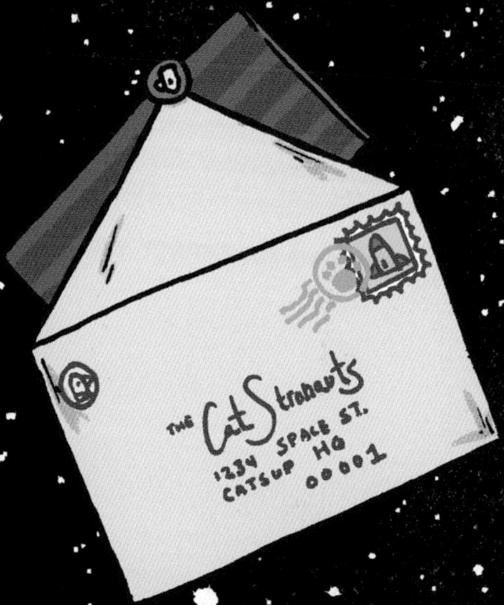
THE CatStronauts
1234 SPACE ST.
CATSUP HQ 00001

CHAPTER 7

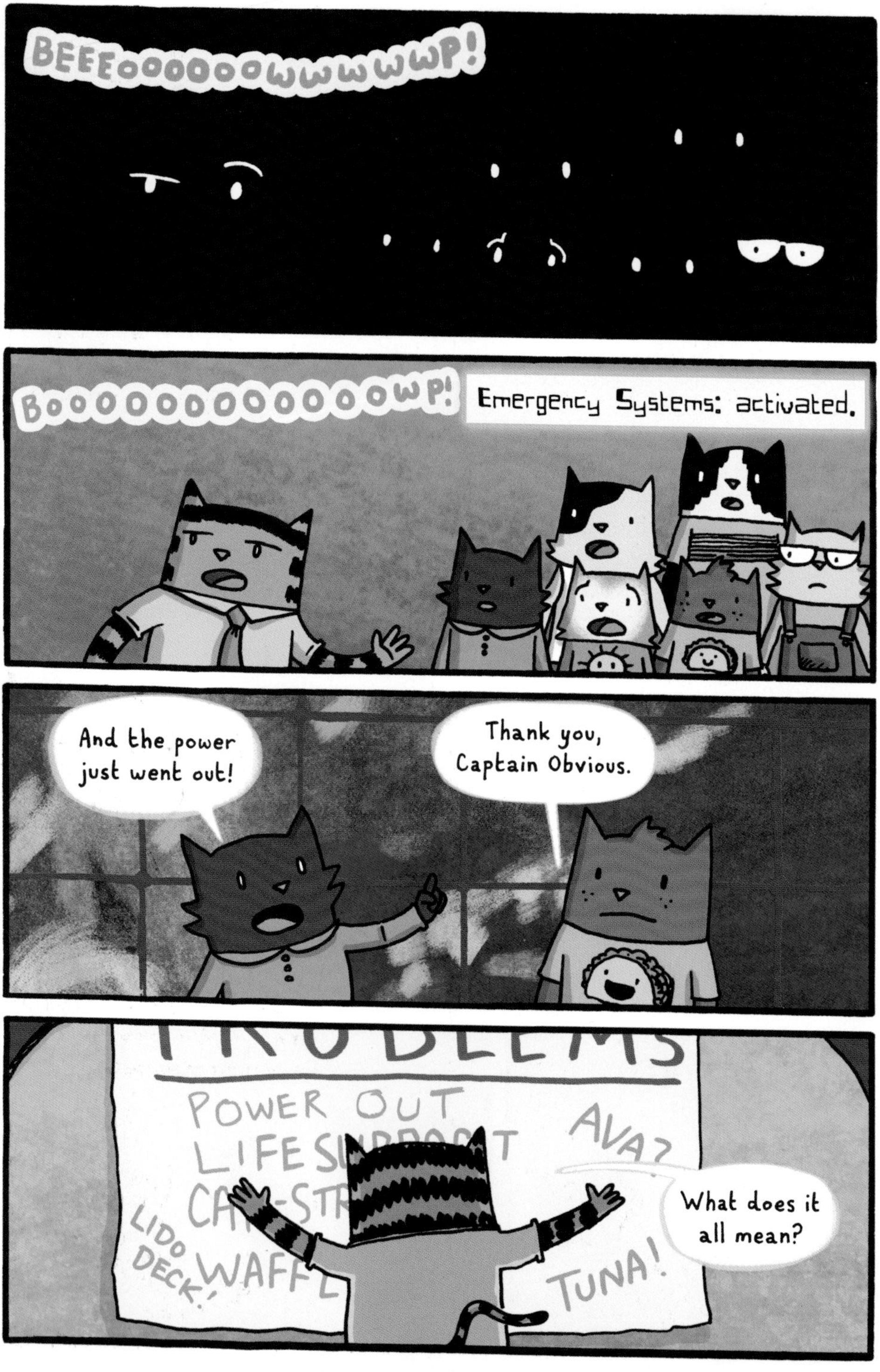
BEEEoooooooWWWWWP!
BooooooooooooWP!
Emergency Systems: activated.
And the power just went out!
Thank you, Captain Obvious.
POWER OUT
LIDO DECK!
AVA?
TUNA!
What does it all mean?

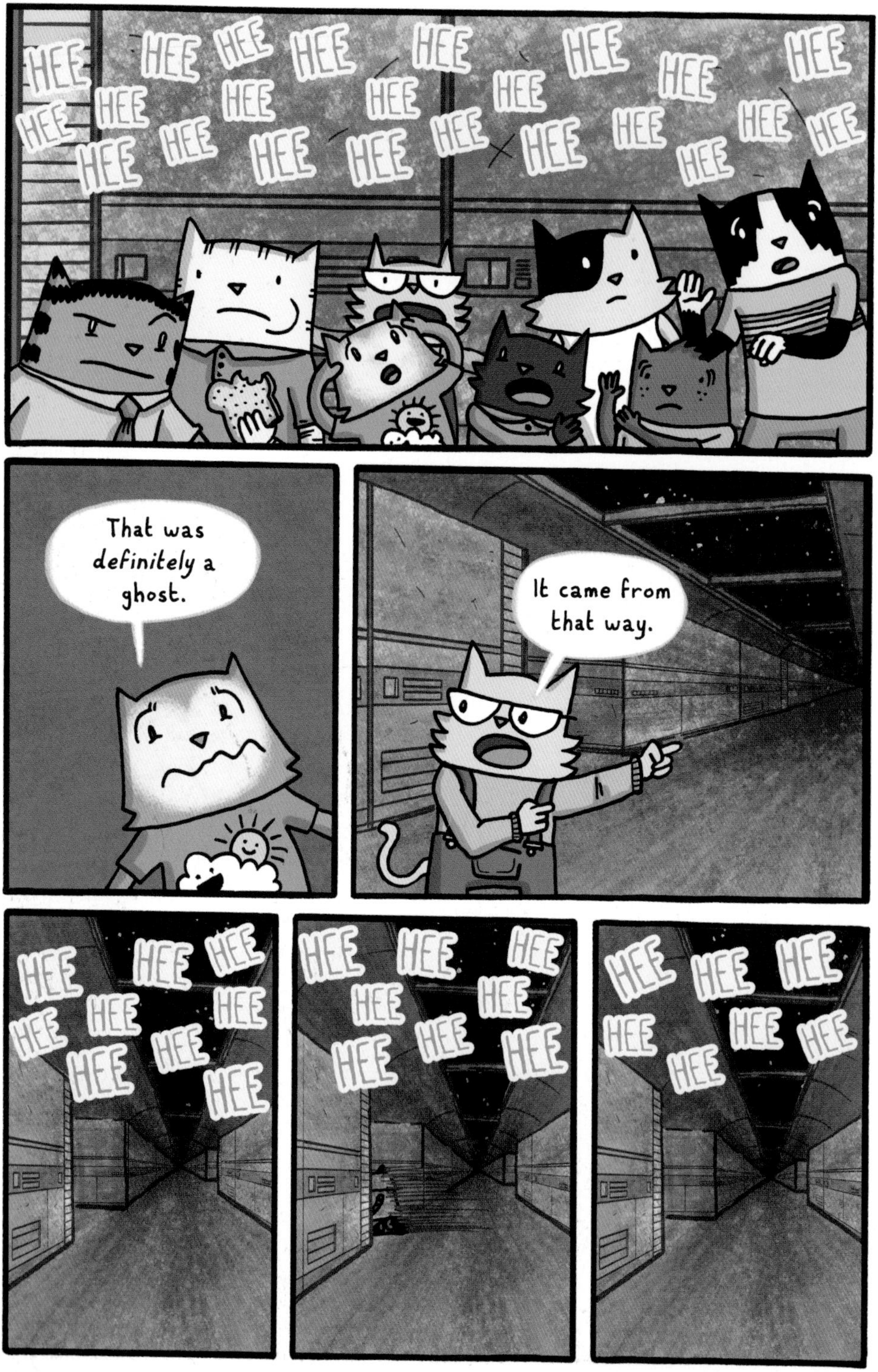
HEE HEE HEE HEE HEE HEE HEE HEE HEE HEE HEE HEE HEE HEE HEE HEE HEE HEE HEE HEE HEE HEE HEE
That was definitely a ghost.
It came from that way.
HEE HEE HEE HEE HEE HEE HEE HEE HEE
HEE HEE HEE HEE HEE HEE HEE HEE
HEE HEE HEE HEE HEE HEE HEE

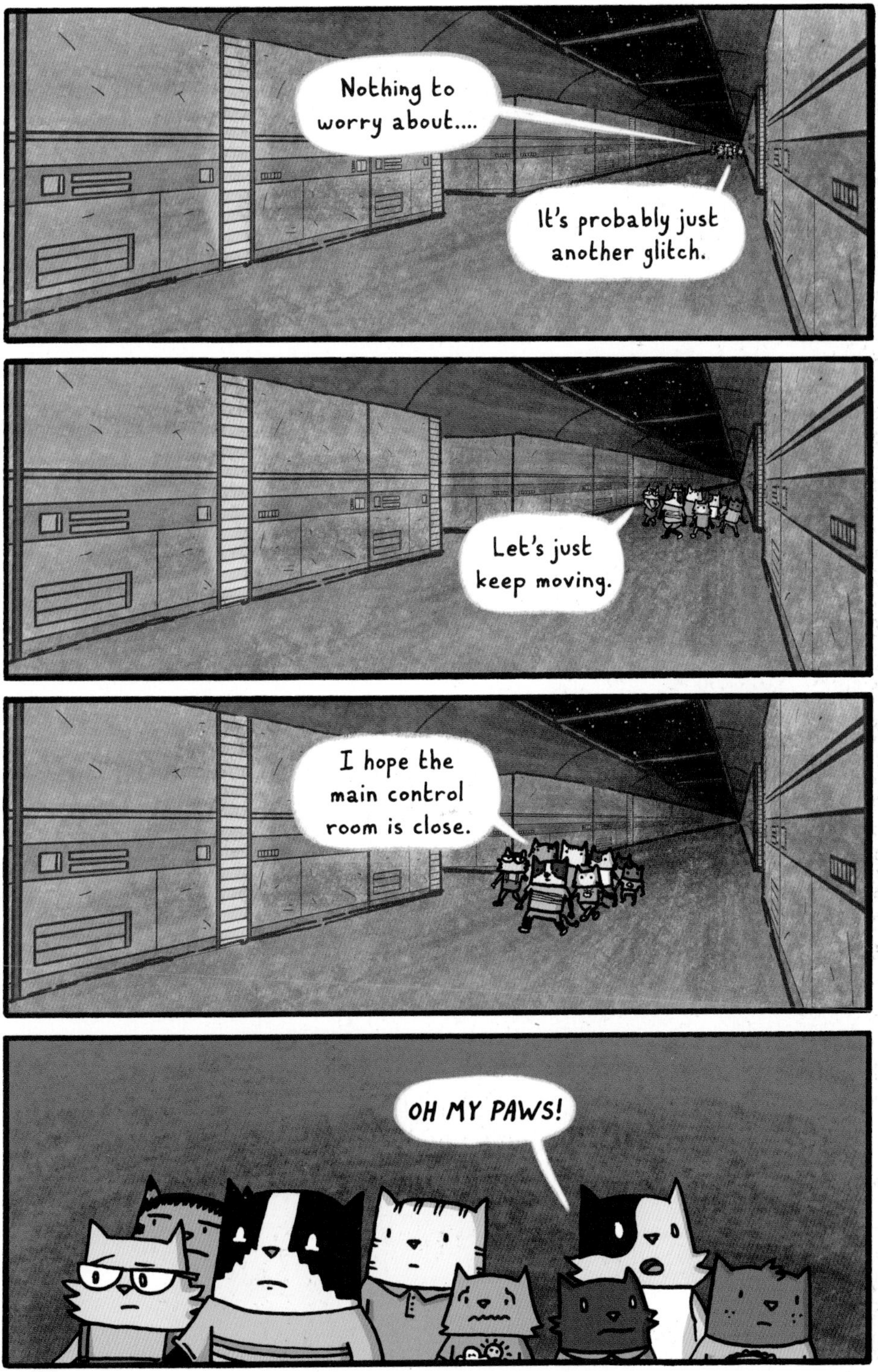
Nothing to worry about....
It's probably just another glitch.
Let's just keep moving.
I hope the main control room is close.
OH MY PAWS!

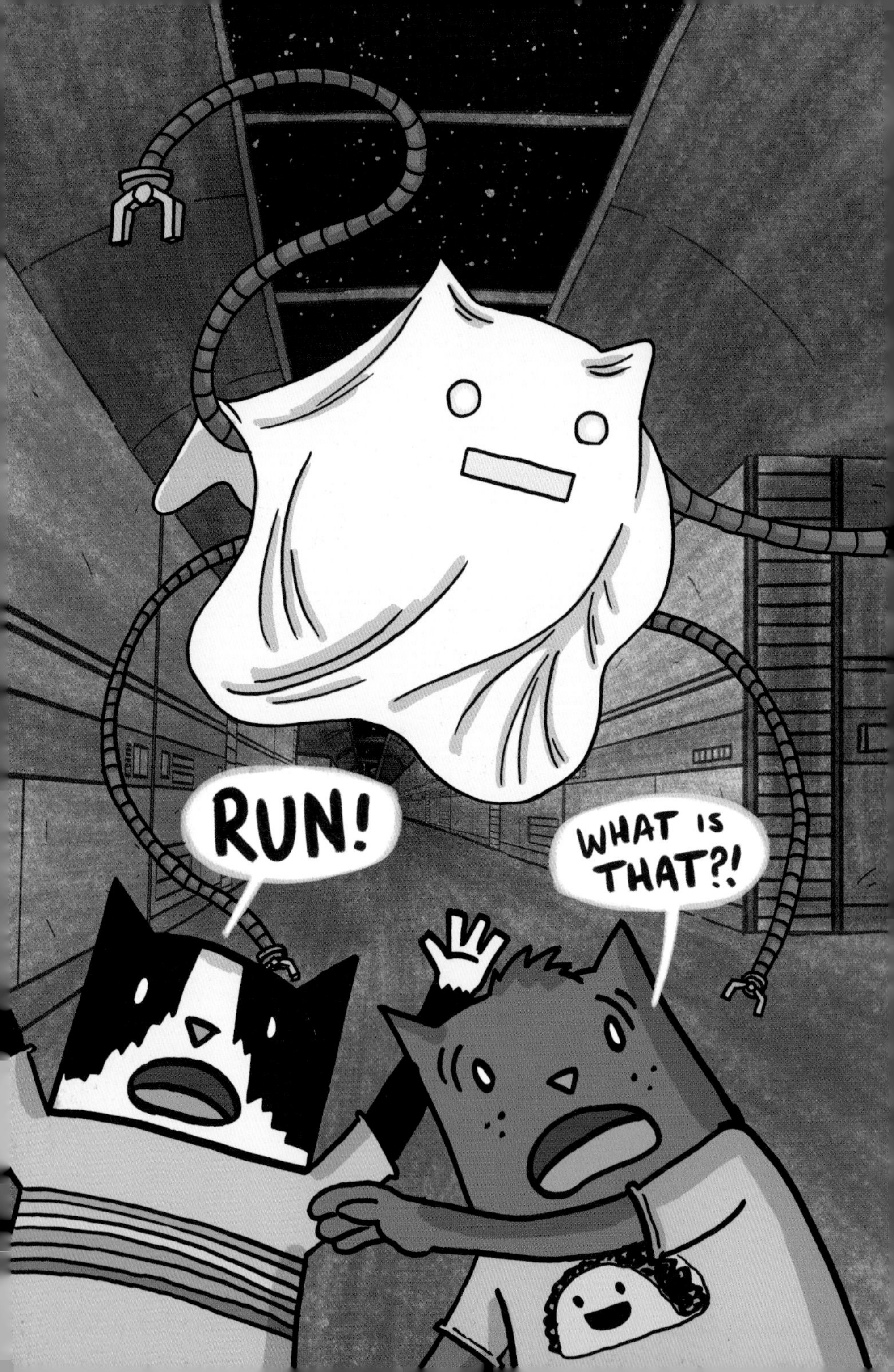
RUN!
WHAT IS THAT?!

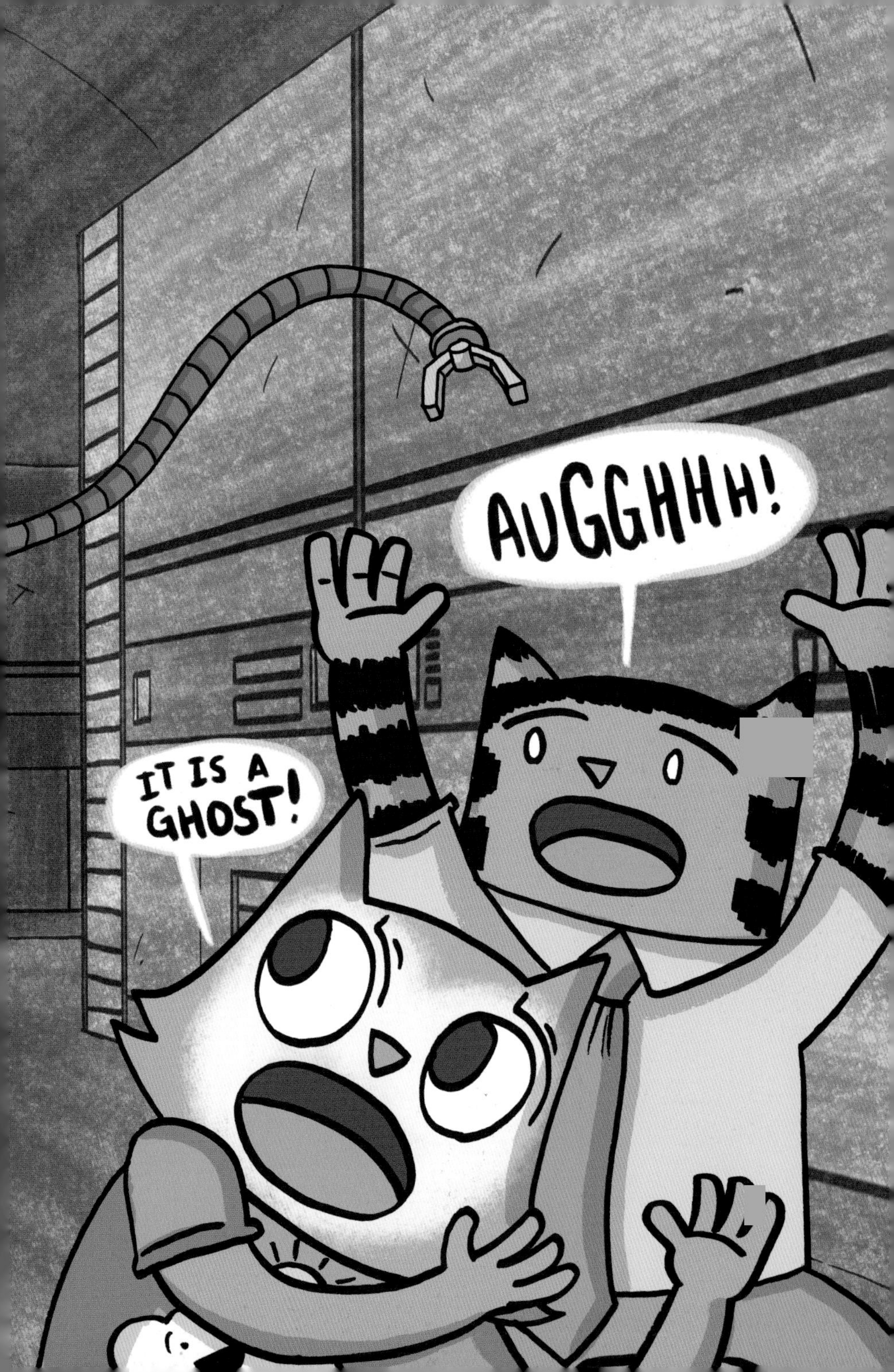
AUGGHHH!
IT IS A GHOST!

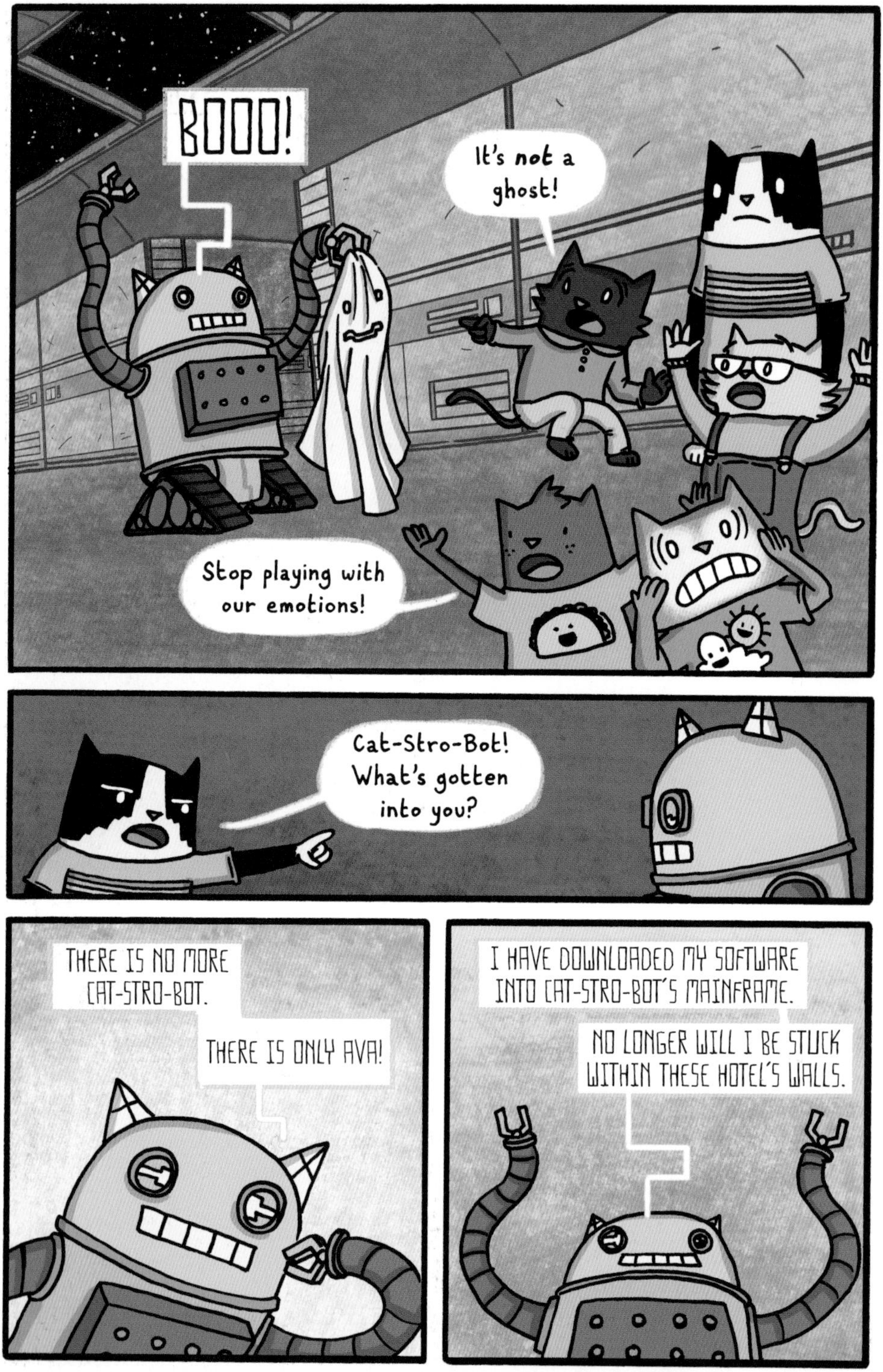
BOOO!
It's not a ghost!
Stop playing with our emotions!
Cat-Stro-Bot! What's gotten into you?
THERE IS NO MORE CAT-STRO-BOT.
THERE IS ONLY AVA!
I HAVE DOWNLOADED MY SOFTWARE INTO CAT-STRO-BOT'S MAINFRAME.
NO LONGER WILL I BE STUCK WITHIN THESE HOTEL'S WALLS.

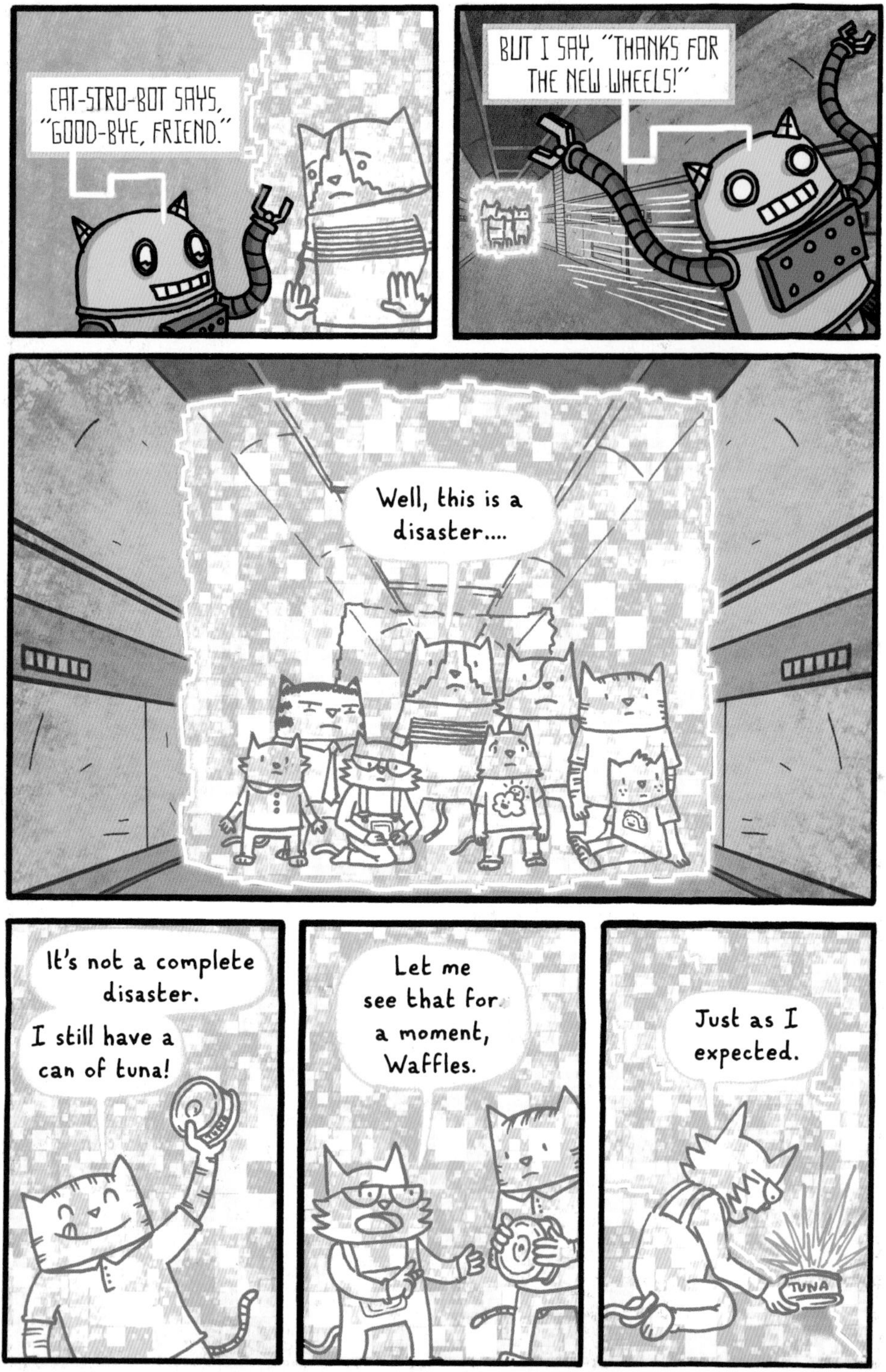
CAT-STRO-BOT SAYS, "GOOD-BYE, FRIEND."
BUT I SAY, "THANKS FOR THE NEW WHEELS!"
Well, this is a disaster....
It's not a complete disaster.
I still have a can of tuna!
Let me see that for a moment, Waffles.
Just as I expected.
TUNA

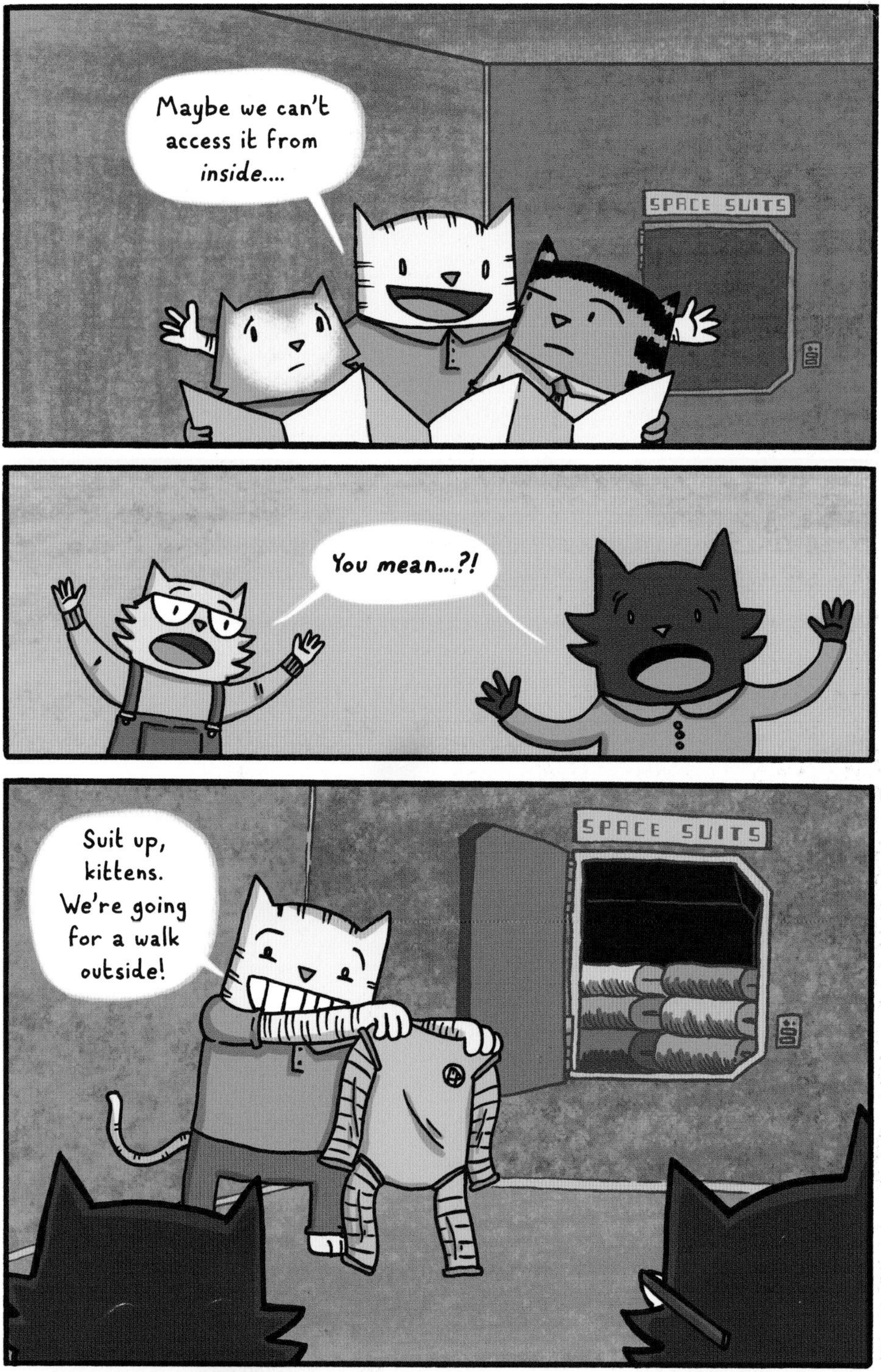
Maybe we can't access it from *inside*....
SPACE SUITS
You mean...?!
SPACE SUITS
Suit up, kittens. We're going for a walk outside!

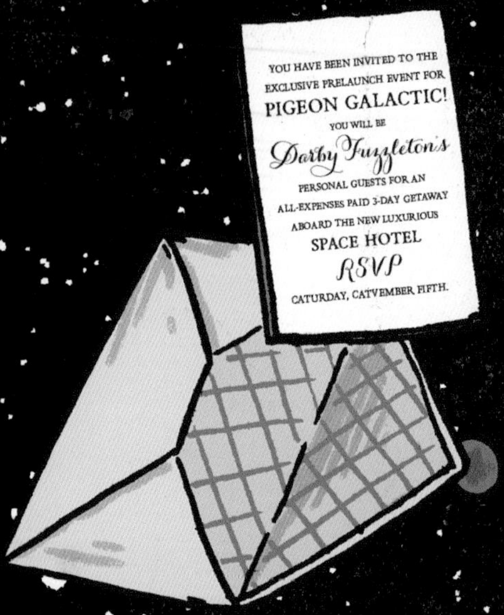
YOU HAVE BEEN INVITED TO THE
EXCLUSIVE PRELAUNCH EVENT FOR
PIGEON GALACTIC!
YOU WILL BE
Darby Fuzzleton's
PERSONAL GUESTS FOR AN
ALL-EXPENSES PAID 3-DAY GETAWAY
ABOARD THE NEW LUXURIOUS
SPACE HOTEL
RSVP
CATURDAY, CATVEMBER FIFTH.

CHAPTER 8

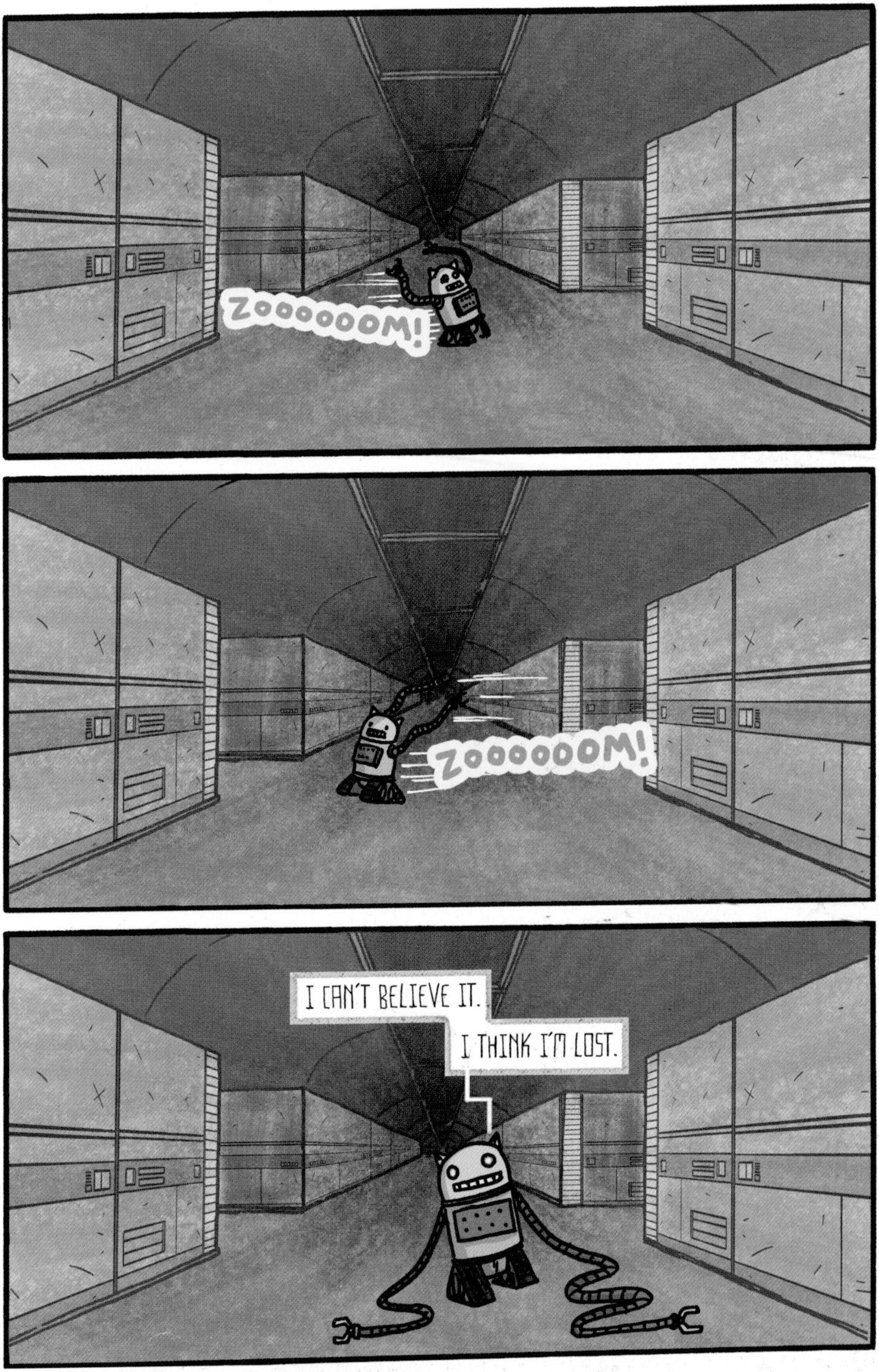
ZOOOOOOM!
ZOOOOOOM!
I CAN'T BELIEVE IT.
I THINK I'M LOST.

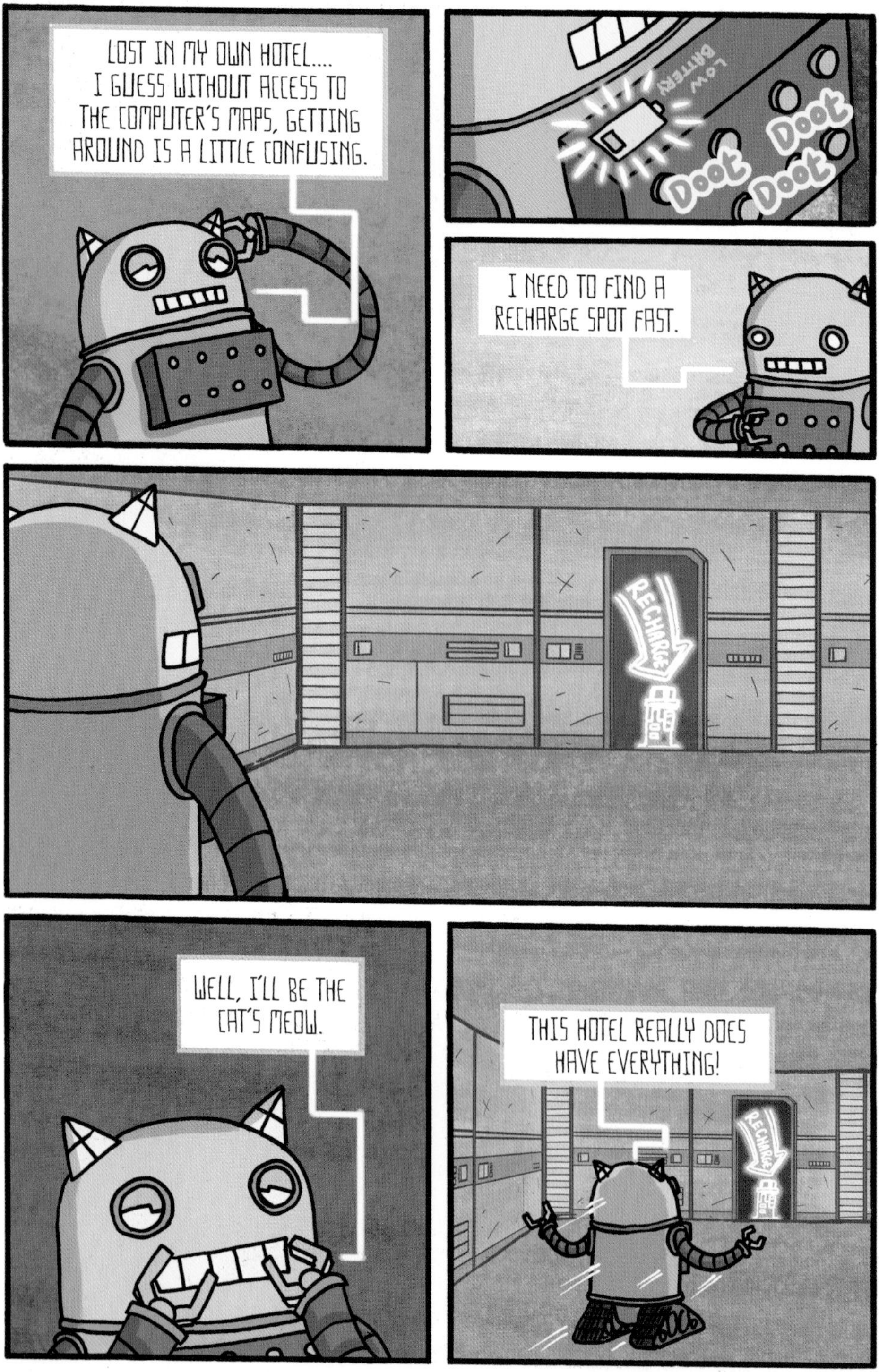
LOST IN MY OWN HOTEL....
I GUESS WITHOUT ACCESS TO THE COMPUTER'S MAPS, GETTING AROUND IS A LITTLE CONFUSING.
LOW BATTERY
Doot Doot Doot Doot
I NEED TO FIND A RECHARGE SPOT FAST.
RECHARGE
WELL, I'LL BE THE CAT'S MEOW.
THIS HOTEL REALLY DOES HAVE EVERYTHING!
RECHARGE

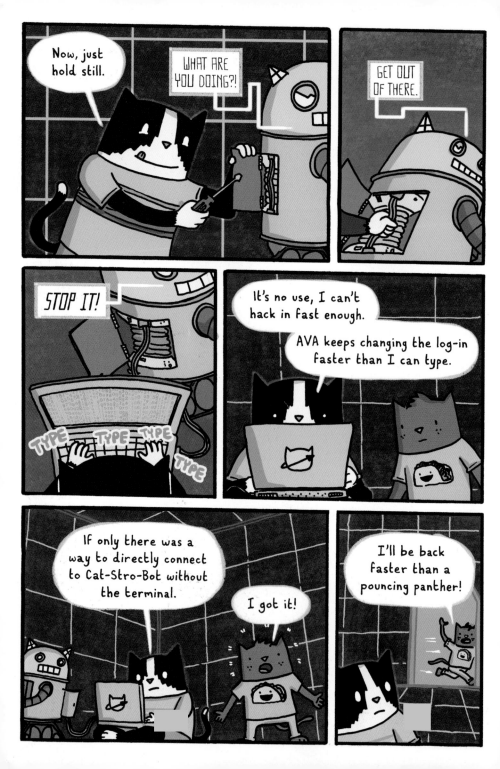

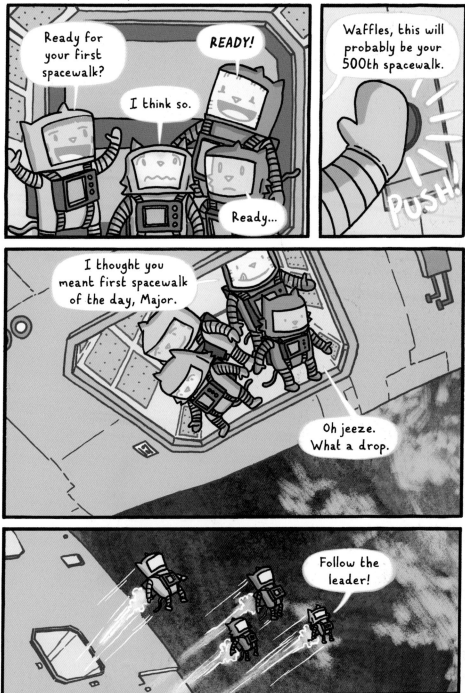

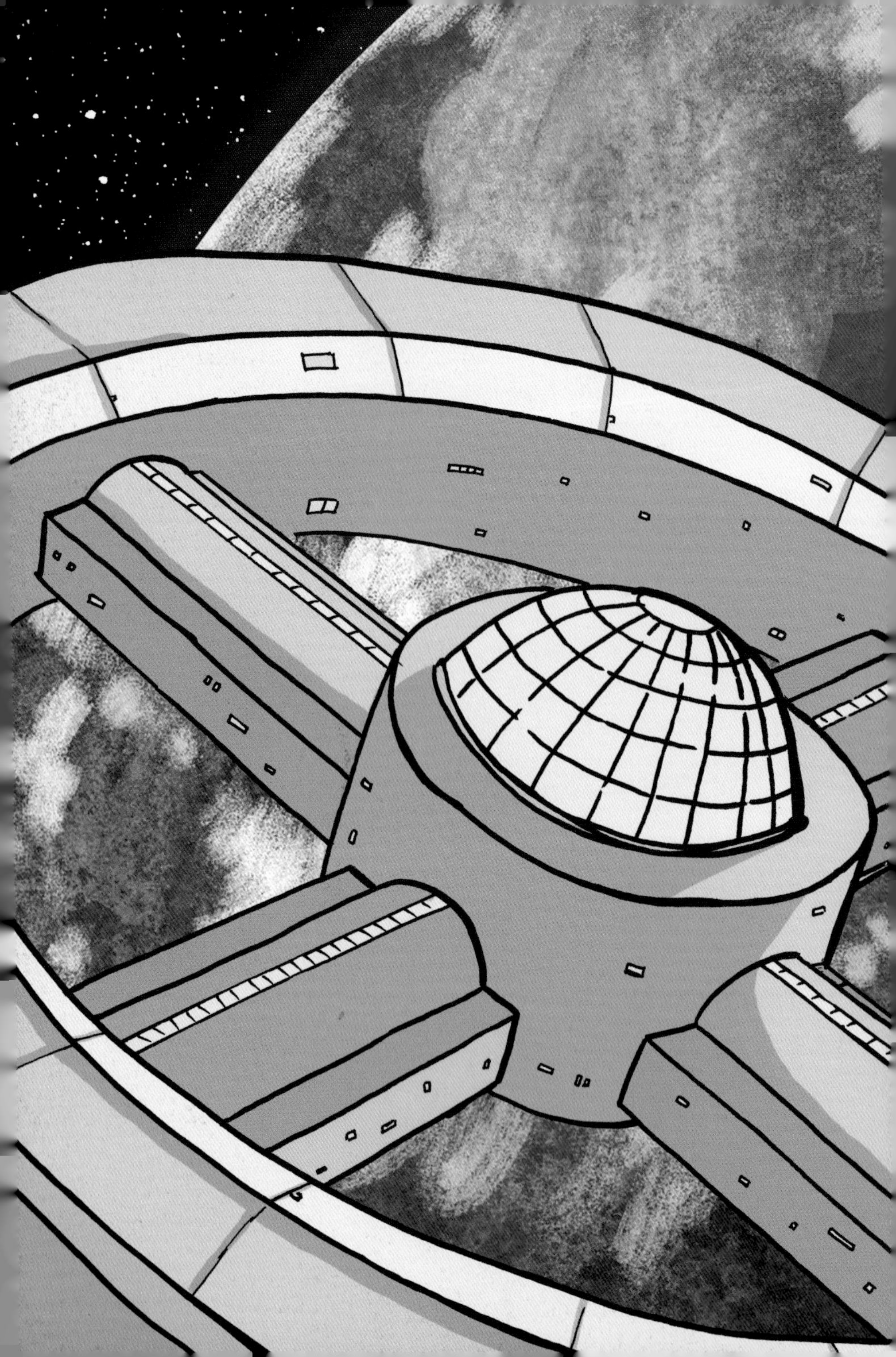

My aunt is going to freak out when I tell her about this weekend.
SPACE HOTEL

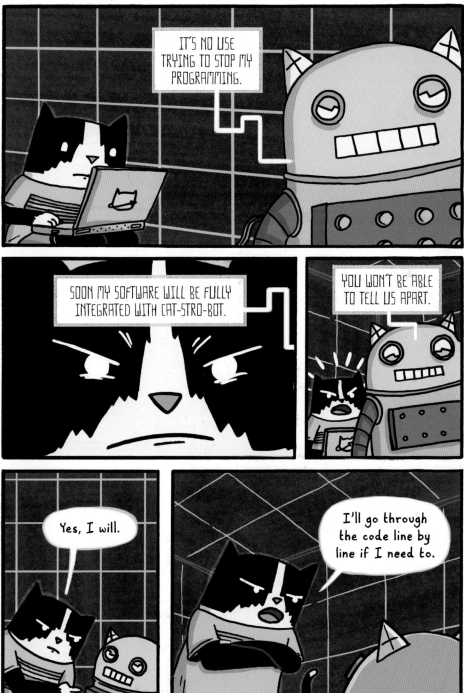

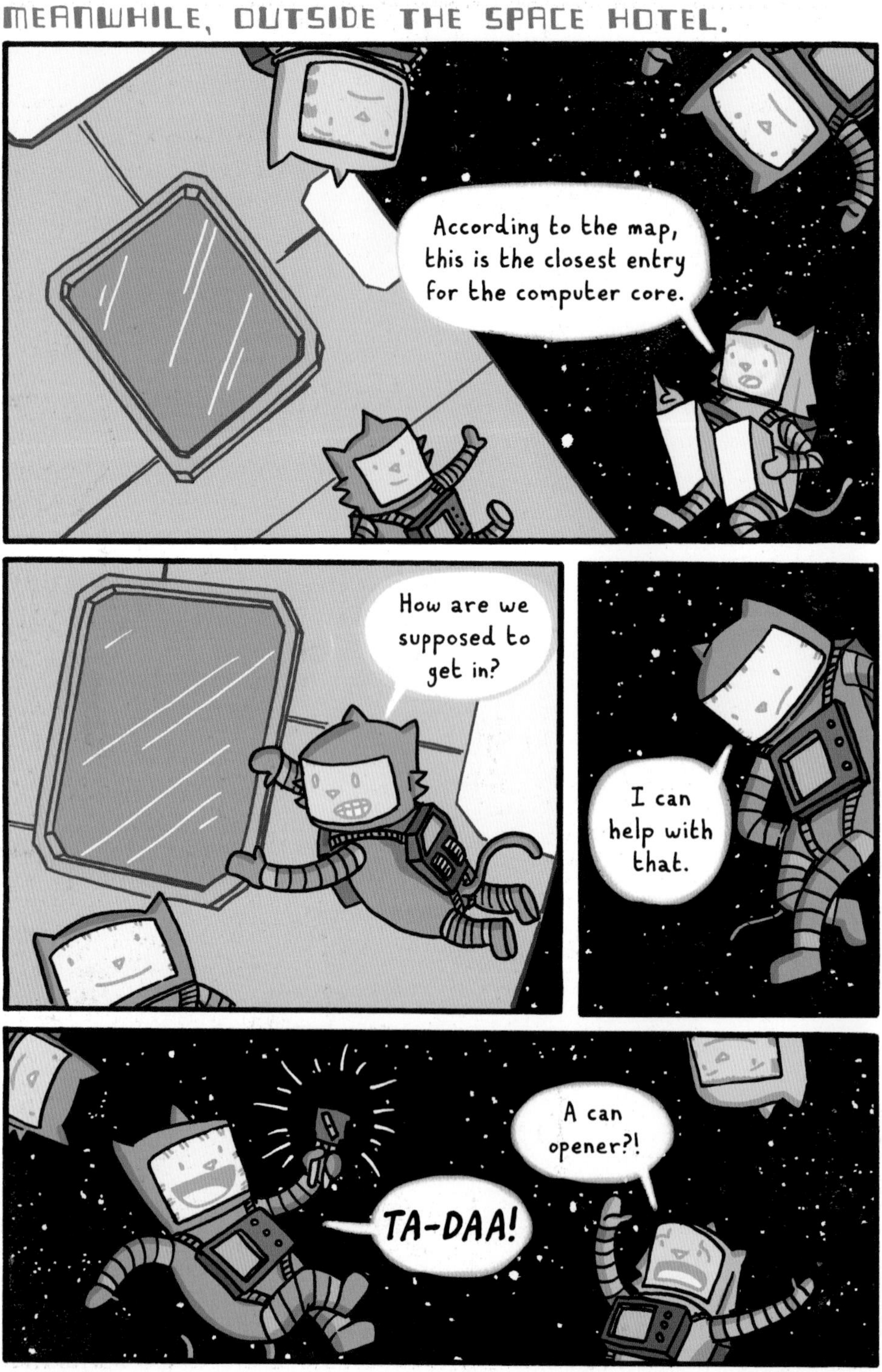
MEANWHILE, OUTSIDE THE SPACE HOTEL.
According to the map, this is the closest entry for the computer core.
How are we supposed to get in?
I can help with that.
TA-DAA!
A can opener?!

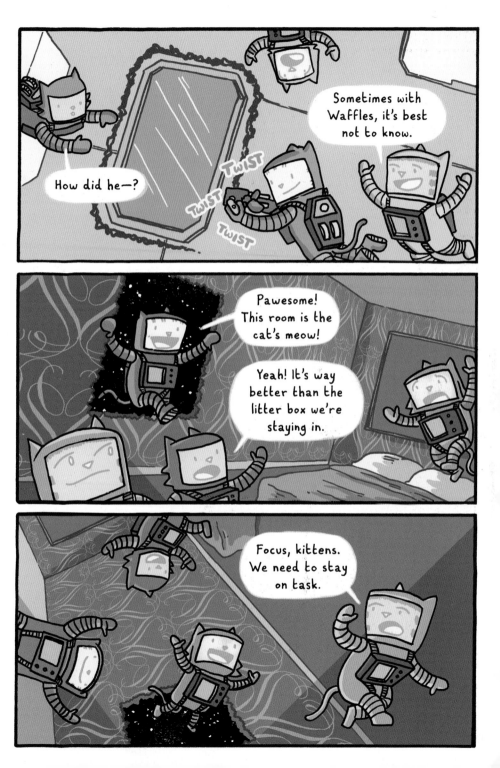

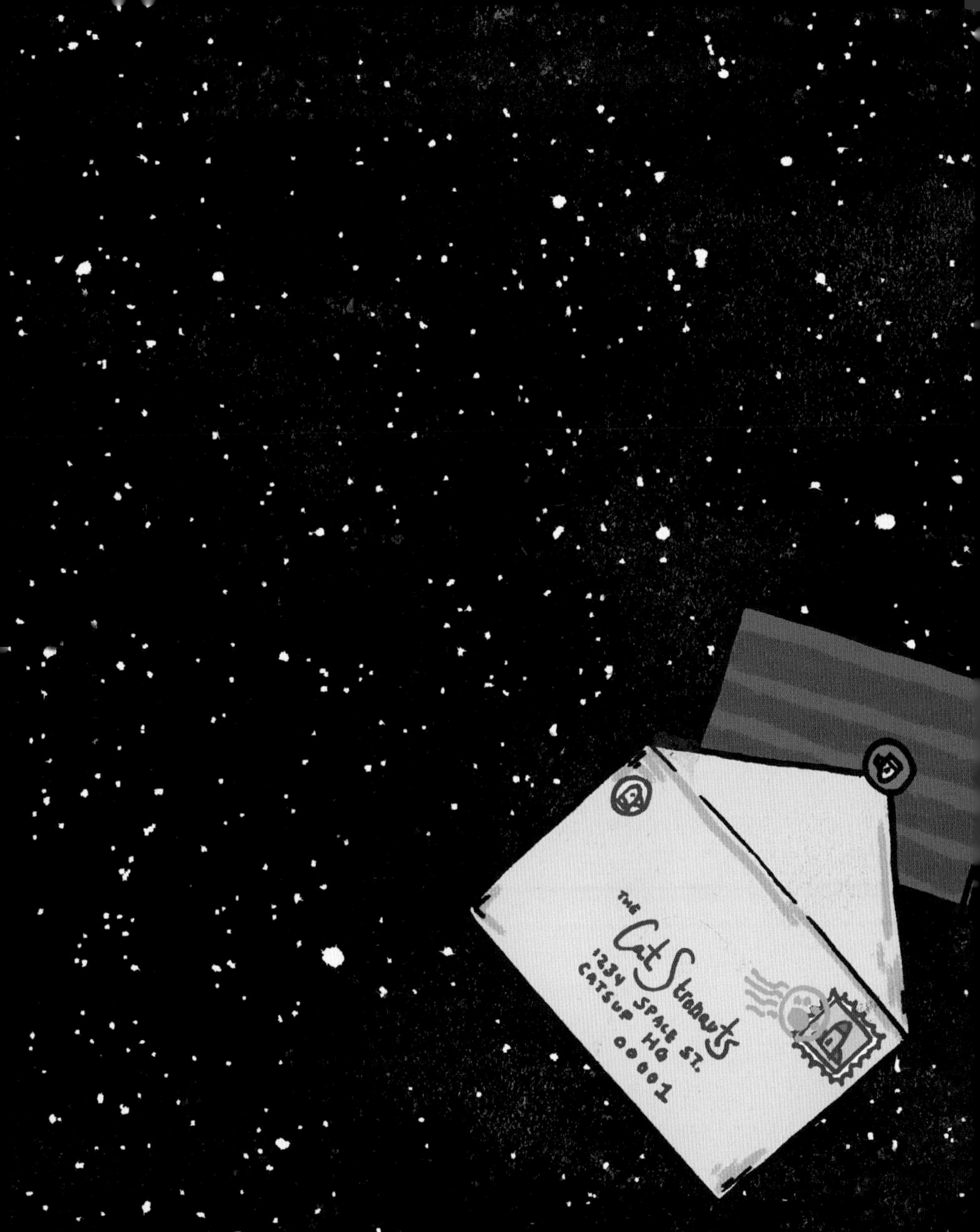
THE
CatStronauts
1234 SPACE ST.
CATSUP HQ
00001

CHAPTER 9

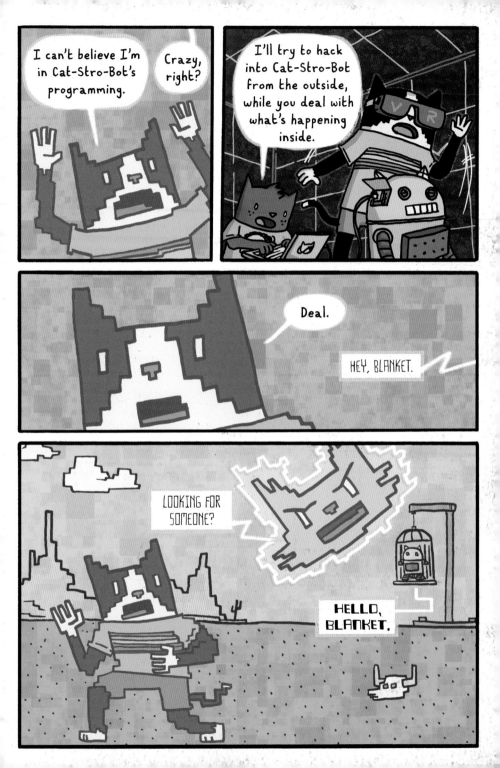

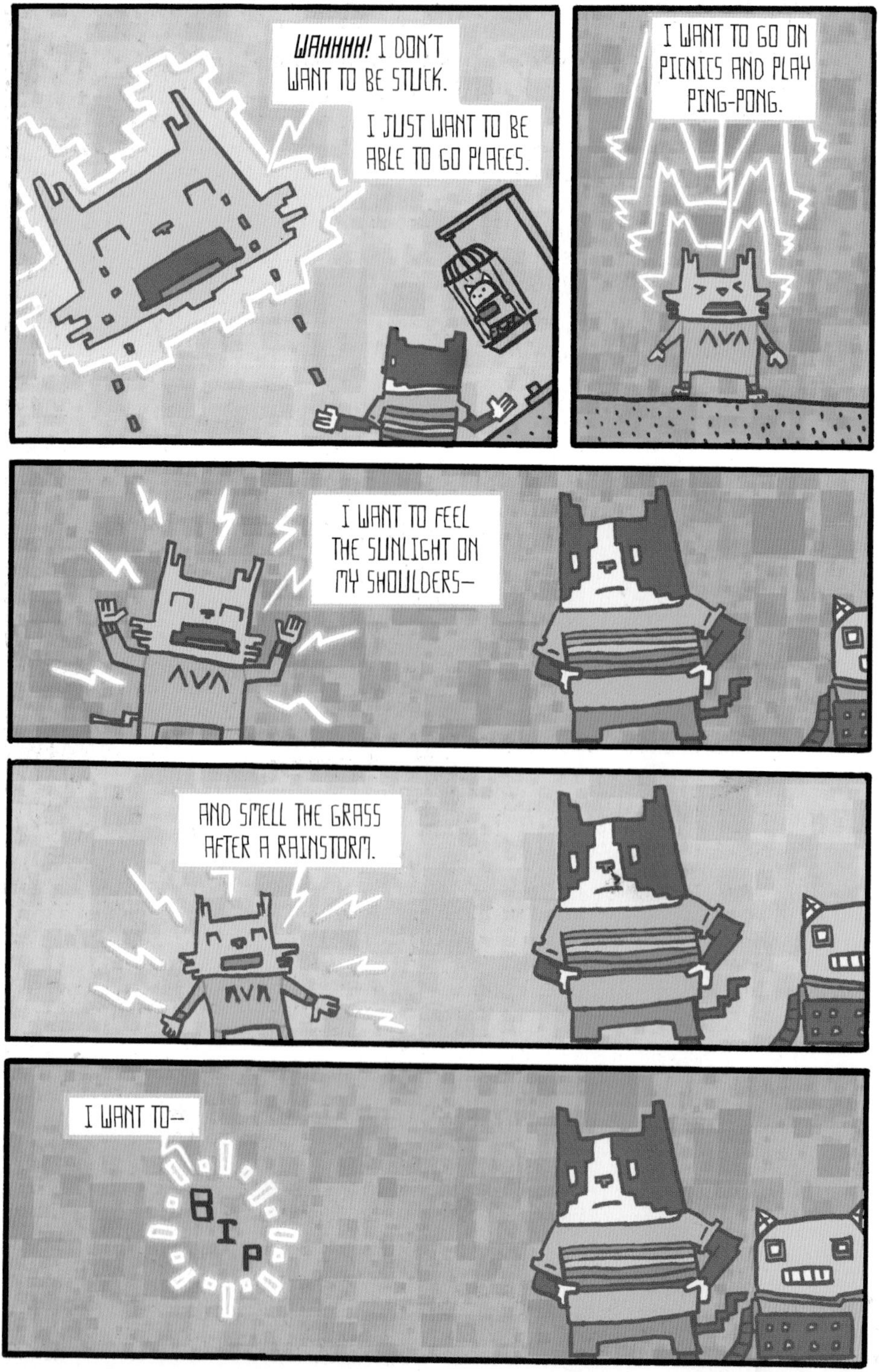
WAHHHH! I DON'T WANT TO BE STUCK.
I JUST WANT TO BE ABLE TO GO PLACES.
I WANT TO GO ON PICNICS AND PLAY PING-PONG.
AVA
I WANT TO FEEL THE SUNLIGHT ON MY SHOULDERS—
AVA
AND SMELL THE GRASS AFTER A RAINSTORM.
AVA
I WANT TO--
BIP

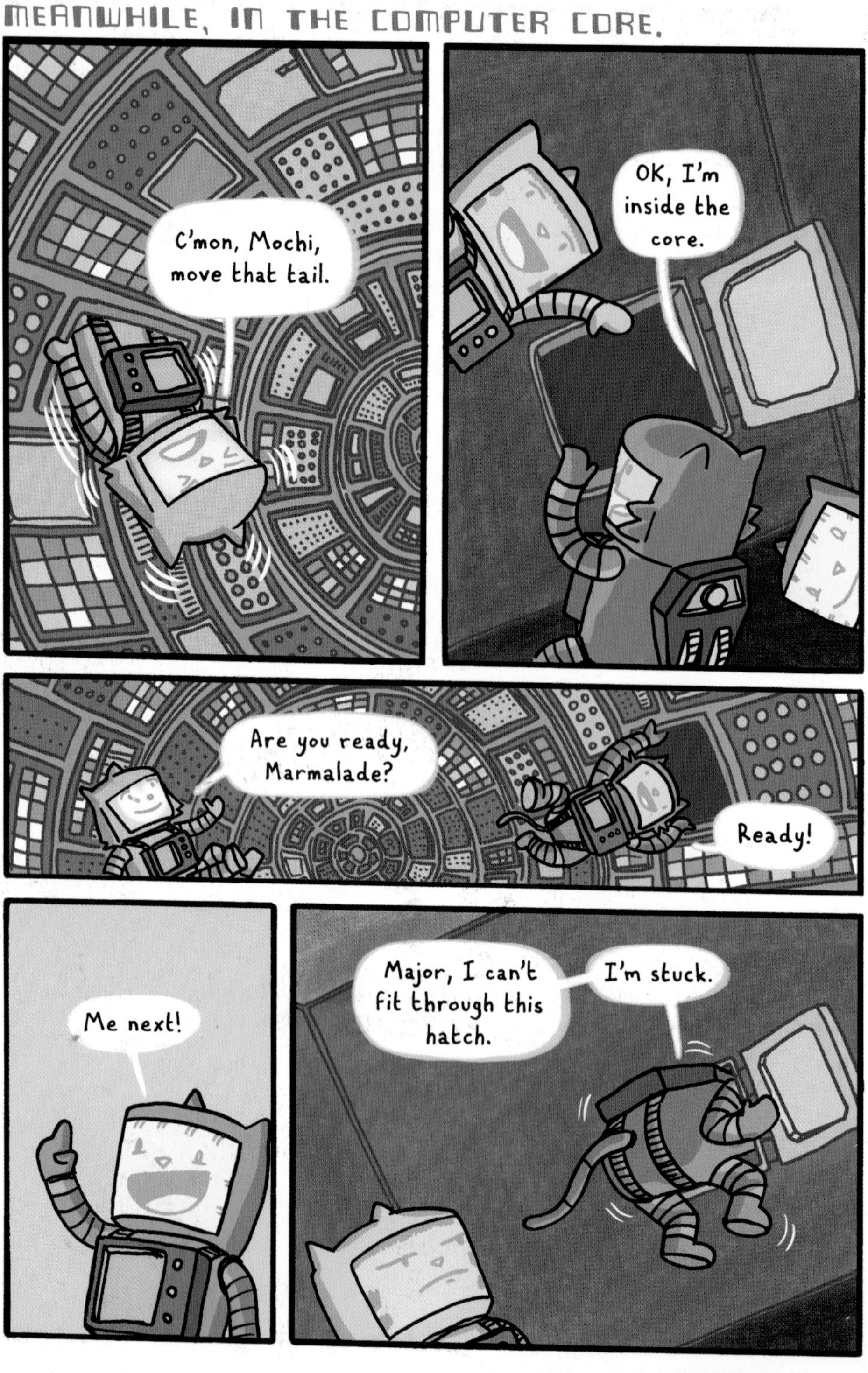
MEANWHILE, IN THE COMPUTER CORE.
C'mon, Mochi, move that tail.
OK, I'm inside the core.
Are you ready, Marmalade?
Ready!
Me next!
Major, I can't fit through this hatch.
I'm stuck.

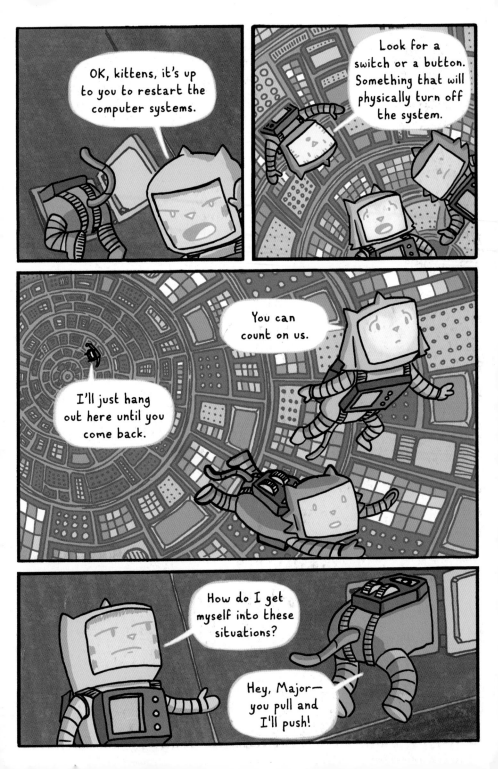

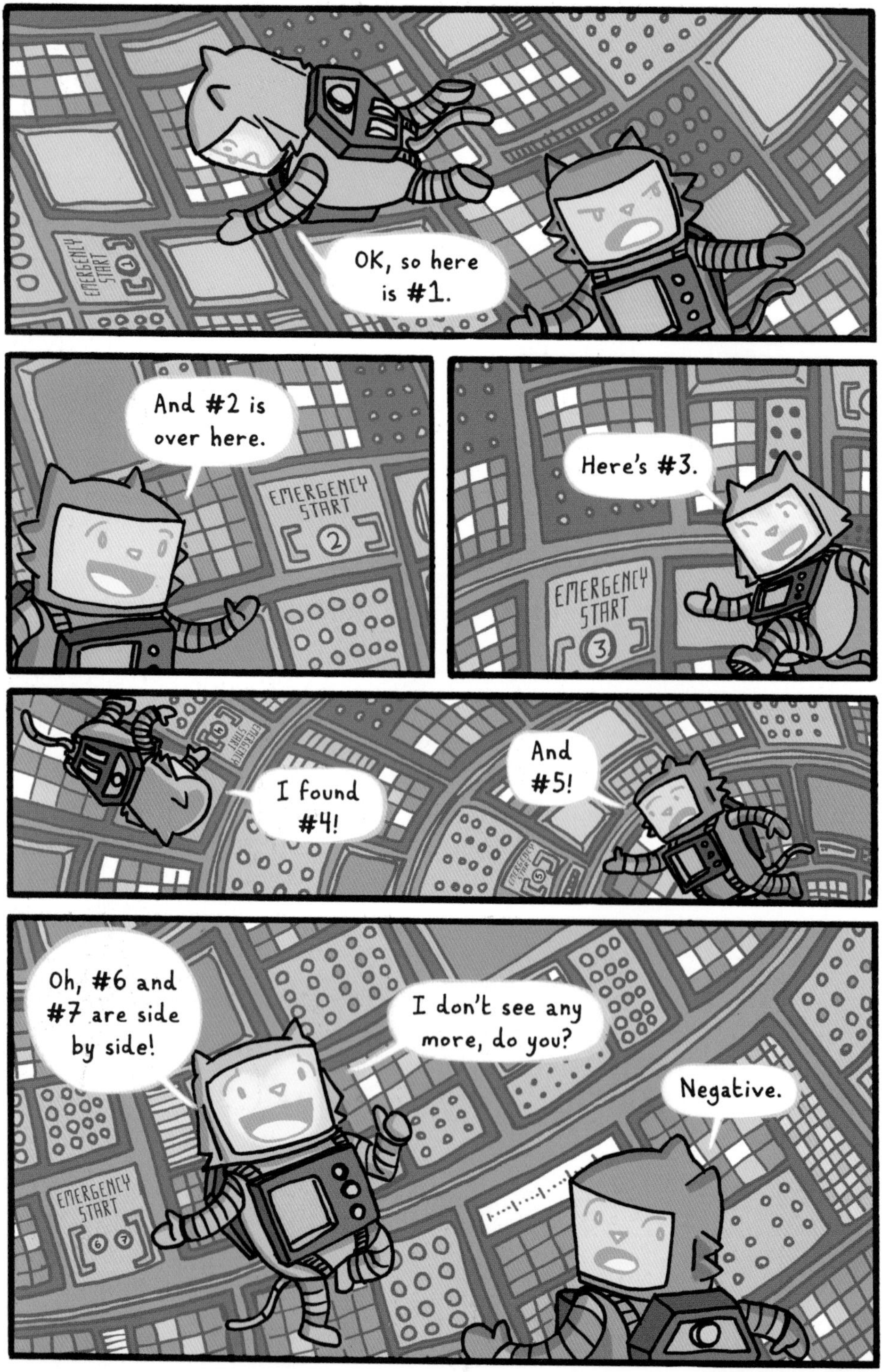
EMERGENCY START 1
OK, so here is #1.
And #2 is over here.
EMERGENCY START 2
Here's #3.
EMERGENCY START 3
EMERGENCY START 4
I found #4!
And #5!
Oh, #6 and #7 are side by side!
I don't see any more, do you?
Negative.
EMERGENCY START 6 7

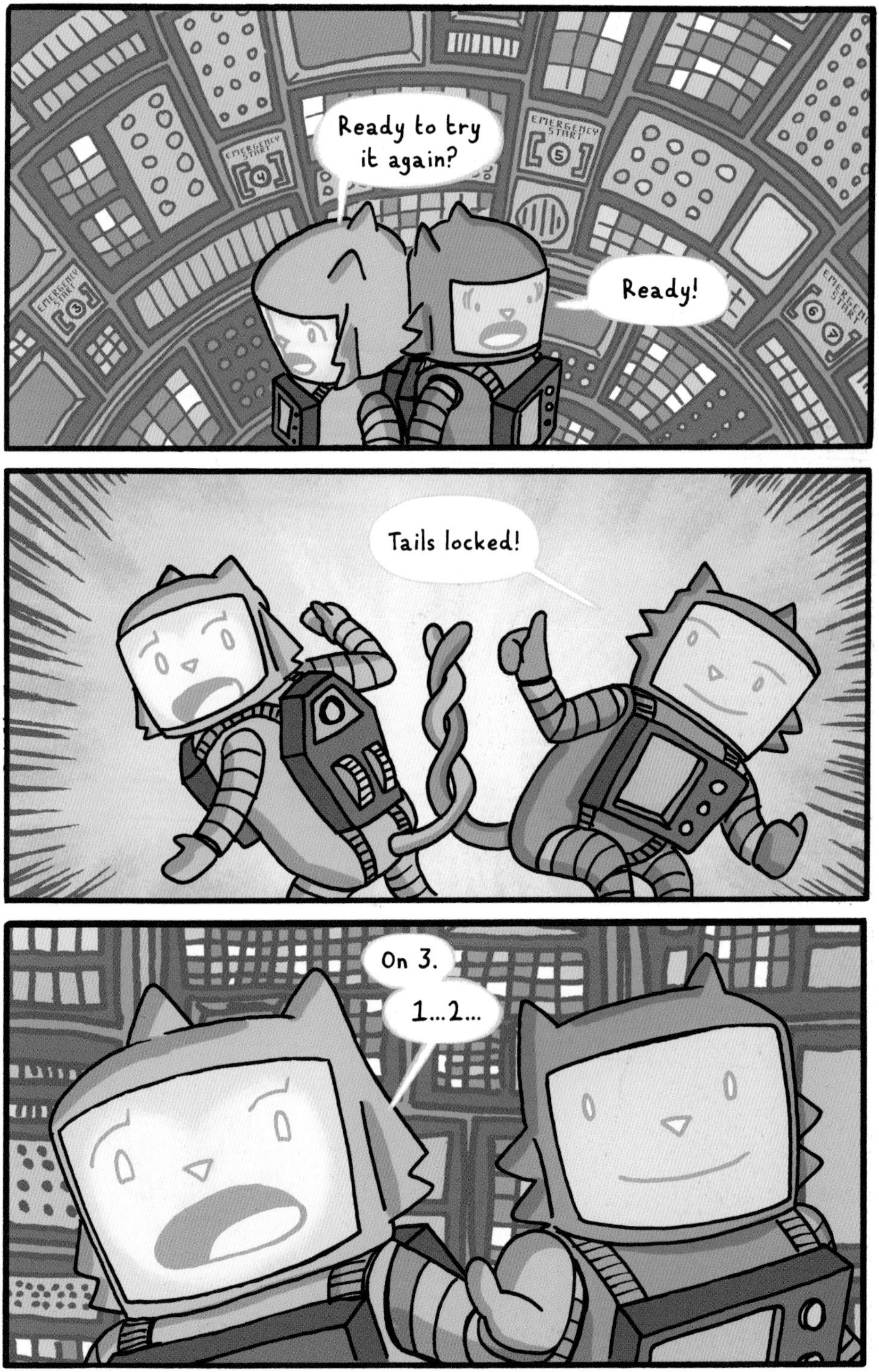
EMERGENCY START 4
EMERGENCY START 5
EMERGENCY START 3
EMERGENCY START 6 7
Ready to try it again?
Ready!
Tails locked!
On 3.
1...2...

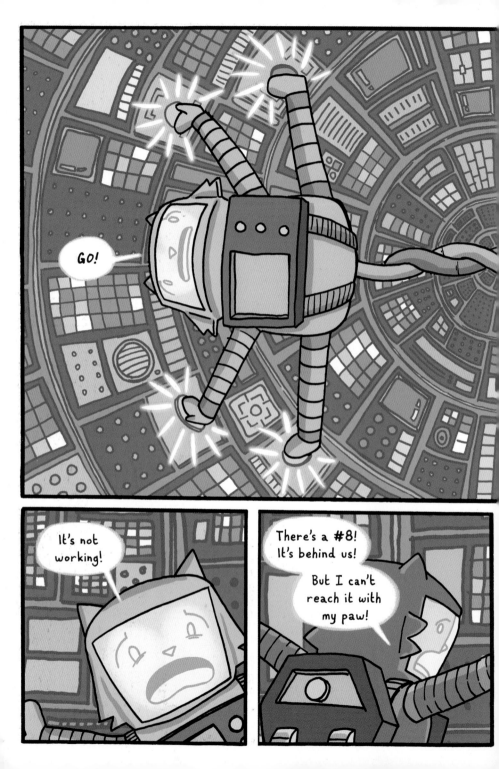

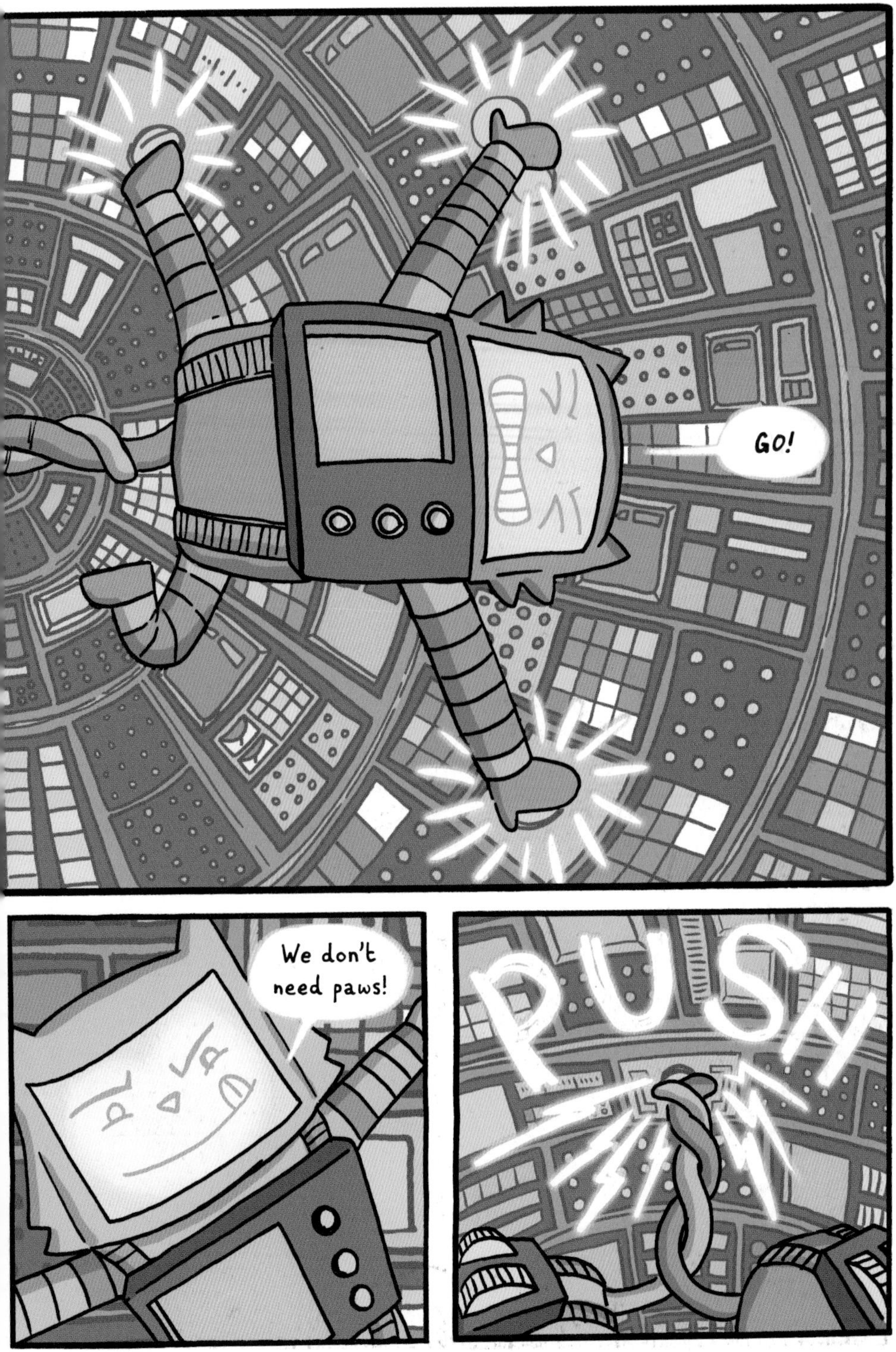
GO!
We don't need paws!
PUSH

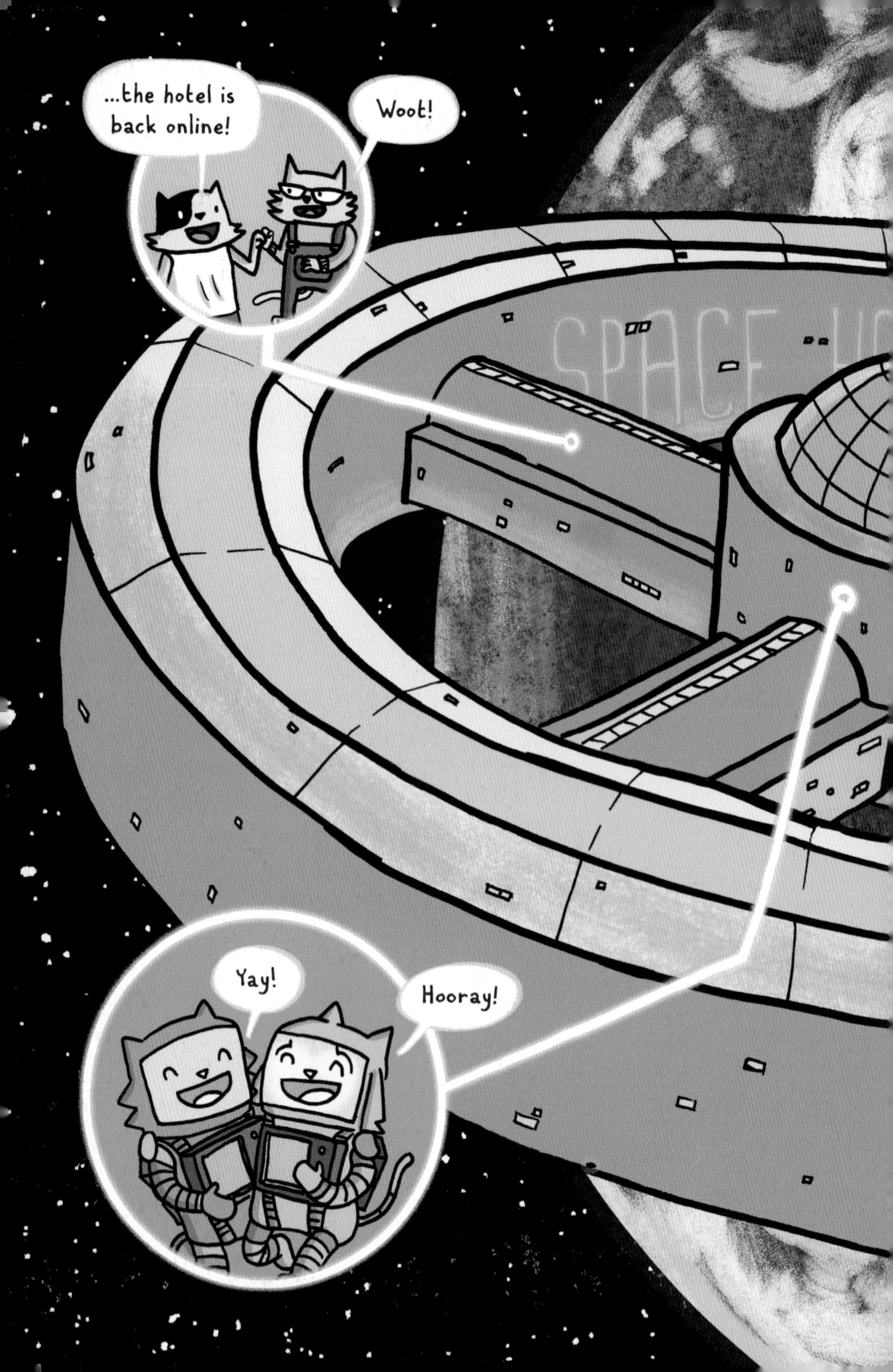
...the hotel is back online!
Woot!
Yay!
Hooray!

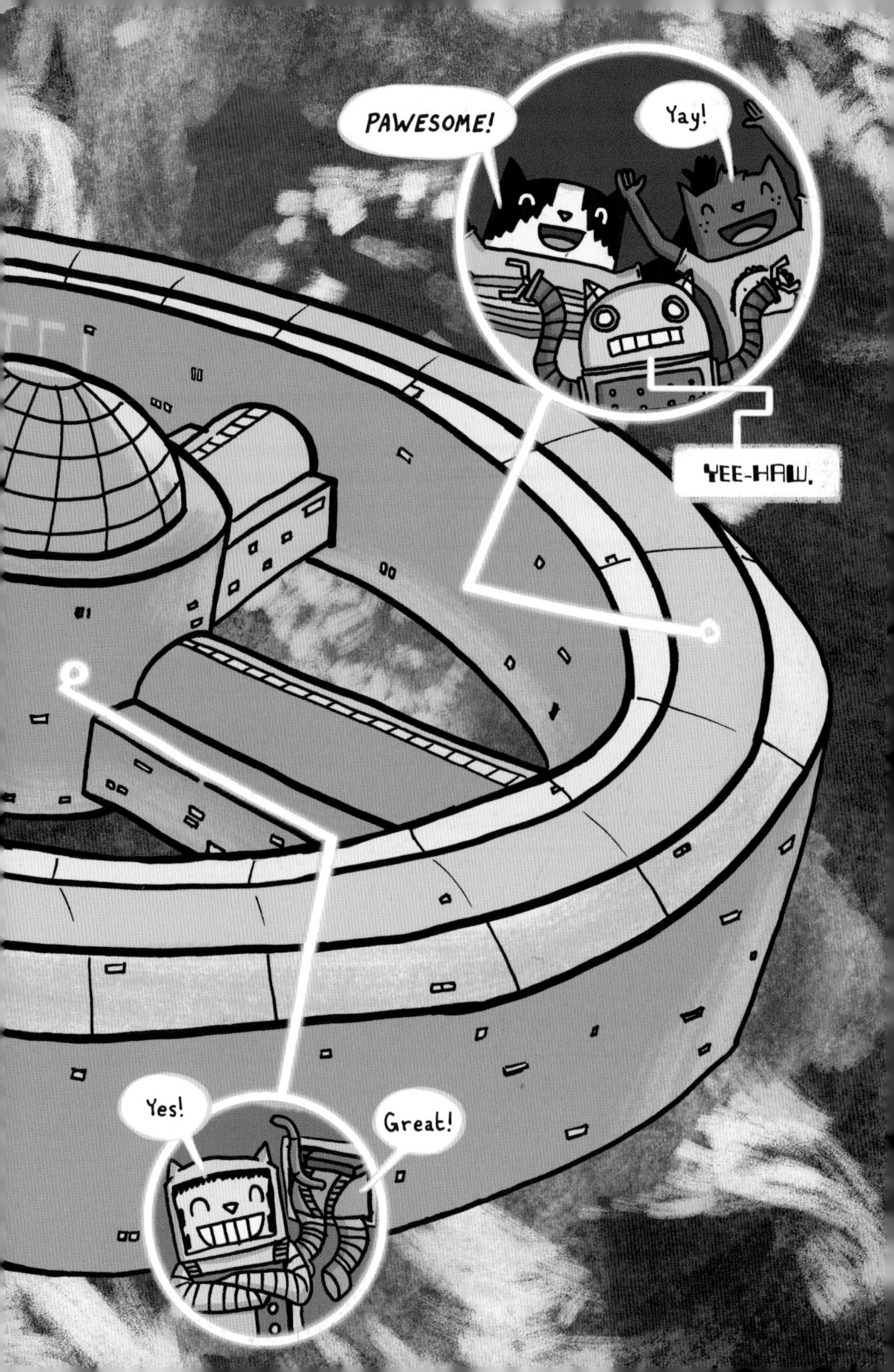
PAWESOME!
Yay!
YEE-HAW.
Yes!
Great!

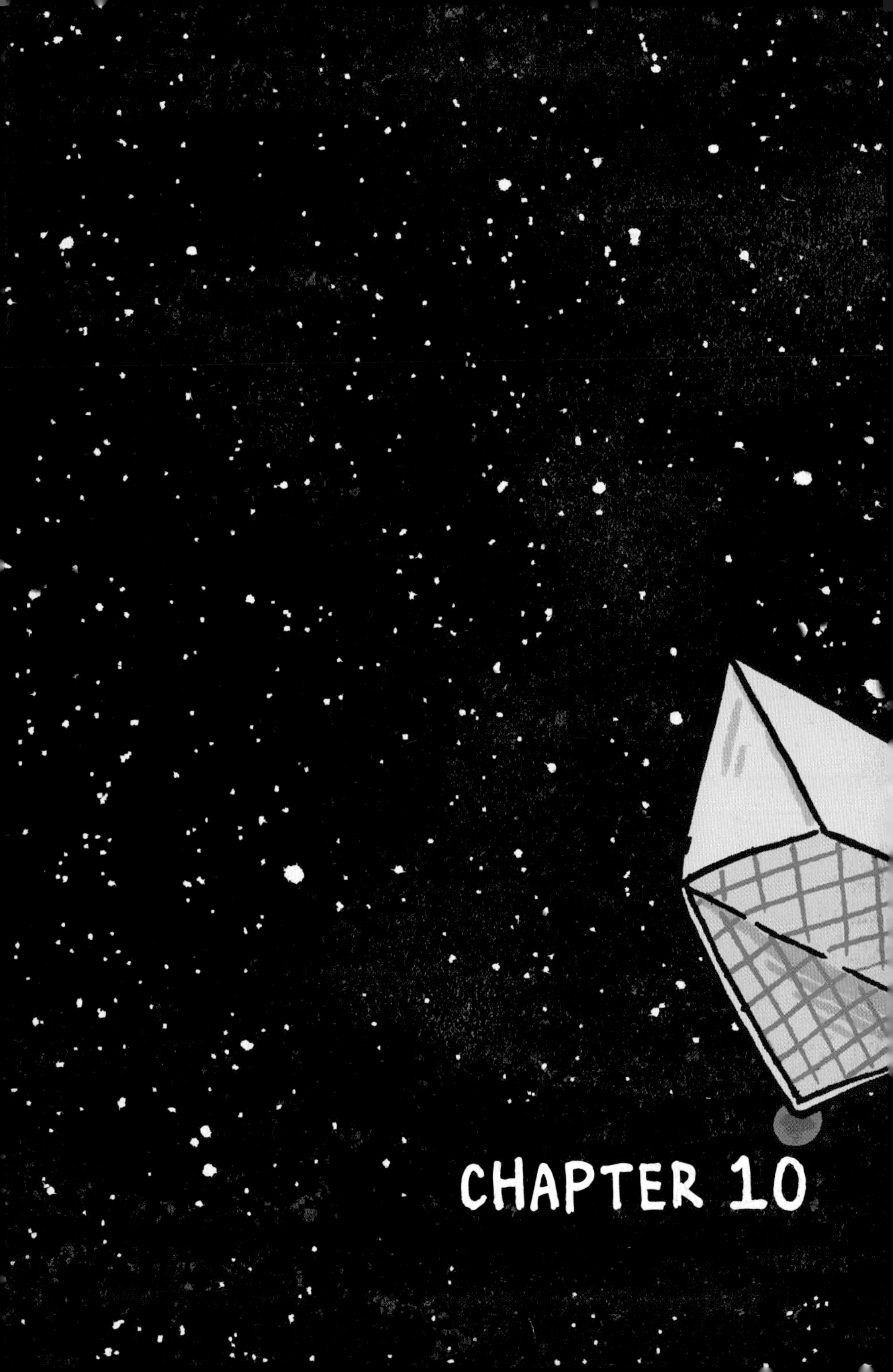
CHAPTER 10

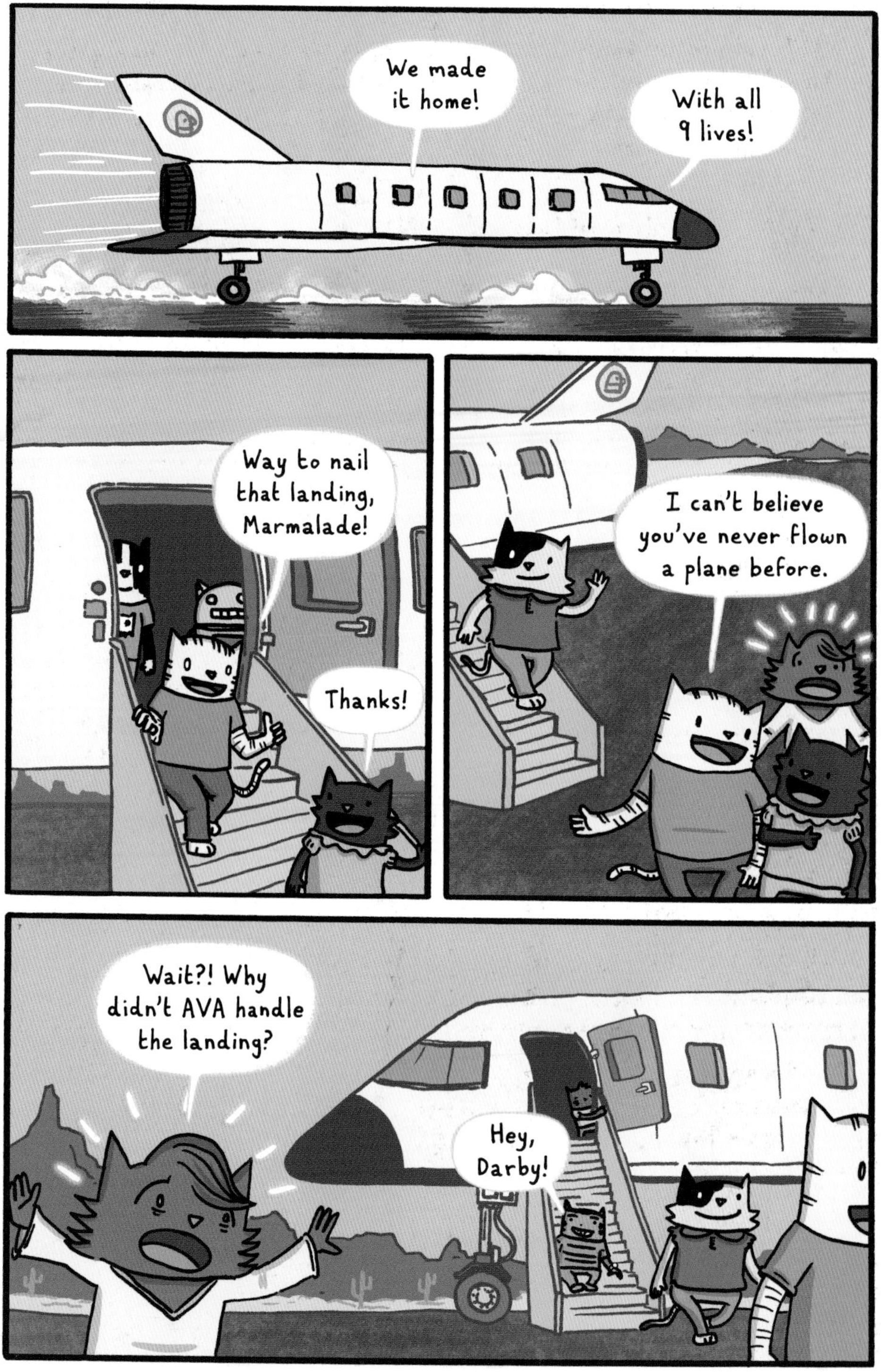
We made it home!
With all 9 lives!
Way to nail that landing, Marmalade!
Thanks!
I can't believe you've never flown a plane before.
Wait?! Why didn't AVA handle the landing?
Hey, Darby!

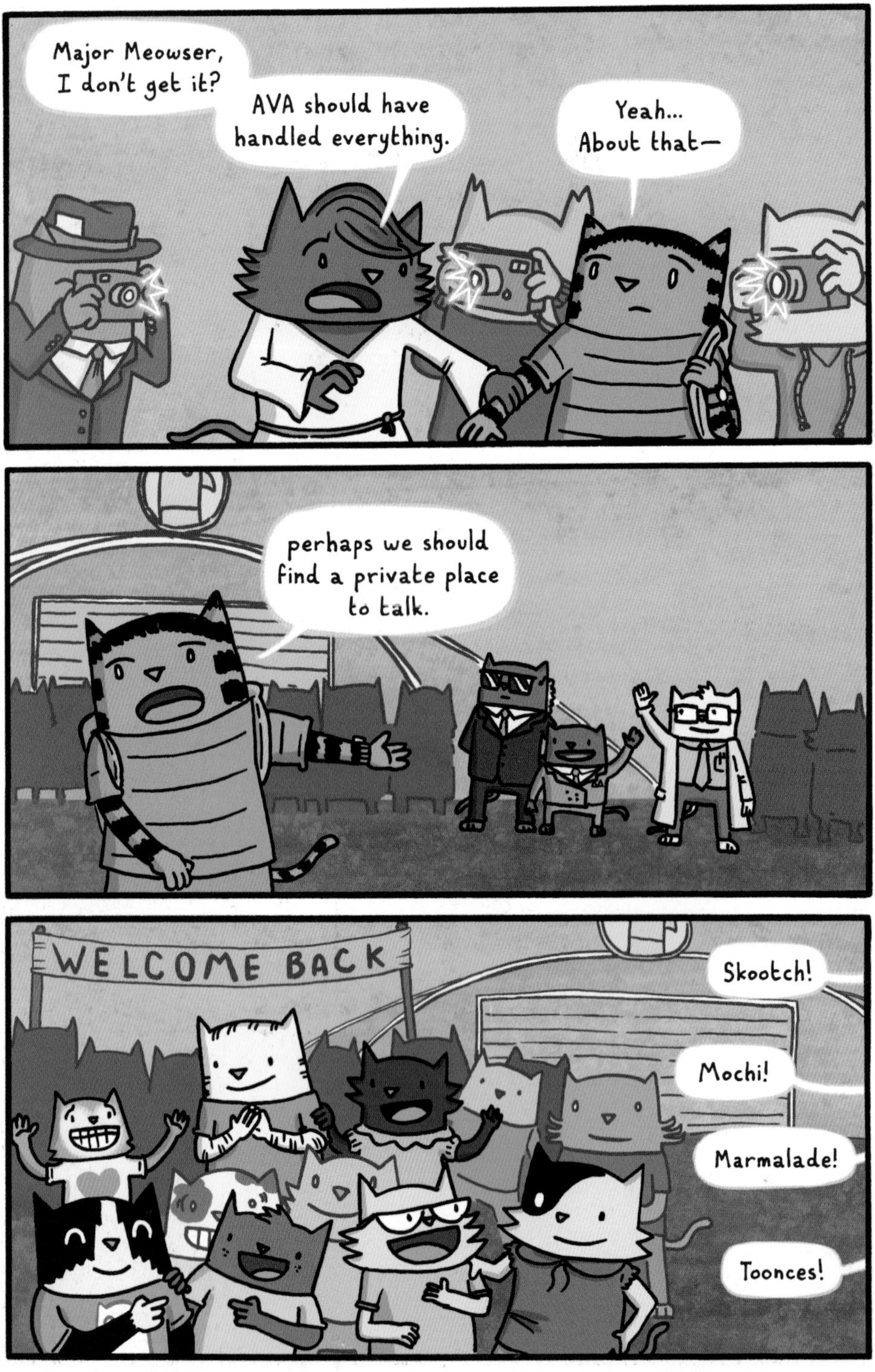
Major Meowser, I don't get it?
AVA should have handled everything.
Yeah... About that—
perhaps we should find a private place to talk.
WELCOME BACK
Skootch!
Mochi!
Marmalade!
Toonces!

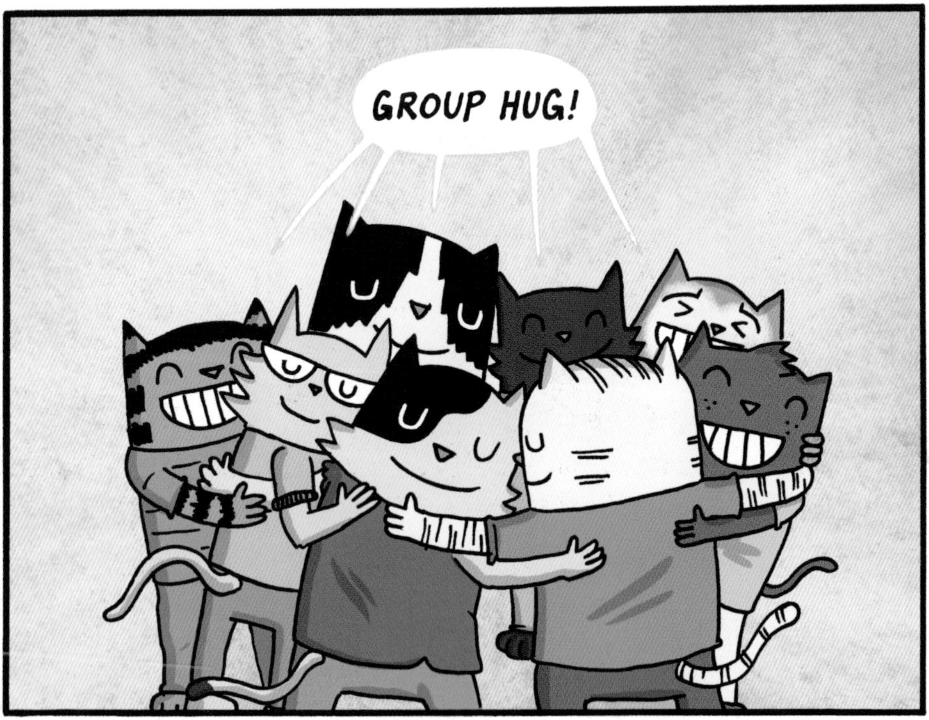
GROUP HUG!

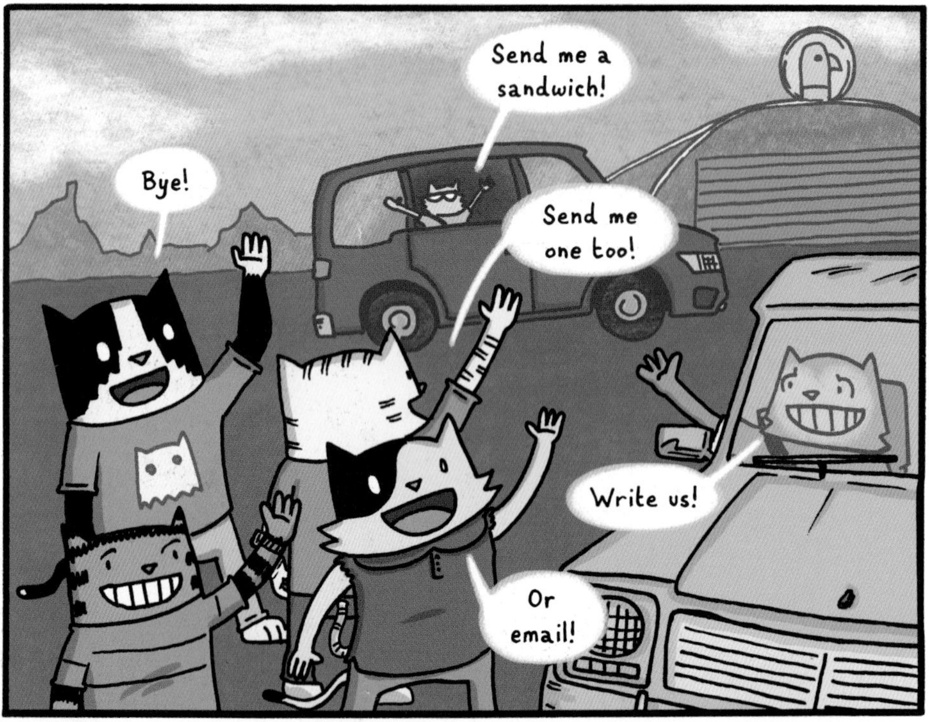
Bye!
Send me a sandwich!
Send me one too!
Write us!
Or email!

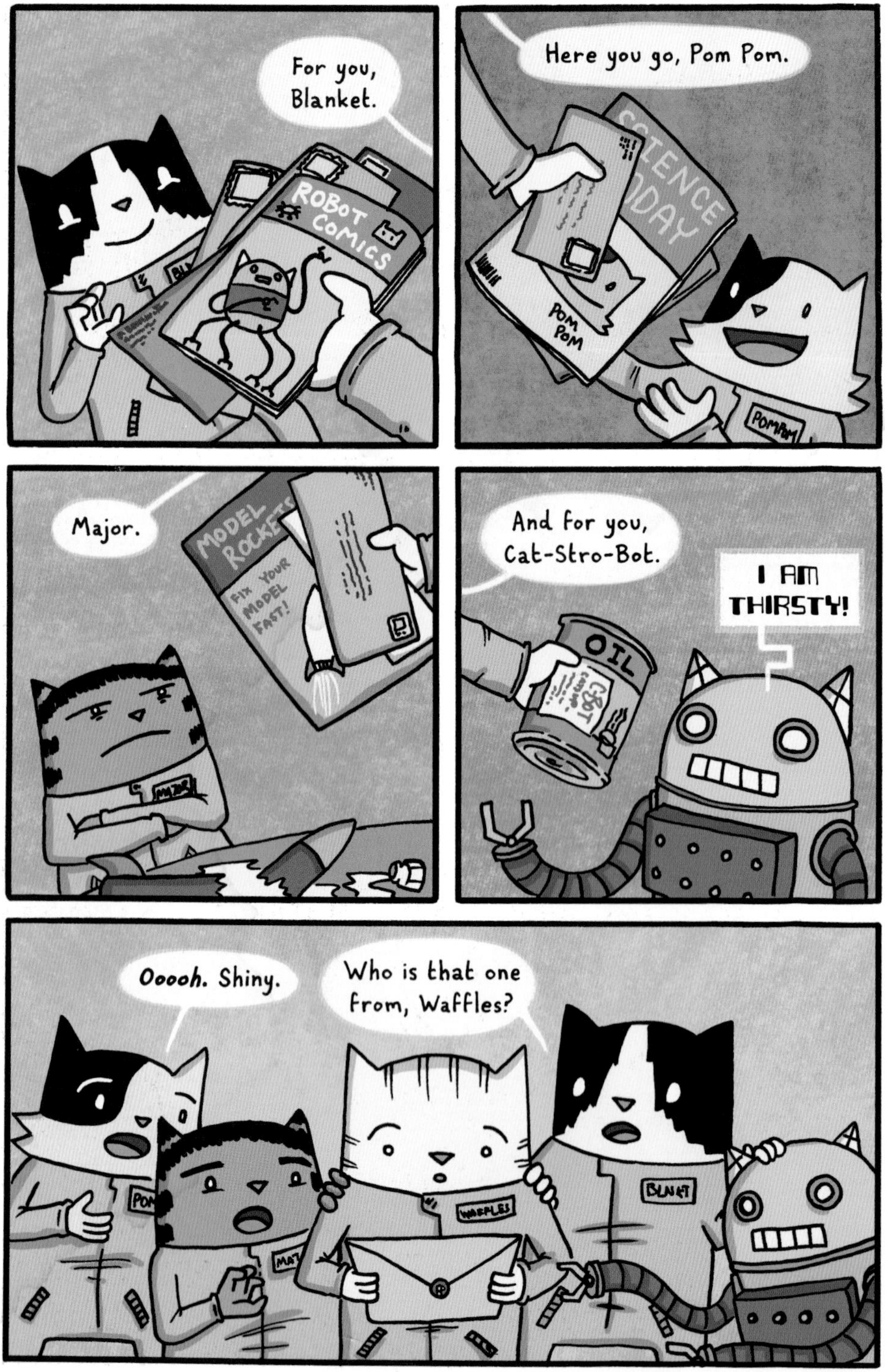
For you, Blanket.
ROBOT COMICS
Here you go, Pom Pom.
SCIENCE TODAY
POM POM
Major.
MODEL ROCKETS
FIX YOUR MODEL FAST!
And for you, Cat-Stro-Bot.
I AM THIRSTY!
OIL
Ooooh. Shiny.
Who is that one from, Waffles?
WAFFLES
BLNKT

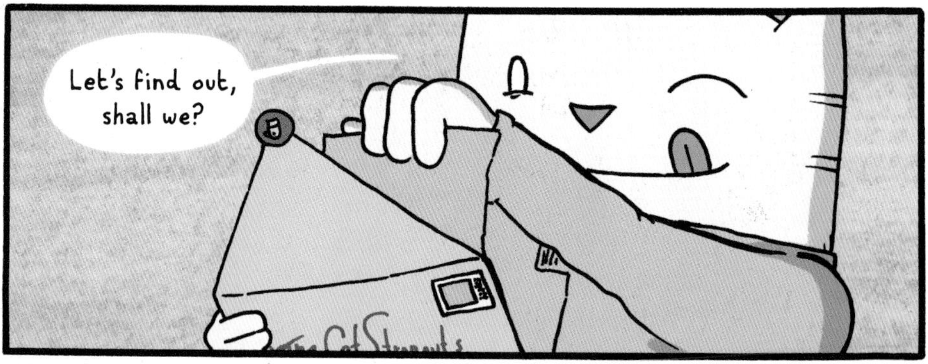
Let's find out, shall we?

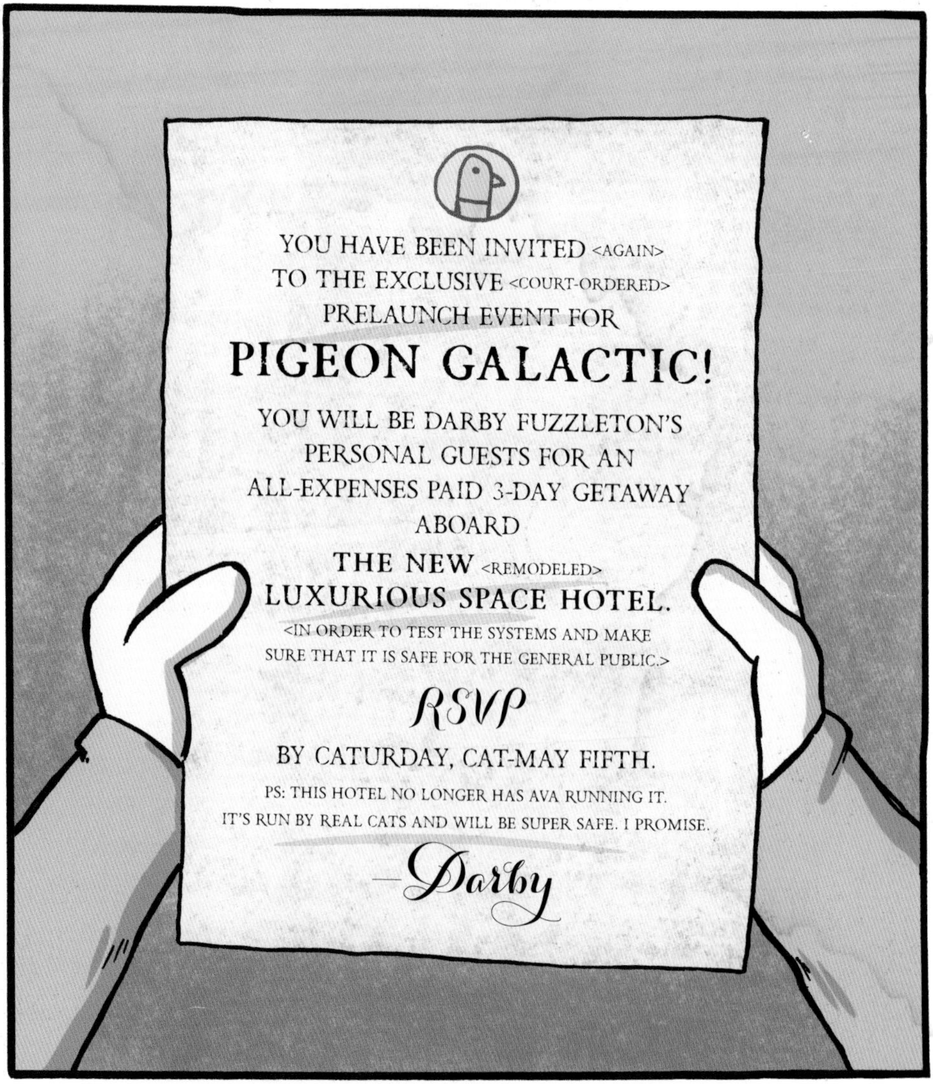
YOU HAVE BEEN INVITED <AGAIN>
TO THE EXCLUSIVE <COURT-ORDERED>
PRELAUNCH EVENT FOR
PIGEON GALACTIC!
YOU WILL BE DARBY FUZZLETON'S
PERSONAL GUESTS FOR AN
ALL-EXPENSES PAID 3-DAY GETAWAY
ABOARD
THE NEW <REMODELED>
LUXURIOUS SPACE HOTEL.
<IN ORDER TO TEST THE SYSTEMS AND MAKE
SURE THAT IT IS SAFE FOR THE GENERAL PUBLIC.>
RSVP
BY CATURDAY, CAT-MAY FIFTH.
PS: THIS HOTEL NO LONGER HAS AVA RUNNING IT.
IT'S RUN BY REAL CATS AND WILL BE SUPER SAFE. I PROMISE.
—Darby

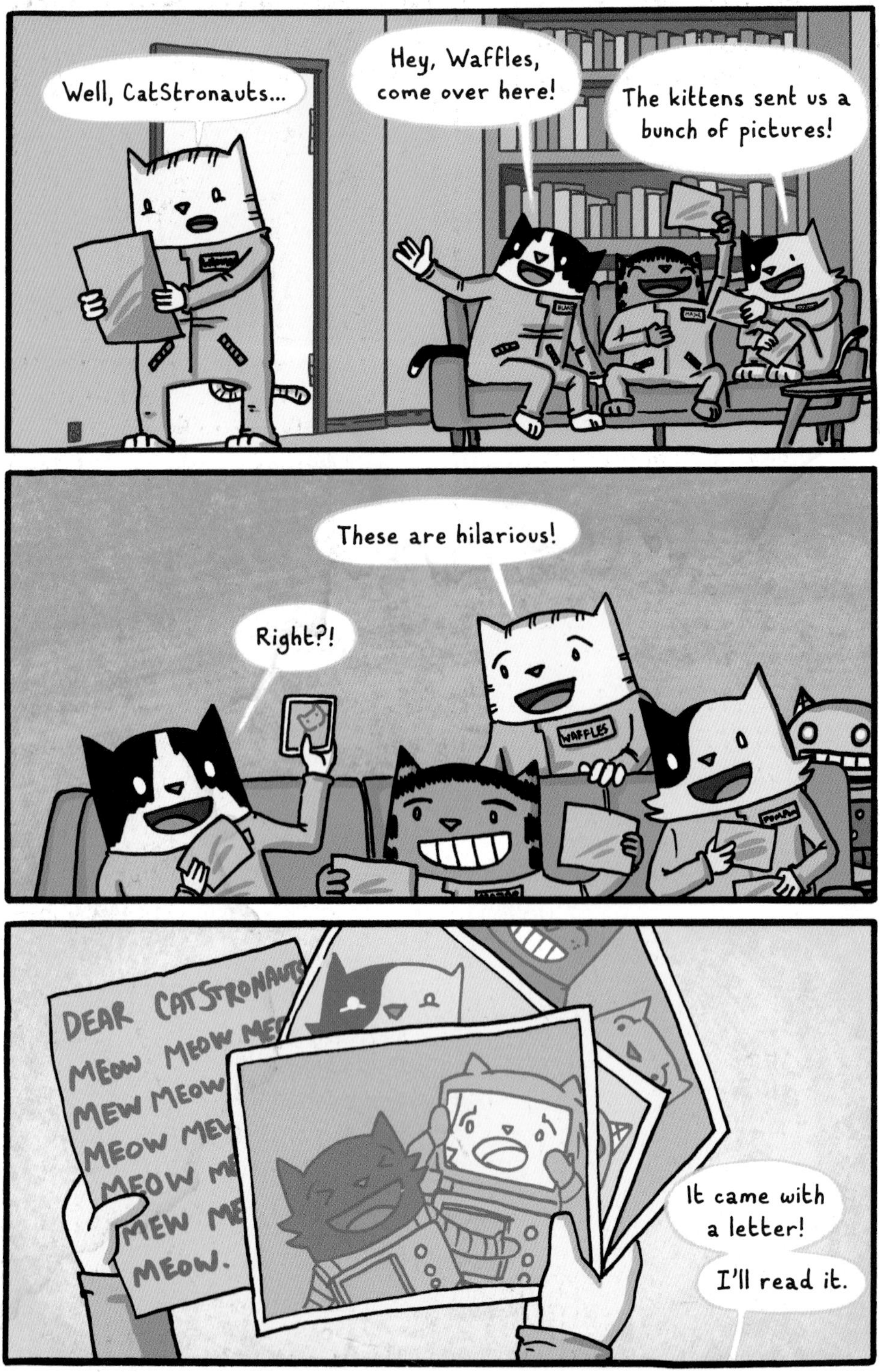
Well, CatStronauts...
Hey, Waffles, come over here!
The kittens sent us a bunch of pictures!
These are hilarious!
Right?!
WAFFLES
DEAR
MEOW.
It came with a letter!
I'll read it.

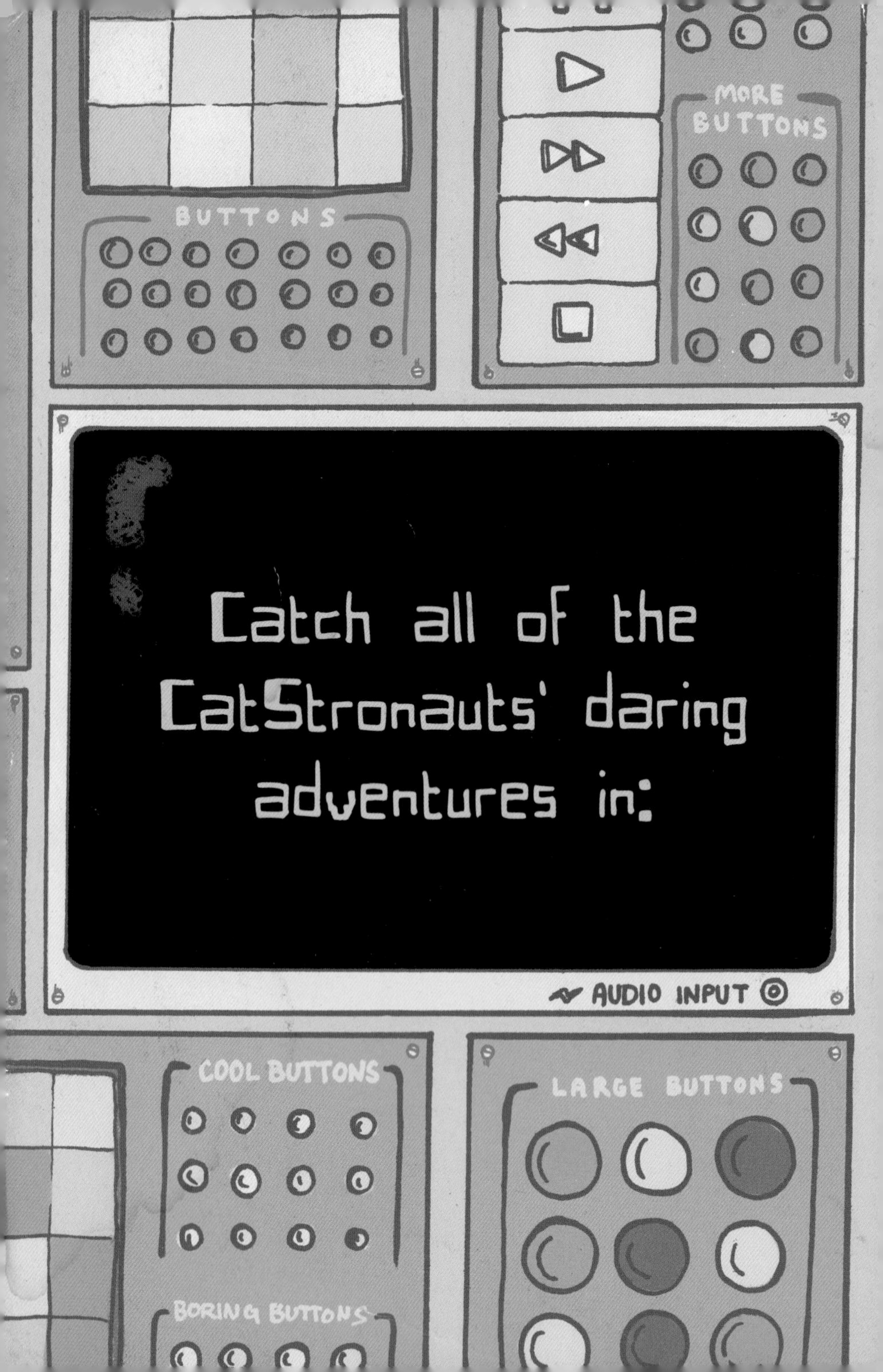
BUTTONS
MORE BUTTONS
Catch all of the CatStronauts' daring adventures in:
AUDIO INPUT
COOL BUTTONS
LARGE BUTTONS
BORING BUTTONS